PRAISE FOR *THE WATCH TOWER*

'Elizabeth Harrower's thrilling 1966 novel *The Watch Tower* comes
rampaging back from decades of disgraceful neglect: a wartime Sydney
story of two abandoned sisters and the arrival in their lives of Felix,
one of literature's most ferociously realised nasty pieces of work.'
Helen Garner, *Australian* Books of the Year

'Elizabeth Harrower's *The Watch Tower* truly feels like a neglected
classic…I think it's one of the most moving books I've read in a
very long time.' Mariella Frostrup, 'Open Book', BBC Radio 4

'I couldn't put down *The Watch Tower*…Harrower's insight into
the nuances of a pathological personality is forensic, and surely one
of the most acute in our literature since Henry Handel Richardson's
The Fortunes of Richard Mahony. At the same time, because of its
complicated tone, her book retains a kind of mythic power.'
Delia Falconer, *Australian* Books of the Year

'To create a monster as continually credible, comic and nauseating
as Felix is a feat of a very high order. But to control that creation,
as Miss Harrower does, so that Clare remains the centre of interest
is an achievement even more rare. *The Watch Tower* is a triumph
of art over virtuosity…a dense, profoundly moral novel of our time.'
H. G. Kippax, *Sydney Morning Herald*, 19 November 1966

'A superb psychological novel that will creep into your bones.'
Michelle de Kretser, *Monthly*

'I read *The Watch Tower* with a mixture of fascination and
horror…[Harrower] is brilliant on power, isolation and class.'
Ramona Koval, *Australian* Books of the Year

'It left me with the strongest sense I have had for a very long time of
the infinite preciousness of consciousness, at whatever cost, and of our
terrifying human vulnerability.' Salley Vickers, *Sydney Morning Herald*

ELIZABETH HARROWER was born in Sydney in 1928 but her family soon relocated to Newcastle, where she lived until she was eleven.

In 1951 Harrower moved to London. She travelled extensively and began to write fiction. Her first novel, *Down in the City,* was published in 1957 and was followed by *The Long Prospect* a year later. In 1959 she returned to Sydney, where she began working for the ABC and as a book reviewer for the *Sydney Morning Herald.* In 1960 she published *The Catherine Wheel*, the story of an Australian law student in London, her only novel not set in Sydney. *The Watch Tower* appeared in 1966. Between 1961 and 1967 she worked in publishing, for Macmillan.

Harrower published no more novels, though she continued to write short fiction. Her work is austere, intelligent, ruthless in its perceptions about men and women. She was admired by many of her contemporaries, including Patrick White and Christina Stead, and is without doubt among the most important writers of the postwar period in Australia.

Elizabeth Harrower lives in Sydney.

JOAN LONDON's collected stories are published as *The New Dark Age.* Her first novel, *Gilgamesh,* won the *Age* Book of the Year for Fiction in 2002, and *The Good Parents* won the Christina Stead Prize for Fiction in 2009.

ALSO BY ELIZABETH HARROWER

Down in the City
The Long Prospect
The Catherine Wheel

The Watch Tower
Elizabeth Harrower

Text Publishing Melbourne Australia

Proudly supported by the Cultural Fund,
Copyright Agency, Australia

textclassics.com.au
textpublishing.com.au

The Text Publishing Company
Swann House
22 William Street
Melbourne Victoria 3000
Australia

First published by Macmillan 1966
This edition first published in Australia by The Text Publishing Company 2012
Reprinted 2012, 2013
First published in the United States by The Text Publishing Company 2013

Cover design by WH Chong
Page design by Text
Typeset by Midland Typesetters

ISBN 9781921922428
Printed and bound in the United States by Edwards Brothers Malloy

CONTENTS

The Only Russian in Sydney
by Joan London

I first read *The Watch Tower* in the library of the
University of Western Australia forty-two years ago.
I must have found it while browsing the shelves of
Australian fiction. I wasn't taking a course on Australian
literature—there wasn't one. Even though I was enrolled
in a course called The Modern Novel and was reading
James Joyce and Ford Madox Ford—Virginia Woolf
was the only female writer to merit a mention—I rarely
read literary journals and had no real idea about the
literary culture of my own country.

In spare moments I always ended up at the fiction
shelves of the library, looking for books that would
speak to me about my life and fate. I relied on random
discoveries. *The Watch Tower*, published by Macmillan
in London in 1966, would have been a relatively new
acquisition.

The novel gripped me like a nightmare. It had the strong, lively, unflinching writing of someone with a story to tell, who goes deeper and deeper into the characters, their feelings and motives, as the narrative races along. Its scenes were vivid, of Sydney in the forties and fifties with its bright air and glittering bays, and the house with the view, and the man who patrols it like an evil dwarf, rolling his eyes and rubbing his hands over some new way to torture his wife. *I didn't know...*I remember thinking that. I meant: I didn't know there was writing like this, in Australia, now, by a woman. I read it as if it were a thriller, obsessively, though no one is murdered. There is only, like the title of another great novel of psychological cruelty, the death of a heart.

The title itself had a contemporary resonance, provided by Bob Dylan's song 'All Along The Watchtower', released a year later: *There must be some way out of here...*

For that is what the novel is about. Entrapment, and finding the way out. Or not.

The novel's opening line, 'Now that your father's gone—', has the ring of *once upon a time* in a fairytale, announcing an eternal theme in the history of storytelling, especially the novel, the fate of single women without a man in the family, or independent means.

Their selfish mother, more like a wicked stepmother, takes her two daughters, Laura and Clare, out of boarding school, to live with her in a flat in Sydney. Laura, the older by seven years, a promising student who wants to become a doctor, is sent to business college to learn shorthand typing and then, according to the rites of passage in those days, cuts off her plaits and becomes a secretary at a cardboard box factory, for the enigmatic owner, Mr Felix Shaw. 'She had a sensation of having mislaid...a piece of herself. There was nothing to dream!'

World War II breaks out, and their mother leaves on the last ship home to England. Orphaned, friendless, the sisters must move into a boarding house and fend for themselves. Sensitive, moral, intelligent, penniless girls, they are heroines worthy of Henry James, Jane Austen or Charlotte Brontë. To save Clare from leaving school at fourteen to work with her in Mr Shaw's next enterprise, a chocolate factory, Laura agrees to marry him.

> 'Mmm.' He moved his mouth ruminatively, never quite displacing that superior smile and its odd suggestion of complicity. Again he hummed out that long reflective noise. 'I don't know if we couldn't fix that up.'
>
> Laura was aware suddenly that her eyes felt strained and sore; the skin of her lips felt taut and cracked with the heat. Talking in this personal way to Mr. Shaw made her feel nervous and giddy, or just peculiar and unlike herself.

Thus the elder sister, traditionally the surrogate mother, offers up her life for a home and security, and to give the younger a chance. Handed over by an unloving mother to a man unable to love, Laura has been groomed for victimhood. Because she is a principled person, she feels in debt to him. 'She had only herself, and out of herself she had somehow to manufacture repayments he would find acceptable.' How she toils! Chores abound in this mansion, as Laura, after a day in the office, scrubs and serves and weeds the garden, and won't ask for a penny for herself. A young woman in wealthy surroundings, she has faded dresses and worn hands.

Mr Shaw becomes Felix, 'a swarthy, nuggety man of forty-four...hardly taller than Laura in her two-inch heels...His voice grated and rasped as if his throat was perpetually rough from shouting.' He has a particular physical presence in the novel, his gestures and speech and 'his restless dark-brown eyes, the pores of his tough skin, his wrinkled sinewy throat and his, in some way, horribly incongruous, imported, impeccable clothes'.

Soon after the marriage he goes back on his word. Clare must leave school after all and go to business college.

Endlessly, as if for sport, he invents ways in which to squeeze the joy out of Laura's life. He insists on Clare's constant presence too, 'to have her there to be knocked down, as it were, by the blows from his eyes and his words.'

Clare, a lover of Chekhov, Dostoyevsky and Tolstoy, isolated in that house, 'where there had never been a friend to call…only ever the indifferent, papery sound of wind in trees, distant traffic, winking planets', feels herself to be 'the only Russian in Sydney'.

I never forgot *The Watch Tower*. The vision of the book, the sense of darkness in sunlight, stayed lodged somewhere at the back of my mind. I remembered the experience of reading it as intense, disturbing sometimes; in the sure hand of the creation of its villain, there was panache, even humour.

It's always instructive to return to a book you admired a long time ago. It carries the ghost of the first reading. Even though we now have words like *misogyny* and *abuse* and *co-dependence* to name the forces that entrap the sisters, the tension is undiminished.

How a well-meaning young woman, brought up to be considerate of others, is harnessed to the demands of a damaged man is still excruciating to read four decades later. Who in the course of a life has not endured, or witnessed, or participated in the attempt of one human being to have power over another? Harrower's relentless observation of this process and its effects is worthy of the Russian masters.

'Little by little,' thinks Laura in a rare moment outside Felix's radar, 'she had resigned away the trust she had been given to be herself—out of pity, from a desire for peace at any price, thinking nothing really lost, anyway, by her silent acquiescence.'

To be herself. Unlike Laura, Clare has never signed away an inner life. Hers is the view from 'the watch tower', on guard for danger but also looking out at the world from a contemplative distance. *Reality.* That is her quest.

> This permanent awareness of what was so, regardless of her whims of the moment, regardless of what it would be pleasant to believe, or not pleasant, this solid bedrock was what she was, what she was about. What could there be in its place if you were differently constituted?

This awareness includes the acknowledgement of otherness, the respect for another's being. Sometimes there is joy, rapture, in light, or trees, or the humanness of strangers, but its practice is as austere as any other form of spiritual exercise.

What I had forgotten from my first reading, or perhaps was not ready to receive, is the strength of this slowly gathering counter-force, the means of resistance to the malevolence of Felix Shaw.

The assistance Clare offers Bernard, the young Dutchman, survivor of the war in Europe, is like the breaking of a spell. Suddenly she sees that 'she and Bernard had traversed the same extreme country'. It had never occurred to her that she could be useful to anyone. 'Yet she felt extraordinarily light-hearted—like a scientist at the very moment of discovery...There was boundless vitality of the spirit, a thoughtfulness beyond words. She could encourage someone to stay alive. And this was what she was for.'

Again and again Harrower defines the ways of the victims, the helpless. *The Watch Tower* is an extended study of suffering, whatever its origin. It is Bernard who has the last word on Laura as he watches her frantic search for the diamond ring that Felix has allowed her to believe she has lost.

> Laura had forgotten him, was unaware of his eyes on her, was so far removed from the light movement of the air, the scent of freesias, the shimmering of leaves, that she suddenly seemed to Bernard, who had seen many victims, to represent them all. She was unapproachable as the condemned are unapproachable and he was responsible, as the free always are.

Where does such knowledge come from? Each of Harrower's four novels is concerned with entrapment of one sort or another, through family or youth or love. But *The Watch Tower*, her last novel, is almost like a distillation in its vision of the forces of good and evil.

Something runs clear and strong through this wonderful, painful novel, the dark and the light. The victim and the survivor. Suffering and joy. The knowledge of both. *Reality.*

The Watch Tower

PART ONE

'Now that your father's gone—'

Stella Vaizey saw the two faces jerk, to an even sharper alertness, and hesitated. What a pair of pedants they were! What sticklers, George Washingtons, optimists!

'Dead,' she corrected herself firmly, with a trace of malice. 'Now that your father's dead, the three of us are going to live together in Sydney.'

The blank receptive faces, the wide-open eyes, turned now to their headmistress, Miss Lambert, who nodded regretful confirmation.

'When I've sold the house and found a flat in the city,' the girls' mother continued, taking in the exchange of looks dryly, 'I'll let Miss Lambert know.'

A magpie or a currawong, or some other bush bird she hoped never to hear in town, gave its careless, beautifully deliberate call from a giant blue gum in the distance outside the school grounds. (Someone sighed.) Closer at hand there were energetic sounds from the tennis courts, and laughter.

'I can't persuade you to reconsider this, Mrs. Vaizey? If we had Laura for her last years—She's one of our best students, you know.' The girl had thought that she might study medicine as her father had done, though Laura had now and then expressed her willingness, in addition, to sing in opera, if pressed to do so. And laughable and unlikely though such ideas often

5

seemed, it was a fact, Miss Lambert had to admit, that human beings did perform in operas the world over, and that Laura had a charming mezzo-soprano voice, was musical, and had an aptitude for languages. However, her poor young father—at forty-five five years younger than Miss Lambert—had had a heart attack at the wheel of his car setting out one evening to visit a patient; and now, in a sense—from a headmistress's point of view—his daughter's life was in danger. (Clare's too, of course, but she was only nine, not at such a crucial stage; was apt to say, anyway, to benevolent enquiries about her future plans, 'I don't know'— unlike some others of her age, who could already answer, with an aplomb Miss Lambert liked to flatter herself the school had fostered, 'A physiotherapist, Miss Lambert', or 'A debutante, Miss Lambert'. Nice decisive little lasses!)

'Laura's career—It would make so much difference. There are scholarships—' Miss Lambert murmured, rising even as she spoke, for Stella Vaizey was murmuring back with a soothing insulting confidence, 'The girls understand. Their father was not very practical.'

Called on for understanding, her daughters looked at Mrs. Vaizey with a probing uncertainty. She cared for them so little they were awed. Their father had translated her to them from time to time; now Laura was obliged to attempt this for herself and Clare. Recently, she had explained: 'She's wonderful, really, it's only that she's unpredictable. But she's unusual because she's not an Australian, I think. You'd be bound to be different, being born in India.'

Clare left her attention and a finger on the blue-ruled page of her homework book, and raised bright-grey eyes to her sister's face. After an empty perusal of this face, which was intently thinking at a pastel portrait of Princess Elizabeth, Clare's eyes dropped deep into the inky problems of trains travelling at sixty, eighty and ninety-five miles an hour between three distant cities.

'Yes,' Laura repeated, frowning at the princess.

'Mmm.' Clare's agreement had the moody, putting-off note of one resisting an alarm-clock, but a part of her mind was grateful to hear: *wonderful, unpredictable, born India*.

But now, just ten days ago, their father, whom they had assumed to be as enduring as the sun, had turned out to be more unreliable than anyone they had ever known. Mrs. Vaizey had come with the news and gone. Their friends had crept off looking sly and sympathetic by turns, whispering at the end of the corridor, acting as if the Vaizey girls had violated the rules of some secret society. Miss Lambert and the other teachers were kind, but their helplessness in the face of events, and the chasm between the sisters and these officially affectionate, familiar people, became more and more apparent to them as their mother shook hands with Miss Lambert now and kissed them and left the school. At a distance and slowly the idea rose on the horizon: it had only been a transaction all the time. They were only money and words and figures on an invoice.

During the remaining days there, the girls often stared into each other, profoundly surprised at the shape their world was taking. There was no precedent for death, and the snapping-off of what they had taken to be eternal friendships with Sheila and Rose, and being left (it felt) at the mercy of their mother with whom they were not very well acquainted. Monuments like Miss Lambert and the school were evidently insubstantial as the vacant creatures moulded in sand to resemble people by the sculptor on the Sydney beach they went to once.

Laura's father—her *father*—was as easily disposed of as the scraps of paper on which she had printed: *Dr. Laura Vaizey*. The taken-for-granted evolution of school life—entering as a 'little one' and leaving as a very senior person who had worked desperately hard and passed a most difficult examination—was apparently *not* inevitable.

Laura had read books. In all except a few dramatic stories set in other centuries, involving characters and circumstances ridiculously far removed from hers, everything ended happily for young heroines. Though their plans were shattered and there was no hope at all, it always worked out that there had been a fantastic misunderstanding. The girls and their loved ones then sped, laughing, to their rainbow-coloured future. Was she not a young heroine? Those other tragedies (Miss Lambert's classics) were beautiful, of course, and very sad, but not like anything real. So what had happened to the Vaizeys couldn't be tragic; it was only stupefying, left the future mysterious and unimaginable. It felt odd to plan only from morning till afternoon till night, with the next day, the next week, a featureless vacuum: and next year, or five years' time, like the space off the edge of the world. She had a sensation of having mislaid a vital pleasure that she could not quite remember, or a piece of herself. There was nothing to dream!

Clare bore her departure from school rather better, since she had always been under the impression that she had been sent there originally as a punishment, or to be got rid of. One night long ago her parents had quarrelled. They had said words she had forgotten that nevertheless had meant what she had understood and remembered them to mean. She and Laura were not wanted. School was a place they could disappear to for ever.

Nor had anyone, since she had arrived there years before, ever explained from the beginning the purpose they were all allegedly pursuing. In another place purposes might be clearer, the beginnings of stories be told—among them, even the reason for being here at all.

'I want you and Clare to take over from tomorrow morning, Miss Muffet.' Stella Vaizey lay back in bed and extended one small, beringed and manicured hand in a final relinquishing gesture. Propped against two pillows, smoking an Abdulla cigarette, she looked tolerantly at Clare, who sat on the dressing-table stool, leaning on her knees, plaits hanging, one navy-blue ribbon untied; and at Laura, who stood, back to the windows, assessing the strange bedroom and its furnishings with quick little glances. Laura hated that 'Miss Muffet'. It wasn't well intended.

'You're fixed up at your business college; Clare's enrolled at her school, and they're both within walking distance. You know where the shops are, and the beach is at the bottom of the hill, so you've got nothing to complain about, have you?'

She was crossing them off her list!

'And now that everything's settled, I'm going to expect you both to take some responsibility. I'm *very* tired. I've had a busy, upsetting time with that oaf of a solicitor bungling everything and selling the house. It's been a great—' her eyes filled with tears. She sneezed, and sneezed again, and groaned luxuriously as if to say, 'There! You can see for yourselves how ill-treated I've been.'

She was a very attractive woman. Her thick creamy skin tanned easily; her face was short and wide;

her eyebrows were dark and shaped with a beautiful, appeasing regularity; her mouth was pretty and her eyes were soft-looking and changed from violet-grey to amber in a way that had been considered fascinating. An Indian languor and grace of movement not always found in the offspring of British army majors had surprised and lured a number of young men none of whom was ever to be famed for his percipience: one was David Vaizey. It was clear even now, even to the girls, that she had been wrought for more congenial circumstances than these.

'Poor Mum!' Out in the kitchen, her tone perfunctory rather than sincere, Clare disposed of her mother and balanced on the white-painted spar of a chair, tipping it up and rocking.

'We'll work out a timetable and make lists. You'll have to help!' Laura was impressed by her own authority. Yet it was a joke in a way. Even her strict claim on Clare was made with conspiratorial laughing eyes. Yet she felt like someone else.

'I *will*. I *will* help,' Clare protested, her lively speculative look fastened on the game of houses they were about to play. Giving the chair an incautious jerk, she landed horizontal on the floor, the breath knocked out of her and a bump rising rapidly on the back of her skull.

'Oh, look out!' Laura whispered, giggling, as their mother called out from the bedroom, 'What on *earth*—?'

They giggled silently as Clare picked herself up, and their mother's voice continued to rebuke their thoughtless noise. And they went on giggling—now that they had started—because of something embarrassing to do with their father, whom they had not known very well either; because this was the first day in their new home, a furnished flat, in an unknown suburb—Manly, in a huge city, Sydney—and they had to walk alone into strange institutions tomorrow.

They laughed, and they had to sit down; and they laughed, and bit their hands, and wrapped their arms round their middles, and started each other off again when the riot seemed to be waning. They laughed till all their laughter emptied out, then almost instantly they felt very tired. They smelt the clean and unfamiliar odours of the flat—new paint, empty cupboards—and draughts of the salty wind that rattled the loose windows.

'She'll get up tomorrow or the next day.' Clare shivered and yawned; and, standing up to go to bed, staggered for no reason and started to laugh again. And even as she laughed a strange silent panic rose up in her and she thought, with a sort of bright rigidity: *I want to go home.* She was trapped here. She wanted to go home. Laura was locking the back door, and her arms looked white and weak. Laura knew no more than she did.

The school, teachers, friends, had cast them off. Their father was nowhere. I want to go home, Clare thought again stubbornly, pushing with her mind against the knowledge that she had really nowhere to want to go. Caught, not safe, cold—There were no reliable people. It was all wrong! She kicked the chair that had made her fall over.

'What were they like at school?' Laura carefully washed the chops that had slid with gentle wilfulness from griller to linoleum.

'All right. One girl said I put on jam. I *don't* talk funny. I *told* her it was only Miss Carroll's speech class. What were they like at your place?' She set out the cutlery on her mother's tray.

'All right.' Laura had learned a number of illuminating facts not connected with shorthand and typewriting: for instance, it was pitiable, awful, not to have a boyfriend; it was repellent to have your hair in plaits and not to wear makeup; it was peculiar to be without a father, yet to have a mother who need not work; it was the very nadir of dullness in a female of her age not to be able to discuss film and recording stars. 'I hope I'll like it. When I get to know them better.'

On one side of the dining-room table Laura was practising shorthand outlines, on the other Clare was brooding over an atlas.

'How long,' she asked, her eyes roaming the coloured world, 'how long do you think Mum's going to stay in bed? Because it's weeks and weeks. *I* don't think she's very sick.' Clare looked through to the kitchen where dirty dishes stood in dismal mounds on the sink; she pushed her face out of shape with her fists and crossed her eyes.

Laura stopped work to sharpen her pencil with a razor blade. 'It's her nerves,' she said loyally, looking into her young sister's eyes, then dropping her own. But it was important to believe that your mother, at least, was truthful, at least. She, Laura, was seven years older than Clare so it was up to her—

'Well, why,' asked Clare darkly, having considered the proposition of her mother's nerves for some seconds, 'won't she let us go out or anything?'

'We went swimming on Sunday and we're allowed to go to the pictures next Saturday afternoon.' Laura pressed the sharp point of her pencil on the page and broke it.

'Yes, but you know what I mean. That's just us. Why can't we go to see any of the girls ever?'

'Because she likes to know where we are and who we're with, *and*'—Laura looked up again from grinding away at the lead pencil—'they can't come here because Mr. and Mrs. Kirby downstairs own the place and they'd ask us to go if you brought fifty noisy little friends home.'

Clare wriggled her shoulders and grimaced at the map of the world. 'Old India!'

'Anyway, when would there be time?' Laura asked, unanswerably.

They were rarely unoccupied. Afternoons ticked into evenings while tomatoes and apples were bought, potatoes peeled, bathroom and kitchen floors washed, dinner cooked, homework prepared; and on Saturday there were groceries to buy, carpets to hoover, washing to be sloshed all over the laundry and hung out; then on Sunday there was ironing, more cooking and homework. Though there was swimming, too, now that it was hot again.

She asked the question and Clare accepted its statement with no trace of grievance. Their rackety housekeeping took time but was a novelty. They were not supervised. Laura aired her pleasant voice daily and liked to stare out of the bedroom window at three huge triumphant flame trees on the slope above the cricket ground, their tangled branches. Clare liked to slide down the banisters to the ground floor. She liked to run, read, swim and sing.

They ran down the steep hill past two- and three-storeyed blocks of flats like their own, and the grey stone church balanced on the incline. Stopping for breath and running again, stopping for traffic and running, their long plaits of hair smacking their backs then curving out ahead, they at last reached the esplanade, the semi-circle of pines and fine yellow sand beyond which there was only the Pacific. If they were uncertain of everything else, they knew this was a boundary. It took them aback. Jolted to a stop, they stared and stared before, in a sense, giving up, looking away, and dropping, stiff-kneed, down the steps to the beach.

'Did you remember to change the books, Laura?'

Stella Vaizey was lying on her dark-blue velveteen sofa under the windows, smoothing her eyebrows with a tiny brush, examining the effect in the oblong mirror from her handbag.

'Yes, I got two of each. Don't know what they're like.'

At her mother's behest she had joined the three-penny lending library and was working systematically along the shelves. Mrs. Vaizey flipped and dipped through the novels and tepid tales of travel Laura produced, but the flat was silent for hours on end while, in private lairs behind cushions and the high backs of chairs, or round in the passage between the brick laundry and the paling fence, the printed pages were taken in by her daughters with such fervour that objects any less wondrous than words would have been permanently enfeebled by it.

'I went to town this afternoon. Some of Daddy's friends from home rang up.'

Laura sat down on the stool, leaning forward, to listen eagerly. 'Who? What did they say? Did they remember us?'

It did not surprise her, as it had the first time, to hear that her mother had gone out. Frequently now when early summer produced mornings of unparalleled transparency, of a significant and singing radiance, she sauntered into them. She window-shopped and pottered and drank coffee. She had her hair set and met country visitors. She sat in the faded canvas deck-chairs facing the ocean and read what the astrologers foretold for the following week, and wrote to her brother Edward in India, and other distant relations in Somerset. More important still, she had begun to play bridge three or four times a week with a group of women who gathered in Mrs. Casson's flat downstairs.

Stella Vaizey was convalescing. She resided rather than lived with her daughters. Languid, detached, she allowed herself to be looked after. She could venture out safely now, because it had become obvious to the girls, without a word having been uttered, that someone so small should not have to labour. *They* were Australian, medium-sized mortals, quite lacking in their mother's fragility and exotic heritage. It was entirely natural that they should leap about, bruising their shins and hip-bones, cutting their fingers, acquiring circles under their eyes, in the process of fending for her and themselves.

In town, apart from her card-playing acquaintances, Mrs. Vaizey knew no one. The uncle whose presence in Australia had been the pretext for her visit to the country, and in whose house she met David Vaizey, had died. David's sister was married and living in Canada. His father, an old man now, whom she had never met, lived somewhere in the north of Queensland with his second wife. No solutions to her future were likely to be forthcoming from any of these directions, yet—

'Something very, very nice is going to turn up one of these days,' she promised herself, speaking aloud to Clare.

Was it? Clare watched her mother rasp a match on the box and light her cigarette. Fascinated, with an almost loving intensity, Clare watched the cigarette smoke writhe. She *knew* her mother, but still, something wonderful was going to happen. Her mother said so.

'Who knows? I might open a gift shop down on the Esplanade or the Corso with that little bit of money Daddy left. Or I wonder if flowers—?'

She raised her face to the looking-glass never far from her hand, and inspected her smooth creamy image. Surely it had a meaning? So accurately designed. Even her hair, which was heavy and smooth, arranged in what Miss Lowe down the street called 'a sculptured Egyptian style', looked somehow intended. A wealthy husband, of course, was the obvious answer.

'Yes, a gift shop! Laura supported her seriously. 'Or flowers.'

She and Clare had risen up with genuine praise and encouragement for dozens of tentative musings of this nature on their mother's part. Unfortunately, though, her mentioning and their support always had the effect of turning an idea for action into buried experience. However—

Laura passed what passed for examinations at the business college and was commended by Mr. Sparks who owned it and had a black moustache.

'As our top student, Laura, you could have the pick of the jobs on the register, but your mother wants you to find something locally, does she? You'd get more money in town.' Jim Sparks, thirty-five, destined to spend his days nursing his own invalid mother, raised his moustache enquiringly.

'It's the travelling time. I help at home.'

'Oh, well. That doesn't leave us too much choice, you know.' His pale fingers went over the card-index with a cycling motion. 'Shaw's Box Factory. Only a fair wage to start. No Saturdays.'

Laura had her light-brown sun-streaked plaits cut the same afternoon, and her hair hung in loose natural waves to her shoulders. Out of startled blue eyes she looked at her new face. She felt a sensation that was hard to identify. She half-thought to put it down to the loss of her hair, which had never been cut before. But it was only that reality, in the sound of a few words, had twisted her heart.

Shaw's Box Factory. Doctor Laura Vaizey—Laura Vaizey at Covent Garden—

She was like someone who, having gone bravely through preparations for an operation that would almost certainly truncate her life, realised with a terrible twisting of her heart just as the anaesthetist's mask descended, that this shocking thing was truly happening, inevitable: shrieking resistance was of no avail.

'Well, if that's the job Mr. Sparks has suggested—' Her mother gently acquiesced in his decision and continued her letter to Edward. Instead of evaporating as expected, Laura remained. Her silent presence made Mrs. Vaizey look up, mildly irritated but constrained to add, 'Something very nice will turn up soon, you'll see!'

She was rubbing her jawline delicately with her left hand. 'Don't tell me I've been bitten by a mosquito!— No, if your father had only thought—But, anyway, you're a born homemaker, a born housewife. And you've got an unusual little face, pretty eyes and teeth and a small waist. You'll—' she stroked her jaw worriedly '—meet some—' she paused again. Laura wandered off.

Mr. Shaw of Shaw's Box Factory was a swarthy nuggety man of forty-four who looked closer to fifty.

He was hardly taller than Laura in her two-inch heels. He usually wore a brown suit with the coat unbuttoned and flapping open, and had a dark-brown hat at a dashing angle on his thick black hair. Heavy untidy eyebrows overhung eyes of an extreme darkness with large irises and almost no whites. In the afternoons, by four o'clock, his beard was beginning to sprout. He looked like a pirate, and people who had never seen a Turk or a Persian thought that he looked like these foreign men, too.

Most of the time he was absent collecting materials and delivering orders. When he came to the factory his attention went with the inflexible fixity of a primitive machine from one object to another—one ledger, one journal, one carton filled with little boxes. He rarely spoke and when he did it was only ever about the particular task that had his attention. His voice grated and rasped as if his throat was perpetually rough from shouting. Since he was apt to speak without indicating which member of his staff he was addressing (by, for instance, looking someone in the face) and since he was inclined to enunciate in the manner of one talking to himself, he was very often asked to repeat his instructions. Occasionally this seemed to anger him, but in general he appeared not to notice the presence of company.

In the one-roomed factory five girls sat at a long bench opposite a row of windows; on the brick wall blearily visible through the glass they read, day in day out, in green letters on a yellow ground: TRY TRIXIE TEA — IT'S TASTY, TEMPTING AND TANTALISING!

Layers of cellophane material pressed into folds and cut into solid crosses by a guillotine were stacked at each girl's right hand. Four strokes of liquid cement and a moment's pressure completed a box. Towers of these colourless cubes were constructed daily, the girls competing against each other for the highest wage.

Florists were Shaw's chief customers, but jewellers and department stores were beginning to place big orders, too. The wireless played all day. The girls worked fast and sang huskily.

After a few hours' inspection they were casually friendly to the new office girl who sat typing at her desk further along the same grimy wall. They genuinely pitied anyone who had to write shorthand and add figures. Especially since they made more money than she did, and worked the same hours. Yes, they felt quite friendly towards her.

'How're ya goin', Laurie? Watcha up to this arvo, love?' They peered over at her typewritten page, at her notebook, laying warm hands on her shoulders. Idle for a moment, kindly patronising, smelling of face powder and pickled onions and liquid cement, they paused to joke with her and tease her.

On Laura's fourth day at the factory, she yelped at the sight of two large rats running not very quickly in her direction along the ledge behind the girls' feet.

22

Aileen and Greta, the senior girls, choked over their boxes, laughing. 'They're our pets! Doncha like 'em? Feed 'em our crusts! *They* won't hurt you! More afraid of you.'

The young ones, Shirley, Diane and Bernadette, cried inextricably, 'They don't like 'em eether, Laurie. They're havin' you on. Dirty big things!—The rats, the rats, we meant!' they shrieked, voices and faces cracking with giggles as their elders threatened to crown them.

Returning to the factory at three that afternoon, Mr. Shaw found a tin of poison on his desk. He read the label, ponderously turned the tin upside-down, then raised his eyes to look at Laura for what appeared to her to be the very first time.

'What's all this? Where did this come from?' His voice was thick and slow.

Laura told him she had bought it, and why.

Mr. Shaw began to laugh in rather a startling way. He looked—jocular, Laura thought, but he laughed the way people did in pantomimes, the way the Dame did, as if he was listening to himself.

Feeling herself blanch, Laura returned his smile conventionally and asked, cringing from the thought, if she could put the poison down.

'Well, now! Well, now!' With a stunning abrupt-ness Mr. Shaw *stopped* laughing, and looked at Laura with a very serious frown, as if she had brought up some entirely different subject, and was asking him to throw away half his assets. She felt, and was abashed to feel, that she had begged a colossal favour. After all, in a way, he did *own* the rats.

Her nerve fluctuated; she could understand nothing. Seeing her waver, Mr. Shaw started to laugh again in a way that was meant to be, but was not entirely, reassuring.

'Okay!' he declared largely, tossing all sensible deliberation aside. 'Out they go! And I'll put it down myself.' This girl had actually spent *her* money to get rid of *his* rats. This fact continued to strike him. No, he was not indifferent to it. 'Save you the trouble,' he added.

After this, Laura felt a vague sort of loyalty to the man. Somehow he had put her under an obligation.

Mrs. Vaizey sat in the sun on the tiny back balcony of their flat. From the rubbish-chute leading down to the incinerator there was a slight, disagreeable smell of burning paper. She stared out peevishly at the blue sky, the red-brick walls of buildings identical to the one in which she lived, at two pairs of striped pyjama trousers animated by the wind performing a sailor's hornpipe on the clothes-line next door.

To her brother Edward, she wrote: 'Something will have to happen soon. This can't go on. One's connections are all at home in England. Suburban life here is out of the question. The girls don't mind it. They are their father's daughters.'

Their father's daughters pushed through the Saturday morning shoppers, their string bags bumping and knocking. They worked their way into the butcher's shop, stood amongst women's backs and sides of beef and waited.

Coming out, Clare was radiant. 'Laura. That girl in the blue shorts in there. She smiled at me. Laura. She looked friendly. I thought she was going to speak to me. Laura? I wish—'

Laura was glancing down her list. She looked about for Clare. 'Where were you?'

'Here. I was telling you—'

No one ever listened. You might as well not have a voice. They walked on together. Clare's fair face was softly coloured and in the heat today as damp as a leafy plant. Again it brimmed with brightness, information, enthusiasm. 'Laura! Laura! Listen. In that milk bar just back there, there was a man who looked exactly like Dad. He saw us, too. He might have said something, if we hadn't been going so fast.'

Laura tutted as they angled in and out among the slower walkers.

'He was probably going to ask you to stop staring at him. You do this all the time.'

'No, he wasn't. I do not,' Clare defended herself and

mooched along watching the ground for a few moments. She knew she was always—not exactly staring at people, but looking out for them. Looking out.

'Well, that's the lot.' Laura eyed the pedestrian crossing up ahead that led homewards across the busy street, then looked down at her young sister, whose thick fair plaits dangled over her shoulders. Obscurely angry, she said, 'People can't just speak to other people in the street if they don't know them, Clare.'

'Why? What would happen if they did?'

In pictures, at Saturday matinees, strangers addressed each other constantly. They also danced on tables and sang in the open air, and no one appeared surprised. As for simply being friendly—there was nothing obvious, that she could see, to stop her from speaking to the very next person who passed.

'Why shouldn't they?'

'I know,' Laura said unwillingly, changing her heavy bag from her right to her left hand. 'Look out for that bus, Clare!' They dodged their way across the street and walked under a dark avenue of Moreton Bay figs. It was true. If you knew no one, Laura thought, and were not allowed to speak to someone till you knew him or her, how would you ever get to know anyone? Because you were unknown yourself, and could not be approached either.

She sighed.

'Laura. We've been in Sydney a long time now, haven't we? I worked it out.'

Laura nodded, thinking of the factory. The sun had an angry heat. They toiled up the steep hillside staring mutely into the bee-catching hibiscuses of apricot and watered-pink that lined the road.

Lying awake in bed, Laura heard the delivery car screech round the corner. Then the four tightly-rolled newspapers were hurled—ill-naturedly, it sounded—into the imitation-marble vestibule.

Clare was still asleep, invisible under the bed-clothes. Laura creaked cautiously out of the room, skimmed downstairs, skimmed up, and in the kitchen at the liver-coloured table, spread open the *Sydney Morning Herald* at the Leaving Certificate results. Curiously elated, she found her school and looked down the list, the omissions beginning to register in her mind. Jacqueline Smith had failed, and so had Paula, and so had Ruth. Yes, there were more names than Laura's missing.

She jumped. In the bedroom the clock clanged frantically. If no one attended to it, it was capable of dancing off the dressing-table with every sign of bad temper. Her heart shook. Silence came abruptly and Laura breathed out and moved her hands abstractedly over the paper, attempting to fold it up.

After her shower she returned to set her mother's tray and make the breakfast.

Even money can't buy everything.

The thought appeared vengefully in her mind as she tipped innocuous flakes of cereal into the three waiting plates. She paused, tilting the packet up, halting the stream.

Money can't buy everything.

The thought came back with a stab of triumph that was not nice: Laura was shocked. Hastily she set the packet down, switched on the wireless and coffee percolator, cut the bread for toast and listened with extreme agitation to a cigarette commercial.

Some of those girls like Jackie Smith used to receive an allowance twice as big as the wage Laura contributed to the housekeeping purse. Paula was one of several who had been promised a car if she passed this examination. She had not even scrambled through!

Crunching cereal to drown the voices in her head, she sat opposite Clare and pretended to listen to advertisements for beguiling brassières and invincible headache powders. The time was announced. Singers sang.

'And now we're going to give you John Charles Thomas and—*The Bluebird of Happiness.* A lovely thing, this.' The announcer's tone, coming through the small yellow radio, suggested that this was a piece of rare generosity on his part.

From chattering on about her history homework, Clare closed up instantly. Both girls buttered their toast and spread marmalade on it, chewing carefully not to miss a word.

Be like I, hold your head up high,
Soon you'll find the bluebird of happiness—

Was this true?

Gravely, they looked at each other over big coffee-cups.

You will see a ray of light creep through
So just remember this, life is no abyss
Somewhere there's a bluebird of happiness.

Really?

They had heard this story so often—almost every day—and it was so sincerely sung, perhaps it must be true. If it was, though, and they could not fail to find the bluebird, why did it sound so—lugubrious? There was another livelier song about a bluebird in your own backyard which was also much-favoured by record selectors.

Blessed with the ability to believe in miracles and magic, Clare had looked down over the brick balcony wall to the small cement square where the clothes were strung up, quite willing to see an actual, but magical, bluebird if one felt inclined to appear. Laura's nature was less elastic than that, but she had tried to imagine once or twice, when she was pegging sheets and dresses on the line, exactly what sort of event, what possible event, could occur in this small yard behind the flats that could change her life for the better. Or even in the flat itself. What could possibly happen?

Unless it turned out that her father had not really died?

Oh, but he must have. When she and Clare had gone home for a day after the funeral, all the neighbours had tiptoed in and out of the house with terrible faces.

You'll find your happiness lies
Right under your eyes
Back in your own backyard—

Unless it meant devoting herself less selfishly to her family? Laura felt dubious, but she did want to be faultless and to please her mother. Oh, especially to please her mother. So she continued to absorb the lyrics of songs, as Clare did, with secret earnestness. They contained news about the world, just as books and films did, and were addressed to them by impartial adult strangers. Apart from these fabled supra-human people who sent communiqués about life to them, they only knew their mother, Mr. Shaw, their elderly neighbours and Clare's teachers—none of whom were conversationalists, strictly speaking, or powerhouses of spirit and imagination.

Clare left her toast crusts and went to collect her mother's empty tray; Laura took back another cup of coffee, then the two rushed round with dusters and brooms.

The factory day started at eight, so Laura was always first to leave the flat. Walking down the hill this morning, for no good reason that she could think of, she began to cry, to produce, disconcertingly, from her chest, slow extraordinary sobs. She had hardly known that anyone *could* cry exposed on a steep hillside in the sun. Luckily there were few people about and none close to her. She wandered over the footpath from side to side, giving awful, surprising groans.

Laura would never know what she wanted not to know, therefore her grief, and that peculiar shifting and weakening sensation in her heart which had returned, mystified her. Tears fell down and spotted the asphalt; Laura blew her nose and looked desperately at the view.

It was very pretty—as suburban views go. There were the three tangled flame trees, and on her immediate right the grassy oval where men dressed in white flannels played cricket at weekends. Straight down the hill at the very bottom were the Norfolk pines and the sea. The shopping centre lay stretched out to the right below her on the flat strip of land between harbour and ocean, buildings mostly of two storeys. Local inhabitants liked to call Manly 'the Village'. Laura thought this sounded quite sweet, but for some reason Clare detested her saying it, and always screeched at her when she did.

'Hiya, Laurie!' Bernadette's cracked voice greeted her at the factory door.

Really, it turned out to be like every other day, except that she never forgot it.

'Well, you've been loafing about the place for a fair while now.' Mr. Shaw studied his wages book, and spoke to Laura without looking at her. 'I guess we'd better give you a rise or something, eh?' His voice grated with the effort of sounding cheerful. He had wanted to give this girl more money for months. He wanted very much to be generous and to have the reputation of being a generous man. He wanted so much to give, and yet he wanted not to, dreadfully. However, according to the law she was entitled to more money so willy-nilly, the increase was given. Laura hoped to keep some portion of it for herself, for her clothes were very shabby.

Clare had been allocated a place at a secondary school in town, and the ferry fares and the cost of her new uniform and equipment mounted never-endingly. Laura spoke about it to her mother when Clare had run down to the shops for some butter and eggs.

'It's hard on you, Laura.' Mrs. Vaizey looked up from her magazine and trailed an arm along the back of the sofa.

'I wondered,' Laura leaned on the mop and picked at a loose flake of green paint on the handle, 'I wondered if—out of what Dad left—you couldn't—'

Stella Vaizey shook her head and gave her daughter an oddly calculating smile. 'I've told you how we're placed. You know as well as I do what your father was like.' Shaking her head again, she lifted a fine china teacup (one of the few relics saved from the sale) from the small table by her side.

Laura left the paint alone and looked at her mother tenaciously, still leaning her weight on the mop.

'You'll break that, Laura!—No, I suggest we put it to someone in the Education Department that we must have Clare at the local high school.' Her small white teeth snapped a little coconut biscuit in two. She ate one half of the biscuit with paralysing slowness, watching Laura all the while in a bright, patient, impersonal way.

Laura took a deep breath through her mouth, pressed her lips together and lunged away with the mop, starting to push it to and fro over the varnished boards surrounding the emerald carpet. 'No. They only give them domestic science courses here. I've got this rise. We'll manage.'

'If your father had thought of this instead of those stupid investments of his—' Popping the other half of the biscuit into her mouth, she dusted her fingertips lightly together. 'Look, I've sprinkled crumbs on your clean floor.'

* * *

In September a war started.

'What are they *doing* it for?' Clare asked, and her mother said, 'You can read. There's the paper. Find out.' And the reasons were listed there in order of merit.

People were dying.

'How does—killing—fix all this? How does it—put this all right? Who does killing people please?'

'Oh, don't *prattle*, Clare!' her sister said.

'Don't be more childish than you have to be!' her mother said.

'I only—'

But it seemed the oldest sorcery to Clare. Strangers rushed out in the night to slaughter each other. Their blood seeped into the earth. Who benefited? In what way could lifeless flesh right wrongs?

'You're only a child,' they said. 'Be quiet. Nobody *likes* it.'

Nevertheless, it was happening.

She only knew she was a person. To be alive felt highly remarkable. She was a world. She felt this to be equally true of the people she passed in the street. Who had been given the power (and by whom?) to extinguish such creations? Who could want to make them bleed? To accede to the view that deaths could bring happiness and peace seemed to her wilful and terrifying insanity, like agreeing that black and white adds up to toads, and three and four make bones. How could she agree to give herself up since, in some way, she was not hers to give? How could she say, 'Yes, torture those people in the street!'?

She was eleven and brooded on the possibility of reaching Adolph Hitler's side. It was very clear that no one had thought to speak rationally to the man. He was terribly mistaken, did not understand. If a great voice from heaven would cry for all the world to hear simultaneously, 'Stop!' and if, in the universal silence that followed, during which all marvelled, mild and joyful and sorrowing, it could then be explained—

Mr. Shaw uttered jovial warnings to Laura from time to time as if, somehow, the calamity might affect her, but not him. (He did actually say that it wouldn't interfere with him. Laura was relieved to know that she would not lose her job.) There were yellow newspaper placards to glance at walking home in the evenings, and activity, and elation, and even something strangely like jubilation.

Mrs. Vaizey shrugged at the great south land's superficial restrictions on the purchase of food and clothing. 'Austerity makes no difference when you're as poor as us!'

At the factory the girls prepared to sacrifice themselves as war-brides and chanted off the contents of their 'glory-boxes' daily. Everyone had a boyfriend or a brother in the forces, it appeared, except the Vaizeys.

Having no servicemen to contribute to the lunch-time conversation, Laura accepted her unimportance and humbly listened.

'For his next leave I'm making this dress. It's sort of *swathed* over the bust like this and very tight under*neath* the bust, and then it's gathered like this at the waist, and—' Bernadette, seventeen, boiled the electric jug five times a day and disappeared to wash her troublesome complexion.

'Jimmy's gonna send me one of them leather bags with all Egyptian mummies on it.' Diane, who worried about her weight and dieted when she remembered not to eat chocolate biscuits.

'I'm lookin' for a dress-length at dinner-time and it's gotta be the exact same colour as this Purple Wine lipstick.' Shirley, who danced five nights at least out of seven, and was glamorous.

Laura liked the girls; they were good-hearted, but even after a long acquaintance it was easy to offend them. Bernadette looked astounded and scowled incredulously when Laura once said the word 'cameo'.

'*What* she say?—Would you mind not talkin' Chinese, love? It's too hard on me brain-box.'

Now Laura was astounded and mortified. She expunged 'cameo' from her vocabulary for ever. But it was almost as easy to inflame bad feeling by saying an attractive but not lethal word like 'San Francisco'.

'Well, what's that?' Diane looked baited.

'The city.' Laura's voice was faint.

'Oh.' A very flat silence. Evidently she had given them a white-hot forty-seven-sided puzzle to pick up.

'Where is it then?' Greta demanded grudgingly. 'Up north, do you mean?'

'In America.' Light-headed, Laura lifted a batch of receipts from the desk. Reality was a child's Meccano skyscraper, and the game was to surprise the toy inhabitants by pulling the floors from under them.

'America! Well, how did that get into the act? *I* wasn't sayin' anything about America!'

Her young tutors forgave Laura much, however, the day she too was persuaded to buy a Purple Wine lipstick, after holding out against it so long that they had deemed themselves criticised.

Mrs. Vaizey smiled. 'Good heavens, Laura! Blue lips! You look as if rigor mortis had set in. You look like a far-advanced heart case.'

There was a war on.

On Saturdays at the pictures, newsreels showed the bombed cities of Europe and later still the deserts of the Middle East and the northern jungles, streaming jungles where trees walked and killed. Callow, shallow, safe, ashamed, the Vaizey girls were part of an audience that witnessed the destruction of the light of the world from cushiony red seats in the lilac-scented disinfected dark. They were pressed back on themselves and their few square inches of knowledge and experience. They felt in themselves and each other the inadequacy, hollowness and frustration of one seeking water at a dry spring.

Walking slowly home they talked with an empty excited despondency. Laura more easily wound herself up to judge, pronounce, and theorise, but Clare only ground the soles of her shoes harder into the footpath and, grated, said, 'What's the use? We don't *know*. We don't *know*. I mean—' She only meant it felt something like blasphemous, something like licentious, for their ignorance to speak, improvise opinions, consider its emotions in this situation. 'I mean—we don't know anything.'

Laura stood in a thicket of people where the bare sunburned arms of strangers touched each other, to watch the soldiers marching down Elizabeth Street to the Quay and the waiting ships.

'It's a shame the kids are all at school. They should give the boys a proper send-off on a Saturday when—'

Trumpets came level suddenly, sopping up voices, eyes, attention, flashing, passing. Drums, boots, a mesmerising march tune that compelled the most blasé-seeming of pedestrians to fall in with the '*left*, *left*, I had a good job but I *left*' of marching boots. Slouch hats, khaki, bayonets glittering, flags performing in the wind.

'North. That's what they say. That's where they need 'em.'

Brown-faced soldiers, and more soldiers. (*Left, left*, I had a good job but I *left*.) Another band playing with pitiless gaiety.

'They look pretty tough, eh? Look like fighters, don't they? Good old Aussies—'

Again the crowd cried out, and again cheered, and soon another heart-wrenching band was heard in the distance approaching.

Laura watched, and was not the only one to glance up and away from the *left, left*, of sparkling tan boots to the high brick walls of the insensible department stores and office buildings opposite.

Pausing over the ironing of a blue cotton dress, she said to her mother, 'Even Clare's doing something at school with these exhibitions the teachers fix to send bundles to Britain.'

'Well, don't tell *me* if you want to send someone a bundle.' Brittle with boredom, Stella Vaizey looked up at Laura, then looked a moment longer than she had intended, and even made a suggestion. 'Since you can't knit, and I don't quite see you entertaining a serviceman,' she laughed a little, 'you'd better join something.'

From an hour's consideration of 'Clubs' in the telephone directory, Laura drew the names of three

39

organisations. At the first one, the enamelled woman behind the desk looked her over with a single intimidating flicker of her eyelashes.

'*What* was it you wanted?' (She could not have heard correctly.) 'To join the club?—I see. Do you know any members? Three members must sponsor your application, of course.—Then I'm afraid—'

An American colonel pushed through the swing-doors and lamps were lighted behind this lady's suddenly beautiful blue eyes. Someone was at home after all!

Laura took herself off, rocking uneasily on her high heels in the rubbery carpet. She had had no conception that the club would be so—rich. Exclusive. They wanted—they *said* they wanted people to help, but—There was a roaring fire of embarrassment in her chest; not only her face but the whole of her boiled and blazed as she staggered knee-deep (it felt) in the asphalt pavement back to the Quay. It was Saturday afternoon. She had hoped to announce to her mother and Clare—

At the next club, a week later, she turned out to be too young; at the next one, she was not a member of the Church; at the one after that, the entrance fee was three guineas.

Not the girl to pass off these rejections with a self-protective and negligent wave of the hand, she stared at her mother for advice.

'Rome wasn't built in a day,' Mrs. Vaizey said. 'Remember Bruce and the spider.'

'Just a jiff.' The greengrocer was a middle-aged, middle-sized man with thinning hair and brown eyes. like small stones.

Mrs. Vaizey had said, 'Find out from one of the shopkeepers where we go to collect our new ration books. Ask anyone.' So Clare asked him after he had served her with potatoes and onions and started to pick over, in the fashion of a browsing animal who has spent a lifetime in one bare paddock, his spotted apples.

'Now, look,' he said, brushing his hands over his canvas apron before using them to point with.

Clare stood with him in the doorway of his shop. He smelled like a fruit salad. Evidently he was thinking hard. He looked as single-minded as a commando. 'See that hill up there? Well, you go *up* there. You turn *left* at the second lot of cross-roads. You keep *straight on* for a block. You go *over*—'

While looking at him more or less rationally, and trying to absorb his brain-bending instructions, Clare began to be aware of a current of charm and joy humming through her. The man kept talking. She wished he would never stop. She herself had become a pinpoint astronomically distant, silence, light.

Oh, man, she thought without words. Oh, man. I love you.

Life was hard. He was harmless. He had forgotten her. He was all concentration, and innocent, and vulnerable. Clare only knew he awed and thrilled her, that she at the same time knelt to him and protected him out of an ocean of warmth she suddenly had at her disposal.

'Well, 've you got that? Do you know where you're going?'

'Oh, yes,' she lied ardently.

'Well, you're set like a jelly!' In his trance again, in his enclosure where the earth was eaten bare, he glanced at the girl and ambled back to his work.

Clare reeled away down the street, not thinking at all. She could have hugged his knees. Oh, how wonderful! Wonderful! The man was beautiful! She could fly. She could electrify the air. She could create—cause—That wasn't it. She knew—had witnessed—understood—felt—

She leapt along the footpath, a new Philippides, alight, alight. Glory!

Twice she lost her way to the ration book centre and finally had to ask for directions again, but she only turned down the volume of joy in order to hear, then swooned up the hill, her head ringing with it.

'Mr. Shaw must be making a lot of money, Laura?'

Stella Vaizey and her daughter were sitting together on the small back balcony. Laura was drying her hair in the sun, and shelling peas into a pot.

'He is. I think he must be.'

'Aren't there any restrictions on that stuff he uses?'

'He has a friend who gets it for him. All the men who come in to see him say he should expand, but I think he'd rather sell out to Mr. Roberts.'

When Laura saw the two men together the following day, however, she wondered if Mr. Shaw did not want more to please Mr. Roberts than to sell him the business. A long-faced morose-looking man with lank brown hair, and perhaps ten years younger than Felix Shaw, Jack Roberts appeared to have appropriated the vacant position of boon companion to her employer. They held muttered conversations in the corner of the room for hours on end. Mr. Roberts was an excellent listener, but occasionally he put in a dry-sounding remark that brought on one of Mr. Shaw's spasms of laughing. Yet even when Jack Roberts was being (presumably) funny, Laura thought he had an almost dangerous, unamused look in his eyes. Mr. Shaw once remarked to her with heavy pride, 'Mr. Roberts is pretty high up in the black market, you know.'

Ron Moffat, the bank manager, was walking past the factory on Monday morning when Laura and Felix Shaw emerged with armfuls of airy cartons to stack in the car.

'If you sell this concern, Felix, I'll pay for you to have your head examined. It's the coming thing! The coming thing! After the war—plastics, all these new materials. You're in on the ground floor. God knows where you get your stuff, and I'm not going to ask you. But hang on to it!'

Jack Roberts pulled a dog-eared contract of sale from his pocket that very afternoon.

Mr. Shaw said, 'Oh, a handshake on it'll do me, Jack. A gentleman's agreement. I trust you!' He laughed very much saying this, and his eyes were moist.

Jack Roberts grinned. 'No, you don't! Strictly legal. You might try and back out. I've got my boy lined up for eleven tomorrow morning.'

A great excessive shrug of acquiescence was torn out of Mr. Shaw. He hardly knew what to do with himself. His smile was unhappy, his eyes searching. 'Right! Right you are, then!' He was asking for a ludicrously small sum which he had agreed, in effect, to lend Jack Roberts, on ludicrously easy terms.

The factory girls went with the stock, but Mr. Shaw said, 'Reckon I might keep the typist. Got her trained to my methods.' He was combing the city and suburbs for a broken-down business to build up.

'Sure, sure. You're welcome.' Jack Roberts slid his cold gaze over the unsophisticated typist.

'You're a grown woman now, Laura, and you can please yourself whether you look for a new job or go with him,' her mother said. 'Mr. Shaw's always been kind to you.'

'How?' Clare asked, turning aside from her homework, looking at them out of her light-grey eyes, and using the end of her long plait as a shaving-brush against her chin.

Laura grimaced uncertainly, meeting her eyes. ('You can please yourself!') Mr. Shaw—She didn't know him. He never had much to say. He had never once called her Laura. '*You*,' he said. She was considerably more surprised than flattered that he wanted her to remain with him, though she *was* flattered. ('You can please yourself!') And then, surely, if he had sold the box factory, it was to invest in some pleasanter, more inherently interesting business?

'How?' Clare asked again, lightly crunching the end of her plait between her front teeth.

'Unless there's anything about the man you haven't mentioned to me, Laura?'

'No. What do you mean?'

'He gave you stockings and chocolates last Christmas. Admittedly, he gave the factory girls a cash bonus, but you wouldn't have wanted to be on the same footing with them.'

Mr. Shaw—Laura stood thinking inside herself. When he did speak it was only ever about work. Sometimes he disappeared for a few days without warning, but he never confided, when he came back, 'I've been fishing,' or 'I've had a cold.' He was a mystery to her.

'A pound a week rise!' Clare said, spreading the

loose end of her plait like a fan. 'Still, it's not worth it if you don't like him.'

'Who said she didn't?' Stella Vaizey was cross. 'Saying to talk it over with her family. He sounds a very nice man.'

'I'll go with him.'

'Please yourself, Laura. I've got no desire to influence you one way or the other.' Mrs. Vaizey's interest in bridge outstripped by light-years any other feeling ever to have moved her.

Clare went up another year at school.

Mr. Shaw bought an almost defunct home-made chocolate factory not far from the site of his former business. ('Might be able to look in and give old Jack a hand.') He expected strenuousness from Laura and she, with mental energy to spare and practice in providing older people with what they expected, buried herself in her job daily. At the very beginning she had found it difficult to think of boxes with the respect due to saleable products, and she had a slight struggle even now to take chocolates seriously; but habit, which had, after all, accustomed her to her life, was training her. *Money*, she began to think, with some reverence.

'Those Americans are chasing us,' Clare laughed, looking over her shoulder as she and her sister ran for the ferry. 'Should we let them catch us?'

'No!'

46

In Sydney there were fifty uniformed Americans on leave to every woman, and the section of the population that felt inclined for exercise was able to indulge in a marathon game of chasings round the sunny streets and beaches.

On the ferry, uniformed boys asked, 'May we sit and talk with you?' and then with great politeness began to collect facts about the girls' lives. Looking out at the harbour's islands and bays, at the fleets of camouflaged ships, the white-painted hospital ships, the submarine boom across the entry to the inner harbour, they amiably described their own homes and families, speaking in Hollywood accents that made them seem like characters rather than people. But Clare often whispered, the warm resonance of her breath like a bee in Laura's ear, 'This one's really lonely, not just kidding. Couldn't we take him home?'

Laura only had to look at her. They had never taken *anyone* home.

At Manly Wharf, when they left the ferry, more than once they drank chocolate malteds or orange juice with some thin tanned American boy, his face and uniform without a single crease. And more than once, not exactly by arrangement, but not quite accidentally either, Laura met the same boy two or three weeks in succession. Leaves were short, however, and boys disappeared. That they disappeared from *her* life was probably opportune. 'No,' was all she could say to every effort to entertain, for she could not endure the thought of her mother's supercilious, 'A-soldier-who-picked-you-up-Laura?'

Besides, her mother was right: nice boys would never speak to strange girls in the street.

Mr. Shaw was crestfallen never to find Jack Roberts in when he called at the old box factory. He had had a lot of time for Jack; he had liked their yarns about the black-market rackets Jack was in on, and it confirmed everything he knew and tickled him deeply to hear how not one honourable gentleman in the continent would refuse to pocket Jack's bribes.

The factory was unrecognisable now. Jack had knocked out walls left, right and centre. He had a swag of females, a packer, a delivery truck, and God knew what else. After wandering in a few times and standing round like a poor relation waiting for Jack, who never turned up, to turn up, Mr. Shaw gave these social calls away. The cheap little bits who worked for Jack sniggered and asked each other, 'Who's Dracula come to see?'

But it was rough, when you came to think of it, not to have clapped eyes on Jack since they signed the bill of sale. And having reminded himself of the bill, a copy of which was always in his wallet, Mr Shaw looked up Jack's address in the telephone book and detoured off up to the North Shore after unloading a few gross of peppermint creams in town. 'Just passing, Jack!'

Lo and behold! (which was rather how it struck him) Jack's house was a two-storeyed mansion in a sort of Millionaires' Row, with a huge garden and a glimpse through big double-barrelled gates of what looked extremely like a swimming pool out at the front. You would have needed high explosives to blast your way into the grounds.

Felix Shaw drove away very fast, chewing it all over in his mind, and sweating with a curious relief that he had not been spotted. Jack was a married man: the place might belong to his wife. No explanation of this sort exactly fitted Jack's description of his circumstances, but there was nothing wrong with *Jack*. Possibly if Felix had known the cove wasn't really on his uppers, he might not—But a deal was a deal. It was a fair price he had received for the factory, even if it erred maybe one decimal point in Jack's favour. Perhaps the house back there was misleading. A businessman had to put up a prosperous front. Also, old Jack definitely was not doing the business that all the activity at the factory might lead you to expect: his payments were falling further and further behind.

'Come and have a look at this.' Mr. Shaw and Laura were in the car together and it was Friday afternoon. Laura had dashed solemnly in and out of city shops delivering chocolates while he kept the engine running. Now on the way back to Manly, he pulled up unexpectedly in Neutral Bay in a street close to the harbour. 'Bought myself a house yesterday.'

It was a lovely single-storeyed colonial house painted white, with a roof of grey slate and long shady verandahs decorated with old wrought iron. There were lawns. There were daphne and camellia and gardenia bushes with dark shiny leaves. In the garden behind the house there were fruit trees, two of which were hung with enormous lemons, sweetly scented.

Inside, the rooms were large and cool, and stood awaiting furniture and embellishment at the hands of their new owner. A pattern of leaves, criss-crossed and winking light, blew and shivered on the empty white wall of the sitting-room as the poplars at the side of the house shook and sent shadows indoors.

'Well, what do you think? And how about that view?' Mr. Shaw was so strangely jocular that for an instant Laura wondered if the house really did belong to him, or whether he was trespassing as a kind of joke.

'It's beautiful. It's the loveliest house I've ever been in.'

She glanced through the bare french windows, over the greenness of grass and flowering hedges to the blue ship-laden harbour, and the city beyond it. She had no idea what she was thinking.

An enterprising young chap (as Mr. Shaw described him) called Peter Trotter, opened a speciality shop in the city to sell Shaw's factory-produced home-made chocolates exclusively.

Peter Trotter said, 'You can sell anything these days, but you can still sell a good sweet easier than a bad, and this line of yours is unique.' He had three languid beauties, predictably blonde, brunette and redhead, attending to his uniformed clients. He himself, spruce and pallid, helped the ladies who drifted in, drenched with perfume, clanking charm bracelets, complaining glamorously to him about clothes coupons (which he had supplies of) and runs in the unobtainable nylon stockings so thoughtfully provided by American friends.

The ladies' hair was often dramatically tinted and lacquered into wicker baskets with a week's life expectancy. Peter Trotter admired these artful arrangements and his scented callers' prosperity generally. Everyone was playing a part that called for a special American or British accent. It was lovely. The Imperial Arcade, where his little shop was, was lovely. There were ornaments like miniature chandeliers or monster pendant-earrings hanging from the arcade walls, and when the wind swept through from Pitt to Castlereagh Street their long stems chinked and tinkled like glass music in the air.

'No,' Peter shook his head, looking through his window at the ladies wearing violets and camellias on their winter suits. (He could never fathom what anyone found to complain about these war-time days.) 'No. These sweets of yours are unique.'

Felix Shaw laughed slowly, but was none the happier for the praise. Indeed, the very reverse was true. Something elusive, something desirable, something Peter Trotter had found in Shaw's Chocolates was passing him by, though *he* had invented them. Practically.

'Do you think you could ask Mr. Shaw if there's some job Clare might have at the factory now that she's fourteen?'

'Oh, no!'

'Why not? It's good enough for you. Not in the factory, of course, but helping you.' Mrs. Vaizey unscrewed her jar of hand cream and looked imperturbably at her eldest daughter.

'We-ell.' Laura paused.

'If you didn't want to work with her, I wouldn't blame you.' Mrs. Vaizey raised her voice a little, and massaged cream into her hands soothingly.

Out in the kitchen, Clare was washing dishes—a fair, provoking, indolent, moody, silent, sarcastic girl.

'Oh, she's a difficult girl!' Mrs. Vaizey shook her head with a sort of indifferent vexation; she had other, urgent interests looming. Breathing and pondering and smoothing her slippery hands together she looked through to the kitchen again. She had never had any trouble with Laura; Laura had never treated her like this. There was a kind of dangerousness, almost, in the girl at times. A fierceness. People talked about caged tigers and, really, Mrs. Vaizey knew what they meant.

Scraping at a burnt saucepan, Clare listened to the ravings of the philosophical *Bluebird of Happiness*.

Laura hesitated before flinging the blue chenille cover over her mother's bed. Then she did throw it over and leaned across to tuck it under the pillows.

'Now don't sulk with me, Laura. I won't have it, you know. You think she should go to a business college, do you? Oh, we all know you were going to be a great specialist or a second Melba, but Clare doesn't want to be anything. You'll both be married in a few years' time. Still, I suppose we could manage it if it would satisfy you both. Clare! Come here!'

'What?'

'I'll tell you. Your Uncle Edward wants me to go back home to England, to Somerset, now that he's retired there. People are asking for me. All my old friends. This country's never been home to me. It's different for you two. You don't know any better.'

Their faces would not even try to express their feelings.

Laura sat down on the end of the bed. 'Leave us? Go to England in the middle of the war?'

'It can't last indefinitely. I'd go anyway.'

'The other side of the world,' Laura said.

Clare stood, feeling dizzy.

Turning from the triple-sided mirror to face her girls and their surprise, Mrs. Vaizey said mildly, 'It's no use saying the war, the war, to me. Uncle Edward's fixing my passage from his end. He knows people. And by the time I go, Clare will be settled in her job, and you can both be bachelor girls together. What's wrong with that?—Laura, on Monday morning I want you to ask Mr. Shaw if he can get me a cabin trunk wholesale.'

'What job?' Clare asked.

'Do they still make them?' Laura brushed a fly off her knee. 'Cabin trunks?'

Walking home past Manly Pool, deserted, seaweedy and bleak, this stormy evening, the girls had agreed to point out the soldier's bus rank at the end of the street. He was from the country and lost. Even Laura felt there was no harm in him. Then Clare had to make everything complicated by asking, 'What will you do when it's over?' and he smiled such a smile, right into her eyes.

'Architecture or design,' the swarthy young soldier said. 'One or the other.'

Clare nodded her belief and readiness to be told more.

'Have you ever watched one of these big buildings going up? My uncle was a contractor. I used to hang round his jobs when I came for holidays. These buildings—if they're any good—you can see how they follow the pattern of any living thing in nature. See this leaf!' He had only to put out his hand and an example fell into it. 'See how the veins grow progressively thinner towards the top where they've got less to support? Wait a minute. Even in cathedrals— Where's some paper?' He was in all his pockets. 'I'll show you.'

They sat on the wooden seat at the bus stop while he drew lines with professional assurance on the back of a yellow travel permit, breathing, half-smiling, like someone quite alone. Laura's interest was neutralised by her formal terror that he might miss his bus. Buses were large important machines that ought not to be trifled with. They would not change their departure times because of any tomfoolery like this. The boy was only doing this to show off or entice them, or—

'Do you see this grid effect?' Using his pencil as a pointer he began his explanation again, stammering in his eagerness, glancing up, quickly side-tracked into further beautiful lines.

Clare was only awareness of him. Her intuition rejoiced. Oh, human! He was human! Unconscious of unfamiliar girls or what they thought of him. Willing to be defenceless. Without the smallest motive. His simplicity was holy. He was wonderful. Mentally she bowed to him. She would have embraced him with her arms and sent blessings from her fingertips but that the quality she saluted could not have existed side by side with a knowledge of itself. Weak with happiness, she sat beside the fabulous boy.

'There's your bus,' Laura said, with shattering commonsense. 'You'll miss it if you don't run. And we'd better get home, Clare.'

The hand with the blunt pencil stopped sketching those dull lines. Laura was glad. 'Oh!' The soldier looked up slowly, as after a blow, and shyly, with regret. 'Oh! I'm sorry. If I'd had time—' he moved off backwards towards the bus, talking, '— I could've shown you what—'

'It's going!' Laura warned him, and with a loose smiling shrug, he turned and ran.

'What's so funny?' Laura asked her young sister as the bus lurched away.

The street lights all came on suddenly.

'Nothing!' Clare sounded indignant. She started off across the road.

'Look where you're going!—Well, you were laughing! Laura said strictly.

'I was not!' (What a thing to say!) 'I was just—' She looked up over the buildings at the flat grey evening sky and with her face turned right away from Laura's, she smiled.

Mr. Shaw listened, then he said, 'Going away, is she? You and Clare'll be by yourselves, eh?'

He and Laura were checking Peter Trotter's order prior to stacking it in the car. The temperature was well over ninety.

Laura started to draw a flower over the tick beside the Coconut Roughs. 'Yes. We'll move into a boarding-house.' She added some thorns.

'What's the trouble, then? Come on. You'd better tell me.'

Startled, Laura looked up from her order into his hot dark-brown eyes. The sensation she had of his eyes' heat half-hypnotised her. His tone was excessive in some way that was disturbing, almost disagreeable to her. He stood over her in her chair, mouth closed, lips down-turned in a smile as if he thought—what he couldn't possibly think! How kind to take an interest in her affairs!

She looked down quickly. 'It's only that—it's unexpected. If my mother had stayed we might've kept Clare at school. Things like that.'

'Mmm.' He moved his mouth ruminatively, never quite displacing that superior smile and its odd suggestion of complicity. Again he hummed out that long reflective noise. 'I don't know if we couldn't fix that up.'

Laura was aware suddenly that her eyes felt strained and sore; the skin of her lips felt taut and cracked with the heat. Talking in this personal way to Mr. Shaw made her feel nervous and giddy, or just peculiar and unlike herself.

'Oh, yes,' he said, smiling his significant, enigmatic smile. 'I think we could arrange something for young Clare, all right.' He looked very merry. His eyes wandered over the yellow calcimined walls as if they were covered with convulsively funny murals.

'What do you mean?'

Taking in her bewilderment, Mr. Shaw rolled his eyes quickly away from hers in an extreme of secret glee. 'Better forget all that Mr. Shaw stuff for a start,' he advised her in his smiling growl. 'Yes,' he said, looking at the dirty wall rather critically now, 'I think we can take care of that little problem. I think you'd better just marry me, and both of you come to live in the new house. I'll fix everything.'

Apart from her father, the neighbours of those remote country days and, more recently, men who sold vegetables, meat and fish to her over counters, and the few young soldiers who spoke on trams and ferries, Laura had never known any men. By this time she had been longer in the company of Felix Shaw than of any other man, but she had never thought she knew him. He was more than twenty years older than she was for one thing; he employed her, for another. Nor had it ever occurred to Laura that he had any interest in her. He had certainly never shown it. He had always concentrated on this particular gross of boxes, or these special

Easter eggs for Peter Trotter. After years of daily contact she knew virtually nothing about his past, his friends, his private life. He was rarely unpleasant to the staff and at Christmas time he gave them bonuses, but his attitude was never familiar in the sense of being relaxed and assured. He was abstracted, ignored them, lost in accounts; or he was gruffly jovial, laughing in a hearty, not very natural manner. When the older women who worked as confectioners presumed to flatter him with a deference that was at once obvious and sly, he took it in good part. In fact, he seemed almost bashful.

On the telephone now and then Laura had heard his voice slur with anger when someone tried to argue with him, but she always leapt out of hearing with conspicuous discretion at these times. What she definitely knew was that to younger men struggling to establish businesses he could be extraordinarily generous—to the extent of penalising himself.

With his hat tilted and his jacket flapping open he sometimes entered the office like a buccaneer with an invisible crew of attendant and loving cut-throats. He had no opinion of the law, Laura knew that, and several times he had boasted of his admiration for Hitler and the Gestapo! But really, she didn't know him at all.

'That's settled then, is it? You'll marry me and you and your sister'll come to the house in Neutral Bay.—What's the matter? You don't want to marry anyone else, do you?'

'No.'

'Well okay then!'

Apparently he wanted very much to marry her. He wanted her to live in his beautiful house. He wanted to help and take care of her, be responsible even for Clare. Mr. Shaw, Felix Shaw, Felix, a stranger who had no obligation to, had all his attention focused on her, hoped for something of her, asked her a favour, wanted to be kind as this to her.

'I'll give you a couple of days,' he said.

'I don't know,' Laura said to her mother and Clare.

The three women sat at the table in the small dining alcove eating lamb cutlets, green peas and tomatoes. The evening was hot and airless; outside, it was still daylight. Flies zoomed and glided near the ceiling, occasionally darting down to raid the table and be flapped away. The electric refrigerator vibrated rhythmically in the kitchen.

'No one else can decide for you. It could be a very pleasant solution to everything, but—' she extended both hands gracefully, eloquently. Chewing composedly, she eyed her younger daughter, whose face was expressionless.

'I don't know,' Laura said again, but smiled and looked down.

'Does he talk to you about anything interesting? I think he sounds too *old*,' Clare broke in.

'One day I'll give you such a box over the ears you'll wonder what's happened to you! Take no notice of her, Laura.—Well, I suppose Mr. Shaw will give you five minutes to make up your mind. I'll talk to him too.'

Felix Shaw collected the Vaizeys in his car, which, Mrs. Vaizey remarked later, closely resembled a hearse, and took them all to dinner at the Metropole. Throughout the meal he held the floor, laughing and joking so much and sometimes so incomprehensibly that his guests looked at each other bemused, as if they had stumbled in in the middle of a comedy performance that was paralysing the rest of the audience, just too late ever to see the point. No one else really talked at all. Laughing was a change, however.

The next family outing was to the house at Neutral Bay, where Mr. Shaw was not yet living. Wandering round the lawns and underneath the trees, standing on the verandah looking over the harbour, walking through the echoing rooms, they could scarcely refrain from assuming a faintly proprietorial manner. He invited them to. Mrs. Vaizey advised the dark-skinned, stocky, laughing man who might marry Laura, to visit auction sales and antique shops.

Clare looked about the pretty room that would be hers if Laura chose for some bizarre reason to belong to Felix Shaw.

In two months' time Mrs. Vaizey was due to sail for England. Clare plaited her hair and watched the

61

arrival of the cabin trunk that meant one change, and the chocolates, nylon stockings, silver trays and wine glasses that meant another.

Because they proved Felix Shaw's regard, Laura was besotted by her presents, though in another indefinable way they made her uneasy. But Felix gave in so ungracious a manner (if she wouldn't take these rubbishy trifles off his hands, the garbage tin or the office cleaner would) that she was half-reassured. All he implied was that they would marry when her mother left because it would be convenient and sensible.

Felix took the Vaizeys to a play at the Theatre Royal after dinner at the Australia. Apart from pantomimes and school productions of Shakespeare, it was the girls' first experience of theatre. Clare analysed the play and the performance for weeks, and schemed to return to that red velvet curtain.

Felix escorted Laura to small restaurants at Kings Cross, and drove her to well-worn beauty spots that she had never seen. The roads smelled peculiarly of wood-alcohol, the use of which was prohibited and impossible to keep secret, but which made cars run, and was handy since the government had decided in its arbitrary way to ration petrol. 'Pure cussedness,' Felix called this act. 'Just what you'd expect from that lousy crew.'

Everything was new to Laura: eating foreign food, riding in cars instead of buses and trams, seeing some trees and patches of open country, having someone notice her, getting to know the city she had always felt shy in, an interloper from the bush. Her mother had always *said* something nice would turn up. Her mother was pleased about Felix.

The knowledge that she could, if she chose, be relieved of all her responsibilities, lifted Laura to such heights that she felt almost literally buoyant. Not to have to worry and plan for three seemed so glorious a collection of negatives that Laura supposed she must be terrifically happy. Evidently, it looked as if, she loved Felix Shaw.

Clare had turned very noisy.

After years of solitary confinement, after silence, starvation, house arrest, nights lurid with dreams of war and death, after school's juggernaut lunacy, lamb chops and the price of peas, new things were happening.

'Do be quiet, Clare. I can't hear myself think.' Mrs. Vaizey had a million details on her mind. The singing stopped.

'Laura—Laura—' Cunningly she tried to wrest her sister from her vast dreamy preoccupation by speaking low. 'Listen to this: *"But for Roderick, on the bridge beside her, this moment had a quite different sense— some sort of assuagement or satisfaction at her having rested even so much of her as her hands, for however short a time, on even this bar of unknowing wood. His pity, speaking to her out of the stillness of his face, put her in awe of him, as of a greater sufferer than herself— no pity is ignorant, which is pity's cost."* Laura? Don't you think that's—'

'What?' Laura sounded asleep though her eyes were open. 'I'm busy. I wish you'd keep quiet.'

'Sure! Who cares?' Clare rushed away, clutching the book she had quoted from, begging its forgiveness. Not she, but something beautiful had been traduced. Oh, but I know what you mean, she exulted, holding it to her on the dark balcony and smiling like someone in love. I truly do.

How she knew, the particular occasion of her knowing, she could not remember. But, yes, the gratitude and relief of the witness seeing those hands on the harmless rail of the bridge—

She knew about pity. Every day, every day, people walked on clouds of illusion. In that play at the Theatre Royal there was an actress who thought herself lovely, and who was plump and too old for the part. The leading actor meant to be brilliant and subtle, yet no single gesture or inflexion was inspired by talent. Clare's heart was wrung. She suffered for them, loved and shielded them. When they bowed before the curtain and beamed at the applause, tears rolled down her cheeks. It was unbearable. They must never know.

Daily, she heard conversations from adults and from adolescents who, starting from some illogical premise in space, constructed gingerbread houses trimmed with *non sequiturs* and stood back to assess their handiwork with pride and gravity. They thought they knew what they were saying! They thought that what they said had meaning! Girls were bewitched by their own ability to curl their hair and embroider hideous daisies on hideous teacloths. Boys boasted because they could eat five potatoes with a roast dinner. Oh, accomplished! Oh, somnambulists! Silence, everyone! Take care!

On the balcony to which she had retreated, forearms resting on its brick wall, Clare summarily called up her dear ones and relations out of books. They knew her. What did it matter if there had never been anyone about to talk to? These others knew the real world was not tables and chairs and meat and vegetables—or that, given food and shelter, you could surely agree to, had obligations to—venture out? With her head on her folded arms, she stood dreaming.

'I tell you what.' Felix and Laura were eating cheese-and-gherkin sandwiches in the office. 'To save rents overlapping, we'll get it over the morning your mother's sailing. She can come and check up on us and you can move into my house the same day. How's that?'

'Yes. All right.' Laura put down her chipped cup. She felt lately like someone on a runaway train: events flashed by like stations, with no reference at all to her.

'Well, then!' Felix jumped up and gave her a boisterous kiss and pretended to punch her chin, and smiled into her face. 'Hiya, Mrs. Shaw! You better put your thinking-cap on. We've got work to do.'

The factory, the flat, Felix's house, her mother's departure, and wedding arrangements, all concurrently required Laura's total concentration.

'No churches!' Felix warned her. 'Morbid damn' places. Give you the willies. A registry office's the shot. You don't want veils and all that hocus-pocus.'

'No. No.' On the contrary. Laura was stupid with relief. Who would want to stand in a church with dozens of friends and relations on Felix's side, and exactly two people on hers? In bed at night she had suffered over this picture.

'How do you account for it?' Felix-the-vision asked, twisting his eyebrows. 'You must be a very unpopular girl.'

All she could ever think of to say, was, 'But no one knows about us. No one has ever known we were here.'

In the course of packing, Mrs. Vaizey sold a few of what she called her 'treasures from the old days'— ugly pieces of silver for the most part—and from the proceeds bought Laura's wedding clothes. Laura herself possessed seventeen pounds, and Clare had five in the bank.

'I'll be in it,' Peter Trotter said, agreeing to act as a witness. 'The girls can look after the shop. They won't eat too many of the best lines. They're all slimming.'

Felix drove between the flat and the house, and the factory and Peter's shop. Carriers removed Mrs. Vaizey's luggage. Her daughters unpacked at Felix's the night before the wedding.

When the ceremony was over, and she was about to board the ship, Mrs. Vaizey said, 'I leave you the mistress of a beautiful house, Laura. You'll have a new life now as a young married woman. Clare won't be any worry with Felix taking care of you both. You're a very lucky girl.'

A little distance off, along the wharf, Felix was talking to an official in a navy-blue uniform. It was half past two in the afternoon.

Mrs. Vaizey glanced across at the men. 'You can't stay to say goodbye, because nobody will tell us when we're sailing. It's just as well.' Her creamy face, her large amber eyes, were impenetrable. She was like a park that had never once removed its *Don't Walk on the Grass* signs. The black veil of her little hat pricked her daughters' cheeks in turn, and their clothes brushed together.

On the sunny windy wharf, beside the big camouflaged ship, with a war in progress, having just been married, saying goodbye to her mother, Laura felt herself falter. None of this—wharf, ship, war, marriage, farewell—was of her planning. Who had constrained her? She felt like an object.

Clare scowled miserably at the tears streaming up from some place in her chest and out through her eyes. She wanted to shriek with indignation, to fall on the ground, to complain loudly in a loud rough voice. They had all been cheated. She and Laura had never been loved, and certainly not by this woman. Nor for years had she, Clare, felt the slightest affection for her. But not to care that they were parting! Not to care! Her heart was torn to think of all that they had missed.

Accompanied by Peter Trotter, Felix joined them. 'What's the trouble, eh? She's safe as houses. The submarines've all been rounded up. You're safer in a convoy than trying to cross Pitt Street!'

Clare gave her misguided comforters a look and, walking away from the ship, extracted her arm from its unnatural, sickening link with Laura's. At times Laura confused what was with what ought to be in a way that deeply antagonised her uncompromising sister. Striding on ahead, laughing loudly at one of Peter's quips, Felix left his wife to follow in her cream silk wedding dress, with a small wreath of olive leaves on her head.

'Well, look, I know it's your honeymoon and all that tomorrow, Felix, but can you get me out a carton of number fourteens before one o'clock?'

'Oh, I guess we can manage that. With all these women to keep I'd better not lose any orders, eh?' Felix looked sideways at all the two women and gave his slow laugh.

'What do we want with holidays?' Felix said in the morning. 'Anyway, I've got to get these orders out and you'd better give me a hand.'

He looked at Laura in much the same way as he had when she was his employee merely. She was almost relieved. Evidently what happened at night was not carried forward like the petty cash balance to the next day. It would not have been proper. Felix was modest and prim. She was glad. If he teased her a little cruelly, smiling fixedly as he pointed out her defects, she would have to learn not to be too touchy. It was true that she was ignorant. He was no more than right when he told her that she was not beautiful. Yes, she was relieved. Things, shapeless feelings, nightmarish and strange as mountains fighting, as landslides and ranges rising out of the sea, were best curtained off by the gold light of day. It was right to keep days and nights in separate compartments the way Felix did. Fortunately, fortunately, people had the sense not to go about in the mornings, in the streets, as if they guessed, or even (the thought really stunned her) had similar secrets. Evidently in Felix's mind, one section at a time was all that could stay open. This could be a useful habit to aspire to. Assume forgetfulness if you have it not—

'The men of this tribe,' the anthropologist had written in that book of Clare's that she had skimmed one night, 'the men of this tribe regard the act of sex as the ultimate insult to be inflicted on a woman. Having degraded their wives by using them thus, they hold them thereafter in the greatest contempt.'

Goodness knew what brought that to her mind!

If Felix teased her a little strangely, almost unkindly, it meant nothing in particular. Against the teasing and the employer's look and tone, she had to weigh the lovely house, the garden and water-views, and the fact that she and Clare were to be taken care of. Yes, against all her silly invisible fancies, she had to set the very real white house. After all, he had bestowed its care on her.

'Oh, it's heavenly!' Clare said effusively, pressed again and again for appreciation. 'There's a lot of space,' she added more sincerely. 'I like the grass and trees.'

'Space!' Laura's hand caressed the blue curtain. Almost, she revered the house. Almost, she loved and feared it with a heavy doting love.

'Yes,' Clare said. There was more space, but no more company. It was extremely nice to look at, she could see, and there were very many new and pretty objects in it, which she had lifted, looked at and replaced. Of course, it wasn't *her* house, which could have accounted for her ability not to be overcome by its value and its lacy charm. (But of course it wasn't Laura's, either.)

'Picked this up for you the other day.' Peter Trotter thrust a parcel into Felix's hands as he was leaving the shop. 'Present. Reminded me of you.' Felix's expression was both touched and suspicious. 'Wait till you get home,' Peter said, when he started to open it. 'Read the label.'

Striding into the house half an hour later, he called, 'Hey there! Where is everyone? Come and see what Peter gave me!'

Laura sped from the kitchen, but Felix looked about, dissatisfied. 'Where's Clare?'

'Cla-are! Cla-are! Come here a minute!'

She came running from the garden, and raised her fair brows and grinned with open optimistic eyes at Felix, who had so recently provided car rides, meals in restaurants, plays, picnics, events. 'What's happening?'

Felix drew the present from its brown-paper wrappings with a magician's hey presto! flourish, and held it up like an auctioneer.

'Oh!' Laura was prepared to be delighted, but looked at Felix for an explanation.

'An ornament?' Clare hazarded.

'Who do you think it is?' Felix was wearing his slyest smile.

'A sultan? A sheikh?'

The china figure, fifteen inches high, represented a swarthy turbaned man wearing rich robes of red and blue, in the act of drawing a long assassin's knife from the low-slung girdle at his waist.

71

'Bluebeard!' Felix cried. 'Me! Peter said it reminded him of me.' He held the small dark china face close to his own and assumed a terrible leer.

Laura gave an indignant laugh. 'What a nasty thing to say!'

'*He* knew how to treat his women! He knew the stuff to give 'em! Is he like me? Huh?' He grimaced more horribly than ever into Clare's face, popping his eyes at her, and she backed away, giggling kindly. She did not really think him funny at all, but she was very obliged that he tried to be.

'What?' The source of Laura's indignation changed. 'He was the one who had rooms full of murdered wives!'

Felix gave a dreadful roar and rolled his eyes wildly. 'Aha! You want to watch out!' He laughed into the smiling, wary faces with glee. Then with the drawing in of a deep breath, he fell to admiring his own china image. 'Nice bit of work. Must have set him back a bit. Where'll we put it, now?'

All three considering together, it was finally decided to put the villain on the shelf above the fireplace in the sitting-room. The dark brilliant eyes looked out from under the curving satanic brows, the malicious smile never tired.

As she left the room, Felix pulled the ribbons from the end of Clare's plaits, and she exclaimed, pretending to be angry. He laughed, his eyes unreadable. He watched her go. If he had had twelve dependants roaming the garden, answering, 'Yes, Felix!' instantly, when he called, 'Ho, there!' he would have found it even more satisfactory—leaving aside the financial aspect, since the whole idea was hypothetical.

'Yes, Felix! Yes, Felix!' It was pleasing to hear his name uttered on demand by these light, girlish voices, to have people dashing in out of the sun with expectant faces.

But, emphatically, he did not want children. It would not have mattered anyway, but neither did Laura.

'Well, am I going back to school? What's going to happen?' Clare was at the kitchen table scraping the big yellow mixing bowl with a teaspoon. Laura had been baking gem scones.

'Yes, of course you are. You have to. You're under leaving age.' Felix was outside digging round the roses at the front of the house, a hundred yards away or more or less, behind walls, round corners, nevertheless Laura's voice was low to furtive. 'I know the holidays are nearly over. I'll talk to Felix tonight.' Glancing at Clare, she wiped the table with a sponge, and something about her sister's full grey eyes and lids drugged Laura's disquiet. For a moment she noticed the girl. 'Do you want to get your plaits cut before you go back?'

'Yes.'

'Well, now!' After dinner, manipulating the clever point of his tongue round his teeth in search of remnants of steak, and dexterously sucking air through likely crevices, Felix slid down in his chair and stretched his legs rigidly in front of him, crossing his ankles. He thrust his hands deep into his trouser-pockets, poking and sucking, somehow philosophically. 'I don't know. I think she better just go to that place you went to.'

Having eaten, they had checked the factory's books meticulously for two hours in Felix's small office at the back of the house. Now he was teaching Laura a game of dominoes.

'The business college?' Laura's eyes flinched away from his calm smiling dark ones. He had said—She had thought—Painfully, she stared at the black dominoes, the green baize—

'Sure. If she does a bit of shorthand and typing she'll be right.' He appeared to think. 'I tell you what. If *you* can't pay the fees and your mother didn't leave anything—' he gave his down-turned smile and made a roguish play for Laura's eyes. '*I'll* fix it. Add it to the housekeeping. How's that?'

She was like a novice tackling a master of jujitsu. Her head swam. All at once she was clinging frantically to what she had regarded as no sort of solution. 'Oh!—Good.'

'Only good, is it?'

'No. It's more than good. It's very kind of you. If you feel—if you're sure—she can't go on to finish high school.'

Easing himself further down, so that he was resting only shoulders, neck and head on the back of the chair, and supporting his spine in the seat, Felix reminded her gently, 'It's two more years, you know. Don't forget that. At least two years—' He pondered over his decision, and Laura waited, silence pressing in on her.

'No one kept *me* there the extra time, and I don't think I've done too badly.' Felix opened his eyes at her, ruefully, whimsically. 'I don't know. Maybe I'm wrong. What do you think? He looked at her suddenly again, with exaggerated alertness, as if her opinion might even yet change the direction of his life.

Laura jumped. 'No, no! You're not wrong. Of course you've done—wonderfully.'

'Do you think so?' he asked keenly, looking at her as if her answer to this, too, interested him tremendously.

'Of course!' Laura was vehement and whole-hearted in his praise. 'It was only an idea. Lots of nice young girls go to business college.'

Felix smiled modestly at his crossed feet. 'I don't mind seeing that she gets there. Later on, if she comes up to scratch, we might find something for her at the factory. Who knows?'

Laura's left hand tentatively buttoned and unbuttoned and buttoned the button at the neck of her yellow cardigan.

'Where is she, anyway?' Felix affected to glance over his shoulder as if he might perhaps have overlooked the girl's presence.

'Reading. In her room.'

'Oh? What's wrong with our company?'

Laura looked at him, not quite comprehending. 'Nothing,' she assured him suddenly. She continued to look at him till, as suddenly, she said, 'I'll go and call—'

Felix rubbed his nose, appearing inattentive, only saying to his fingernails, 'I don't know if you've ever had to pay an electricity bill in this district, but—ah—' He raised his eyes very quickly and laughed.

'I'm getting her.'

'When you come back I'll beat you at dominoes for the fifth time running. I hope you know that. I hope you know what a fourth-rate brain you've got. Do you?'

The telephone rang in the office and Laura padded rapidly to answer it, and half-ran coming back. 'It's for you, Felix.'

'You're puffing like an old crone,' he said with distaste. 'At your age.'

'I'm sorry.'

Clearing his throat portentously, he rose and, head down, abstracted as a bishop on Easter Day, he moved out of the room like a procession while Laura stood aside. Then she went to recruit Clare, drawing nourishment through her eyes and fingers on the way. Home.

'What? Are you moving again?' Peter Trotter climbed into the car with the disengaged air of one who knows he is granting a favour accepting a favour: his own car was being greased, Felix was dropping him off in North Sydney. He turned his long pale face towards Felix and jerked his head at the roof-high collection of ledgers, cash books, stationery, IN and OUT trays, adding machines and books he could not identify, in the back of the car.

'Yeah, I'm thinking of running the office from the house. I've been carting this stuff home a bit at a time.'

Felix drove with the steering-wheel pressed to his chest, his strong arms hooped round it, hanging on for dear life as though it were the neck of a mad bull.

'This is the last shipment.' He laughed consciously.

Trotter barely opened his trap of a mouth. 'What's it in aid of?'

'Saves a heap of rent, you know. Might as well kill two birds with one stone. She's got to look after the house and it saves time if she does the typing and phoning at home. Then I've got everything handy to work on the books at night.'

Trotter flicked a platinum lighter and applied its flame to a cigarette. He stared, bored, through the windscreen, felt the back of his patent head. Felix drove in nervous, angry spurts as some feeling of his one-time partner's elevation in the world and his own opinion dawned on him. Old Pete had taken steps up out of his range. Look at his suit!

Felix continued laboriously, 'A man's got every-thing he wants at home: plenty of space, view—No sense paying rent for an office. I'll still be pushing this thing round most of the time.' He continued doggedly in this fashion, his voice cracking occasionally so that he could stop to clear it. 'What do you say?'

Expressionless, Peter Trotter gave him a shilling to pay the bridge toll. 'I say it's a lousy idea. You save a few quid subletting the office at the factory (inciden-tally, I'll be your tenant) and drop a packet.'

'How do you make that out? Drop a packet!'

'If you can't see it—In your shoes, I'd be branching out, not closing down.'

'Oh, would you? Who's closing down?'

Peter Trotter shrugged. His indifference was bottomless. Pennies and dimes. Pennies and dimes. Why was he persecuted by the natterings of small-time no-hopers like Felix Shaw with his paltry manoeuvres, when he had real plans cooking?

Tiredly, he made Felix a further donation of his opinions. 'That's how it gets round. "Shaw's doing the paperwork at home. Can't afford a two-by-four office." I'm not saying it's a fact. Only how it looks to the trade.'

Thickly, defiant, Felix said, 'So what? Who cares what the trade thinks? Mr. Shaw's not too worried about them.'

'Yeah. Well. This is where I get off. See you.'

'Would you like to ask Peter and his girlfriend—I think he's got a girlfriend, don't you?—ask them for dinner some night?' Laura looked up brightly from her plate. She had begun to think that Felix was as friendless as she and Clare. Till now she had assumed that everyone else in the world had families and hosts of loved ones, but this was evidently not so. Of course, Felix had known a lot of people in his day and, strangely, when she asked of twenty different people, 'What happened to him?' Felix would answer, 'He's still kicking about. Caught sight of him the other day, as a matter of fact.'

Why were his friends all so irretrievably in the past?

Laura passed on to the next question. Why not start entertaining in this house made for happy gatherings? She could not doubt that Felix wanted that: his purchases of silver, china, glasses, decanters and liquor made it obvious enough. He had insisted on these luxuries at the expense of many a homely article for the kitchen. The only small difficulty was—who in the world could they invite?

'Oh, I don't know,' Felix said indifferently and, at the same time, critically, looking up from his rockmelon. 'No, I don't think we'll bother with Mr. Trotter.'

He *had* asked Peter to dinner some time ago. Peter had intimated that he was permanently tied up. Felix had kept this from Laura. He was rather miserly about any new facts he happened to acquire. He hoarded them in secret as though they were personal wealth, only popping one out occasionally to give Laura a feeling that this poor sample was the very least of all he hid.

Felix spooned up cold, mouth-watering curves of melon. God knew he'd had dealings with thousands of fellows in the course of his several business careers. (Who could he ask to dinner?) He had had Chinese dinners in Dixon Street with four other coves twice a week when one big sale was pending. Other times he'd eaten and drunk in cramped Kings Cross flats while documents were signed and books taken over. (Still, who could he ask to dinner?) In pubs all over the city he'd had sessions with a vast variety of boys from one trade and another. Friends? He'd had them by the gross.

He began his nightly analysis of the Allies' blunders. Easier to win the war than think of a fellow to ask to a meal. But business is business and time is money. When they were mutually useful, Felix and his comrades pounded backs, 'shouted' drinks, and mirror-eyed cried 'friend' as often as the fabled boy cried 'wolf'. Let the ink dry, however, bringing the instant degeneration of all golden partners into mere people, and a sort of blindness set in so that they all became, almost at once, invisible to each other. Passing later in the street, signalling across a bar, whether winner or loser, they experienced a common revulsion. He was only a husk, that fellow. Had been sucked. There was nothing more to be done with him. Out of my way there! Stand back! If I have no further use for them, people should go to the wall.

Clare glanced out of her window up past the garden-beds and the pale camphor laurels under which in their season freesias and daffodils grew in the grass. She looked to the gate in the distance. No one was coming. The gate remained wilfully, so quietly, closed. The white path was untrodden. Leaves and plants moved in the hot spasmodic wind. No one coming. All the colours of the bay translucent. Sunday. Silence. Warmth. Lying on her bed, propped up on both elbows, Clare looked down from the open window, path and gate, to the printed page between her arms. *The Cossacks*. No one coming yet. Patience.

This window was her look-out tower.

All windows were part of the look-out tower. All of the girl looked out of the windows almost all of the time, wherever she happened to be, whatever she might be doing.

'Aren't you sorry about not going back to school?' Laura asked her, perversely exasperated.

'No.'

'Don't you want to *be* something?'

'No.' Exactly what reaction did Laura want to extract from her? And why?

Laura insisted, 'Felix isn't so very rich, you know, Clare. He's put a lot of money into this house.—But isn't there anything you wanted to *be*?'

The girl regarded her. Laura was pressing her to be unhappy. Well, she would *not* be. Or if she would be, she would be in her own good time for her own reasons. Across the harbour was a brick building where she had charged about and shouted in the company of other uniformed girls. In abandoning it and them she felt nothing whatever. Nothing remotely painful. Brought together as haphazardly as sardines in a net, as slippery and indifferent, she and her associates parted almost without noticing they did. As for the future, and learning—Facts did not exactly represent themselves as the key to that magic mountain—And, anyway, she had no choice. Her hair was cut so that it hung straight to her shoulders.

Laura and Felix were very, very busy. They talked about staff, and taxation, and money, and Peter Trotter, and bills, and absenteeism, and competition, and hampering government regulations, and new chocolates, and overdrafts, and the difficulty of finding parking space in town, and money, and the price of food, and money. Clare was not meant to contribute— she thought the subjects too dull to bear consideration, anyway—but Felix did like her to listen, did like to have her there to be knocked down, as it were, by the blows from his eyes and his words.

It was difficult to get away because, apart from Felix's desire for her listening presence, Laura expected constant assistance in the house. And it was a big house, and Laura's standards of perfection in cleanliness were very high. Clare did nothing to Laura's satisfaction; jobs were no sooner allocated than withdrawn; but if she was useless, at least she should be there to witness what went on. Sometimes, though, she escaped to walk round the suburban streets for miles, looking at people, weeds, traffic, flowers and clouds.

She learned to use the adding-machine, and sat at the desk with the goose-necked lamp shining on the ledger. Every Saturday night she went to the pictures at Neutral Bay Junction with Felix and her sister. Unfortunately the responsibility of having conceived, written, performed in, produced and directed the film, which she and Laura, shared, was apt to taint their enjoyment of the programme. Nevertheless, for a few hours she was sometimes in the celluloid company of people who, like people in books, concerned themselves with subjects of more intrinsic interest than the sale of chocolates, or the dust on the dining-room table. Often they were quite awe-inspiringly sane in their habit of attaching importance to what was important and none to subjects like, for instance, a crack in a cement path, or flaking paint on the eaves. It was a relief. More often than not, really, these people regarded, thought about, were involved with one another in a way which struck

Clare as very reasonable, natural and lifelike, though fantastically unlike life.

Meantime, all the time, she watched out.

Jean Robertson, her shorthand teacher, was married, small, sallow, had dark curly hair, a pointed nose and prodigious commonsense. She took a social worker's interest in her girls.

'What these kids don't know would fill the Public Library,' she said at morning-tea time to her assistant, an older woman, Mrs. Cochrane.

'You'll think so when you see these general knowledge papers,' Mrs. Cochrane said with some disgust, stirring her tea. '*Question*: Name the mythical person who turned men into swine. *Answer*: Shakespeare. Jesus.'

Rationing had soured Mrs. Cochrane. She abominated letter-writing, but so many of her neighbours indulged in black-marketeering that she was obliged to keep in touch constantly, anonymously, with the Government. Mrs. Cochrane was patriotic, and described herself to new acquaintances as 'a war-bride of the First World War'.

Unmoved in her down-to-earth nature, Jean Robertson campaigned amongst the girls. Her statements on all matters not pertaining to shorthand and typewriting were gifts of apple from the tree.

The typing speed-tests ended, and the day was almost over. The teacher sat in front of the class, thoughtfully poking at her curly hair with a pencil. 'Have you started up any social life for yourselves since you joined the college?' she asked them abruptly.

They looked at her.

'For example, have you, Clare, invited Ruth home for a record session at the week-end? And Jill, have you and Erica thought of joining a tennis club or the dramatic art society?'

No one answered. Further scales fell. Jean Robertson crossed her legs. The girls waited, agog. To be given secrets, the key to the code, by a grown-up not related, was—

'How do you think people make friends? How do you think adults get to know each other?'

They had no idea. They appeared to struggle to work it out. They still had no idea. They hardly really even yet expected to turn into adults. They were born *children*. They had begun to see that they might have to turn into taller, older children, but when they were warned about changing into adults it was so farfetched they had to giggle and giggle. Because they knew that just as they had (luckily) been born young and children, grown-ups came into being old and made that way.

Mrs. Robertson shook her head despairingly. 'Adults all start out as strangers. Then they're either introduced, or they're brought together in some group, and if they take to each other they arrange to meet.'

'This is elementary even for them, isn't it?' Mrs. Cochrane bent to murmur in her ear, passing through the room.

She looked back over her shoulder at her superior assistant while the girls giggled and chirruped in subdued voices like very young and early birds at dawn. They crossed their legs like Mrs. Robertson and waggled their high-heeled shoes.

Later, Jean Robertson argued, 'With the war and the changes, they're absolutely adrift. Families split up—' She had read, recently, about people having roots.

'Well—' Laura looked up from her typewriter, leaving all her wound-up concentration on her work. Her blue eyes were stinging with strain. It was eleven o'clock on Thursday night. She and Felix had been lost in accounts and correspondence since dinner, and back before that the day and its labour and duties and worries receded to sunrise. It was a matter for wonder to Laura that *any* business required quite as much vigilance, as many letters, as many stock-takings and balances, as this: but Felix was preternaturally thorough in all he undertook, and thoroughness, of course, was a virtue.

'Well—' Laura was half-whispering. 'I suppose you could ask the girl over on Saturday. But what would you do? I don't know if Felix wanted us to go out in the car or anything.'

Standing by the desk, Clare snapped a bulldog paper-clip open and shut. 'I could stay home. I don't have to go, too.'

'He does like you to. You can't very well—'

Clare dropped the metal clip slowly, and looked into Laura's eyes in so peculiarly level a manner that though her face was expressionless, Laura turned back to her machine, distracted.

'Well what would you *do*, for goodness' sake! All this fuss!'

There was a sound of the bathroom door unlocking and opening.

'Does that *matter*? I don't know. She might bring some records over, or her stamp collection, or we could just talk, or go for a walk.'

Laura drew a long-suffering breath through her parted lips. 'You don't even know her,' she objected, beginning to type again. It was so irregular and unnecessary, asking a stranger to the house. Also you had to remember that it was Felix's house and it was only right that he should be consulted.

'But I would *get* to,' Clare reasoned with her at a frantic rate now that Felix was tramping down the hall. She leaned the palms of her hands lightly on the desk.

They stared at each other. Footsteps were approaching.

'Good night!' Clare kissed her sister's jaw and darted off. 'Oh!—Good night, Felix.'

87

'Off to bed, are you?' He offered his face and she kissed him. He surveyed her with a very mixed expression. 'Half your luck! Look at us—still slaving.' He was serious, and teasing, and reproachful, and forbearing, and boastful, and resentful, and amused.

'Do you want me to help?'

Laura said, 'I told her to go to bed.'

'No, no. Off you go. Another night I'll rope you in, though. All hands on deck!' Laughing abruptly, Felix banged her on the back, and then because they did not know each other very well, the three smiled and waved, oddly wary.

In some new way, since they had come to live in this house, it seemed to Clare that words, silences, gestures and the absence of gestures, being present, being absent, had all come to seem more meaningful than they were, to mean something other than what they meant. There was the effect of striking C natural and hearing B flat, so that the mind registered small disagreeable shocks constantly, as if a scientist with a new machine was playing tricks on it.

It just goes to show, as Laura said later. Ruth's Saturday visit was a staggering success. A lively conventional girl, five feet tall, overweight, with a pretty pink-and-white complexion, Ruth was as arch and polite to the Shaws as they were to her. Rarely had she been deferred to as much as this by adults!

The credit for the day belonged chiefly to Felix. After simmering indecisively all morning and keeping his household mesmerised with uncertainty and alarm, he unexpectedly went to shower and change from filthy gardening shorts to new grey slacks, silk shirt and scarf. Then he sauntered into company and exhibited himself to be beamed on, praised and admired.

'Make some of your melting moments and a chocolate log, why don't you?' he asked Laura, giving her permission. 'I'll go up in the car and get some ice-cream, if you like.'

Her eyes questioned his to discover his meaning. He smiled, giving nothing away, so Laura thought she would try being jubilant. 'Our first real visitor! Yes, little girls love ice-cream, Felix. That would be lovely, wouldn't it, Clare?' Never taking her eyes from his face, she added coyly, 'I know some little boys who like ice-cream, too, don't you, Clare?'

Felix cast his eyelids down and gave a sheepish smile, seriously.

Clare raised an unwise eyebrow (something she had only recently learned to do) but no one noticed.

Ruth came and brought records and her bicycle, intending to teach Clare to ride it. When this had been declared quite beyond any talents Clare might possess, Felix lay down on the carpet to adjust the radiogram. Then he danced in turn with Laura and the two girls, who could not dance, swinging them off their feet.

Short, solid and weighty, he was gratified to surprise them with his physical strength. Laura had to say, 'Don't be too rough with them, dear!' In his hands their wrists and arms were feeble, their bones fragile as chicken-bones. Felix danced daintily on tiptoe with a good deal of elegant arm flourishing and tiny extra steps that were sheer inspiration. The carpet was such a handicap it was an asset, making them stumble and laugh till they were quite disabled by their hilarity.

During and after a period of enjoyable eating and drinking, Felix performed card tricks, asked riddles and juggled—all with a disarming congested glee that made Ruth say, sentimentally, as she and Clare walked up the hill together carrying records, pushing the bike, 'Gee, they're lovely! Uncle Felix's funny! I nearly died. That was a scrumptious chocolate cake. I'm just about bursting. Gee, it's a terrific house, too.'

'Yes.' Clare looked into an intense afternoon sky of savage, almost clamorous, blue. At a great height a few vaporous streaks of cloud stood between the earth and eternity. She had a vague desire to scream, and thought she might be dying.

'I'm starting my new dress tonight,' Ruth said, with another freshening of vivacity. 'It's going to be gathered on to a wide yoke *here*, and then—at the *waist*—'

Cars passed. Gardens were being hosed and sprinkled. Two dogs were barking a duet somewhere in a distant street.

'Well, wasn't that nice?' Laura asked, washing the dinner dishes in her brisk and competent way. 'Ruth's a very pleasant little girl.'

Clare nodded two or three times. 'Yes.' She dried a handful of cutlery and sorted it out, clanking, into its drawer.

'For heaven's sake, Clare, I thought you'd be bubbling over.'

Considering a pile of saucers judiciously Clare said, 'No.' To deny the day's gaiety seemed churlish and unreasonable. They had laughed and talked incessantly, in loud voices, shouting each other down. A feeling of being somewhere precipitous had exercised apprehension and excitement. Yet the absence of a fatal accident had hardly been sufficient to set her heart alight with joy, nor had she any particular feeling that it should have been.

Even while Clare was contributing her fair quarter of smiles and exclamations, balancing a plate of ice-cream on her knees, flashing her long fingernails in animated talk, her self inside her lay injured and drained. This was unreal. This was artificial. 'Go away, go away,' her voice silently exhorted the three whose easy eyes and glances, easy satisfaction, easy amusement, divided her from them in some way more profound than that in which black skin is divided from white, sickness from health, age from youth. 'Go away.'

They desired and expected nothing more of themselves, each other, the afternoon; they were not, with those eyes, aware of anything more to be desired or expected. Even Laura, with her husband, house, visitor and cakes, was well content.

Clare recalled Ruth wandering, inquisitive, about her bedroom, pausing to admire the impersonal array of covers, brush, comb, Royal Doulton pin trays and small crystal vase that Laura and Felix had bought for the dressing-table. Ruth examined and saw every expensive artifact with an acuteness of interest that fascinated Clare. Clearly, Ruth would remember for months, years, perhaps for ever, the thin blue-grey china trays that she had turned about in her plump white hands. She found them worthy of coveting.

'Ruth's a very nice little girl,' Laura said. 'What did you expect to happen?'

'Nothing.' But of course something had. A small explosion had revealed to Clare that she was a person to whom one *thing* was much the same as another, interchangeable because unspeakably unimportant. Another explosion had revealed the alarming fact that this was the way her companions regarded *people*. That her own singular expectations came from the springs of her being and might be the source of her life's experience came to her intuition cloudily, chilly, like a portent.

'Well then—' Laura had finished wiping down the stainless steel sink, and now removed her rubber gloves and washed her hands and dried them. 'You're never satisfied, Clare!'

'No, I'm not,' she said viciously, clinging to her dissatisfaction as though it were her only virtue, the only spar of timber to clutch in a shipwrecked sea.

'When I think of all those poor people in Europe and Asia—' Laura's voice was warm, her manner matronly. She gave her sister a severe look and went off to play dominoes with Felix. If people did not make the best of things and look on the bright side, it was frightening to think how discontented they might be. Here they were—lovely house, lovely autumn weather, a superlative view, cupboards and refrigerator stacked full of food, safe from bombs, cold and hunger, which was more than many, many poor people could say, so why Clare could not be content, why she had to be so—somehow, remorselessly expectant—

Laura opened the door and Peter Trotter asked, blank-faced, 'Where's the boss?'

'Felix's collecting the car from the garage, Peter. He won't be long.'

He frowned at his watch. 'I'll give him five minutes.'

Without removing his hat, he lounged through the house to the office, bestowing condescending glances to right and left. Recently, by one means and another, he had become rather rich. It was irksome enough to have to address Felix, who was a man: Felix's simple wife he ignored, grunting a refusal to her offer of tea or coffee.

'I was doing some ironing in the kitchen,' she confided next, hovering in the doorway.

Peter Trotter looked up at her stonily. 'So what?' Then pulling some papers from his pocket, he cracked his knuckles, found his Parker pen and hitched his chair closer to Felix's desk.

In the adjoining kitchen, Laura started to thump perplexedly at her ironing. She could never, would never, believe that anyone deliberately intended to be unpleasant. This meant that much of her time, even while she bowed conscientiously over the factory's accounts, was spent rationalising the apparently nasty behaviour of people who *could* smile, and had been known to, and who had formed ordinarily amiable words with their lips, and who therefore must be, really, nice and well-meaning like everyone else.

Even Felix who, since he had married her, must care for her, was off-hand and not altogether faultless in this direction. When Peter or any perfectly strange man called on business he was apt to ignore her, never to call her by name, hardly to acknowledge her as his! He knew it, too, she could tell, from the little smirk he gave when they were alone again.

Stretching another white shirt on the ironing-board, Laura continued: but he didn't realise how his attitude influenced the attitudes of other people towards her. But then again, how could she take it personally? Neither Felix nor Peter had a high opinion of women as a sex. Felix on occasion had even seemed to taunt her with being female. Being so much younger was a disadvantage, probably, if she hoped for respect and inclusion in discussions. Only to be allowed to listen! But she did throw all her energy into Shaw's Chocolates and was dedicated in her desire for the company's success, even though she could not believe in it exactly as Felix did. *He* felt the eyes of the world were on Shaw's Chocolates. He would not have been unduly surprised to find Shaw's Chocolates headline news in the *Herald* any morning.

'That's how businessmen have to be,' she explained to Clare so that she herself might begin to understand this monomaniacal approach to life.

Still, even Felix had broken down once and admitted that no one could work harder than she did, and if he would only not treat her like a spy from whom state secrets had to be guarded, she might be even more helpful.

Oh, she remembered she was a woman! Not a member of the human race to Felix and Peter Trotter. Except, she recalled, turning the shirt on the board, that they all had a radically different way of treating the diamond-studded ones who frequented Peter's shop. *Rich* women they respected. Or their money. Peter liked flashy-looking women, too. Felix never noticed women in that way.

She folded the shirt. If she allowed it to be, this reflection about money could be galling. *She* owned a few washed-out and repaired pieces of clothing. Now that Felix was keeping her (and Clare) she naturally received no wage. This was quite right, and all right, as long as her worth as a person was not equated, even by her husband, with her bank account.

In the office, Peter Trotter cracked his knuckles again.

Peter now owned four shops and took the factory's whole output. He also rented but had no obvious use for the office Felix had vacated.

'If he wants to waste good money—' Felix grinned, thinking himself a devil, rubbing his hands together.

'He can afford to—the profit he makes,' Laura said. Felix had set his own profit quite peculiarly low, and expected miracles of household management from her.

'It would not occur to you to consider his rents, wages and overheads, I suppose?' Felix was too pleasant.

'It just doesn't seem fair. We work so hard, and yet—'

'And yet? And yet?' he prompted her, smiling with what looked like intense pleasure into her eyes. As suddenly his face changed and appeared to register intense hatred. 'What do you know about work, anyway?' His hand tapped rapidly at his chest. 'When I was your age, I didn't live in a house like this. Don't think it! *I* didn't have it handed to me like you two. Mr. Trotter and I know what a day's work is, so kindly don't poke your nose in where it doesn't concern you. If I want a friend of mine to get on, he will. I'll see to it. So shut your face!'

'Felix. Oh!' She rushed away, stricken.

Later she worked it out that he had been joking, though very roughly. Her inability to comprehend Felix with any certainty often fatigued Laura. But he did need her; he was her task. She supposed he must be an enormously subtle and complex man: he was not, obviously, what he sometimes seemed—His look had actually said: *you're jealous of Peter.*

'Hi, boy!' Peter looked up from the divan where he had retired to study a racing-guide. 'What say we clinch it?'

'Oh!' Felix laughed falsely. 'You're on to that again, are you?' He sat at his desk and swung the chair round on its revolving base to face the divan. 'I've just been up collecting the car.'

'You know what I've offered. It's the best you'll get. Better close that door.' Peter paused. He watched Felix sit down again. 'Because if I withdraw my orders you've got no goodwill to sell anyone else. You've had it.'

'Ah!' Still smiling, Felix leaned back to drag his tobacco pouch from his trouser-pocket. His hands trembled as he began to roll himself a cigarette. 'But where would you be without Shaw's Chocolates?'

'With my shops, and my reputation, and the publicity I've bought, and the clientele I've built up, I could sell dog biscuits and make a packet. Don't think *I* count on you.'

Curiously, every remark the man made amused Felix. Nothing could have offended him. He had an extraordinary air of indulgence. He seemed almost charmed, as if a baby had hit his face with a baby hand.

'What if I don't want to sell?' Felix parried, his arm wavering as he lifted it from his knees, drew on his shaggy cigarette and replaced it.

'Look, boy, I can give you ten more seconds. I'm late as it is. What's in it for you? Stuck at home. The thing runs itself.' He jerked his head at the closed kitchen door behind which the wireless was playing and the iron thumping. '*She* could run it. I've got the shops, the personnel, the clientele. If I can't get your place, I'll get a better one. So it's the end of the line.'

Felix laughed heartily, his short square brown face, on which the skin drooped in loose folds wrinkling all over. 'You've got it worked out, all right! Well, I don't know, young fella—I wasn't thinking of getting rid of it just yet, but—' he caught Peter's eye 'if that's how you feel, it's a deal.'

He stubbed out his mangled cigarette, dashing at flying sparks and shreds of tobacco with his left hand. Peter Trotter almost smiled. He pulled from his pocket a contract which would be, he said, 'legal enough' till they saw their solicitors.

'What was the joke?' Laura asked, looking up from the ironing-board, smiling tentatively, when they appeared. She had been so glad to hear them laughing together; Felix needed men's company and light-heartedness.

'Were we telling jokes?' Felix drawled. 'I thought we were talking business.'

Trotter met Felix's eyes, looked at his watch.

'In good time you'll be told all you need to know,' Felix said to Laura, and in his expression there was an element at once sexual and sadistic. Clapping her on the back with a firm hand, he chuckled dryly, secretly, across the room, into his friend's flickering, evasive eyes. 'How about a cup of something, eh?'

'Not for me, boy. I'm off. See you. Ring me.' With a brief salute, he was across the hall and gone.

Laura woke to a cheerful bull-frog version of *Happy Birthday*. It was only Felix, up and dressed, come to serenade her, holding parcels wrapped in pink paper: a silver tray, teapot, coffee pot, sugar basin and milk jug, pewter mugs and theatre tickets.

He had roused the unconscious Clare at six and now she stood singing a duet with him and breaking into giggles as he strained after subterranean notes and jumped about the room with bearish playfulness. Laura uttered little squeals of delight.

Clare now handed over her packages: a pair of pretty red sandals, a cotton skirt, a leather handbag.

'Oh, it's too much. Both of you. Everything so smart and well chosen! You both always give me beautiful presents.'

Considering her income, Clare certainly gave lavishly, saving for months. But nothing was too much for Laura, nothing could be enough. You had to make it up to her, somehow. Had to try to. She said, 'I'm going to make breakfast. I'll call you.'

Sitting in bed with the morning sun shining over her shoulder, Laura was visualising herself in this situation in order to feel a proper reaction to it. Shortly, it became evident that she was in a luxurious setting, surrounded by a small but loving family, and enviable. If she had known years ago that all this was before her, how gladly (she thought) she would have waited!

Rather more girlishly than she had acted and spoken when she was younger, certainly in more youthful a manner than Clare's, she kissed Felix and thanked him and drew the very last dregs of gratitude from herself to please him. After all, she owed him *something*, and at times it pleased him to have her childish and excessive. When you thought of it, he was a stranger, under no obligation to provide for or feel anything towards her! Of his free will he had chosen her. The fact held her. Her mind's core stood in meek and helpless subjection before the idea of herself as someone singled out.

This was a safe and inviolable fact, not to be bent or broken by any amount of thought. Therefore no return that was in her power to give could be too great. It stood to reason. Alas, though! Poor Felix valued beautiful presents, too, like the ones he gave. And she had only herself, and out of herself she had somehow to manufacture repayments he would find acceptable.

'Come in. He's gone to bed.'

Clare hesitated.

'The rain's blowing in, Clare. Come in and close the door.'

With a jerk, Clare obeyed her sister and walked past her into the small sunroom while Laura shut out the noisy night. Then they both stood.

The small steel catch of the cupboard door against which she leaned dug into Clare's spine meanly. Its sharpness penetrated and she levered herself upright on her feet. Rain dripped from her hair.

'What was it?' she burst out. 'What happened?'

Laura shook her head, eyelids lowered. She had thought Felix had lost his mind. Even now, for all she knew, he might be mad. 'He broke everything,' she said.

'That huge—decanter.'

'Your face is cut. There's blood on it.'

'Is there?' Clare stirred and in the instant of stirring lost interest. 'Didn't hit me. Whatever it was he threw.'

They were silent again.

'We can't stand here for ever,' Clare said, as if they easily could, and Laura met her eyes with a sort of consumed look, an extraordinary look, and boldly opened the glass doors leading to the shut-off house and started to inspect it like a tourist at Pompeii. She noted the deep scratch across the surface of the dining-room table that Felix had deliberately carved into it with a piece of glass. Every piece of china and crystal he lifted had smashed with marvellous simplicity against the walls. Steak and beans and a mush of vegetables had somehow submitted to being arrayed peculiarly over the larger part of the carpeted floor.

'What did we do? What were we saying? Oh, Laura. What's the matter with him?'

Laura shook her head. Her excitement was mounting dreadfully and with it came a blind, obsessive look, tight fists, sudden automatic activity.

'What were we *saying*? Was he drunk?' On her knees beside Laura, Clare collected splintered glass.

Feverish, glittering, Laura rose and sped to and fro with dust-pan and broom, hot water and washing-cloths. The house contained a connoisseur's selection of liquor, but Felix had never so much as opened one bottle. In the past he had evidently frequented hotels, but now he never drank. 'No, it wasn't that.'

'Well, what?' Mechanically, Clare helped her restore the devastated rooms, her mind surging and brilliantly alert and lighted, running the scene again and then again in search of clues.

For neither she nor Laura had said anything remotely provocative, had only sat eating dinner, artlessly good-humoured and ready to smile, listening to Felix, the wireless softly playing. Then he had suddenly vomited words at them, his manner extraordinarily agreeable, so that for seconds he might have been speaking Chinese for all the sense he seemed to make. Then with small smiles that were all at once painful but immovable, with unswallowed food turning poisonous in their mouths, they understood him.

He lurched to his feet. Oiled strands of his brushed-back hair fell over the jagged scars on his forehead. His face was contused, his gestures terrifying, his expression ogrish.

Staring-eyed and with a deep fearful incredulity they felt his voice beat against their heads. He lifted and threw and crashed and overturned.

'Go outside at once and don't come in till I call you!' Laura cried over the noise to her sister.

'What about you? Come, too! Come, too!'

'Go outside, Clare!'

'Don't stay! Please don't stay!'

Working for an hour they removed as many signs of Felix's outburst as could be washed away and disposed of in garbage tins. Now they stood in the kitchen.

'What made him go to bed in the end?' Clare asked listlessly.

Laura shook her head. 'He had no choice. He'd been—raving—for hours. It's after one. I'm going to lie down in the spare room. Go to bed. In the morning, we'll see. Don't say anything.'

'I don't ever want to say anything to him again!' Clare assured her, then added, her look incredulous, 'Do you want us to act as if nothing has happened?'

'Yes. Till I've seen.'

'Seen what? He'll remember. Anyway, how can we pretend?'

Laura reasoned to herself, 'It was a sort of—brain-storm. It won't happen again. If we act as if nothing happened, he will, too. Do as I say. Do you hear me, Clare?'

'Oh, I hear you.' She wrapped her arms about her damp head.

Laura rattled two white tablets out of a tube on the window-sill, and swallowed them with a drink of water. Shutting cupboard doors tight, and pressing drawers in, she glanced all about and then switched off the light.

Downstairs on the ferry, and outside in the open air, Clare inattentively cast her eyes over the skyline, the shimmering dark-blue harbour, the over-familiar ships, gardens, red-tiled roofs and commercial buildings whose meaninglessness had begun to perplex her expectations.

Still, it was a pleasant novelty to be abroad on a weekday afternoon, away from college and the stationery smell indigenous to all such clerical places. (She had a mild allergy. The local doctor was passing her on to a Macquarie Street man.)

College—As people often do, she proceeded to muse about the place she congratulated herself on being absent from. College—Mrs. Robertson—Practising what she preached, Mrs. Robertson invited four girls to her flat every Saturday or Sunday for afternoon tea, and Clare went in her turn to indulge in some social life. It had sounded desirable and sensible when Mrs. Robertson had first expounded its workings—social life—but what it turned out to be like was waiting at a bus stop, a grimy bus stop with grit and traffic tearing past. She was desperate to be gone and had been waiting, it seemed, since her life began. She was staring through the grey light and grit and monochrome press of traffic and crowds, waiting for (she supposed) a bus, with longing and anxiety.

Then, because she happened to be standing in the queue, voices addressed her in unending soliloquies, burrowing like parasites for space inside her brain. 'I've told him again and again not to shape my hair in like that at the back of my head. It's old-fashioned—The skirt's going to have six yards in it, and underneath there'll be this petticoat with layers of frills—Ten cartons of Nutty Roughs—With all this funny weather our suitcases were covered with green mould—Hitler's got the right idea about the Jews, they can say what they like—Napoleon, there was a man! Where's your female Einstein, your Rembrandt? Women! Why were all the Greek and Roman statues of men? Because male beauty is superior in every way—When I win the lottery—The neckline's down to about *here*—After the war this block of land'll be worth three times what we gave for it—*Till you find the bluebird of happiness*— It's very important to keep your typing even.'

Gently, mildly, she responded. Politely, she replied.

Glances were thrown at her now and then to solder chains on her attention, since she happened to be there. She smiled and raised her eyebrows with interest. For how could you hurt people's feelings? And it was no one's fault. What it was she expected (and so much time had passed that she could barely remember what it was exactly) was long overdue. To her heart's blood she craved its arrival. In the midst of this curious kind of anguish, people cheerily addressed her at life's bus stop as they would have addressed any wooden post with ears on it.

Without the least doubt, either, Mrs. Robertson, and Ruth and Noelene and the other girls at the college, and Laura and Felix (and these were all the

106

people she knew) found their needs in this direction easily appeased. Yet she was grief-stricken, bleeding to death, because of these daily encounters. If she lied or acted all her life, no one she knew or ever had known would recognise the fact; alternatively, when she was herself, no one recognised that either. If their satisfaction and selves were apparent to her, why not her reactions and self to them? And that she knew and was not known were facts of a piercing intuitive force whose truth was not to be doubted.

For courtesy's sake, and from frustration, she often acted as if she felt herself at one with the company, but since no one assumed that she was *not* one of them, since she never convinced herself in the role, since no one else would have known if she had been Bo-Peep or the man in the moon, it seemed pointless to struggle to grind out genuine lightheartedness and interest, when ears and a display of teeth and any sort of speech contented her associates. Except Laura and Felix, who usually expected silence, but sometimes wanted her to entertain them. Oh, the trouble was there was not *enough* of anyone.

The Russians—Now with Chekhov's, Dostoevsky's, Tolstoy's Russians, who were all more recognisable as people than people were, you could sit on a fine day, or a day of storms, and discuss the very topics that were so lethal in other mouths. You could discuss even the weather with exquisite joy in the company of fully-grown human beings who had eyes set straight in their heads. Peace on earth, goodwill to men! To be always, in whatever circumstances, with people whose ways were instinctive to you.

But alas, alas! Clare sighed and stared at the ever-lasting harbour. The lost tribes of Israel, the wandering Jew, had nothing on the only Russian in Sydney. Where are you, my treasures? Where are you, my darlings, angels, sweethearts, truthful, laughing ones?

A bell rang. The ferry reduced speed and drew into the wharf at the Quay. It was necessary to rise, wait for the gangplank, walk off among the other walking bodies—joggling, jostling, wearing the tin button of charity in lapels, with puckered mouths and brows and out-of-joint lolloping movements and fancy gawky hats; and servicemen idle on leave with yellow faces from atabrin, loafing about the Quay; to be washed about with the sweet startling odours of the country and flowers and wood alcohol; sprinkled with dust, pursued by litter, thrilled by the light in the sky, depressed by the asphalt—Aie, aie!

'Go behind that screen and take off your clothes,' Sir Ronald said gravely. He was a specialist, tall, immaculate, with greying hair and a sun-lamp tan. Having surveyed the patch of hives on the left side of Clare's throat, he was now surveying Clare.

'Ah—' she hesitated, uncertain that he had heard her, but unwilling to have him misjudge her hesitation.

'They aren't anywhere else,' she mentioned again, reassuringly.

'Nevertheless.' Fiftyish, urbane, accustomed to deference, the specialist looked down at her.

'Oh!' Clare went behind the screen and undressed rapidly till she was left in high-heeled black shoes, leg paint, and a white petticoat. She stood considering what it would be sensible to do next. It might have been wiser to have left on some other piece of underwear than the petticoat? Almost certainly he had not meant her to remove literally everything. She had no objection: that would be stupid. If only, though—She wished he had been a little more specific, so that she could have appeared clothed exactly as he expected her. She could hear Sir Ronald moving about.

'Ah—everything?' Her voice went casually through the heavy floral curtain.

'Yes.'

Oh. He had no doubt about what he wanted. Well. Now she knew. Off with the petticoat. She laid it over the back of the chair with her other clothes. So. All she had to do now was emerge. She brushed at the curtain with her fingernails then paused and looked down thoughtfully at her high-heeled shoes. With the rest of her naked, perhaps they looked a trifle—overdone? Slipping them off, she looked at her bare white feet. They seemed not quite fitting to the situation either. Too informal? As if she was about to have a bath? Mrs.

Robertson said, when she heard of today's appointment, that Sir Ronald and his wife were always in the social pages shaking hands with famous visitors from overseas. He probably expected *some* ceremony from his patients. She slid her her feet back into her shoes, drew aside the curtain and stepped composedly out into the surgery.

There were no buildings opposite this long cliff of doctors' rooms in Macquarie Street, and in Sir Ronald's apartments, ten storeys from the street, a wall of windows faced the sky and overlooked below the barbered greenness of the Botanic Gardens and distant views of the harbour and the eastern suburbs. The light was truly dazzling.

Sir Ronald had been waiting. Since he was evidently disinclined to move, Clare approached him and stood in the middle of the dignified room in her high heels.

Not looking into her eyes, Sir Ronald cleared his throat. Clare watched his downcast eyelids, then stared past him through the windows at a cloudscape of wondrous beauty.

'Hmmm' Sir Ronald touched her left breast lightly and cleared his throat again. He walked slowly round her. A clock ticked on his desk, otherwise the room and the city were marvellously quiet. Almost, Clare could have slept, standing there with her eyes open on the clouds.

'No,' the specialist murmured to himself, standing in front of her again and slightly to one side, 'there's no trace of it here.' He touched her other breast lightly with his fingertips.

In the sober, dignified room, Clare's body could have felt conspicuous had she not perceived some years before that she and it were by no means one and the same person. Though she had been dissected and her skeleton and vital organs exposed to a multitude, still, it did seem to her, they would not have seen *her*. No, it was not difficult to be detached. Just the same, her body was extremely white and smooth. In the brilliant daylight, it glowed with the pearly phosphorescence of the clouds she was staring at so assiduously. Her vanity was a considerable support to her. Which of her classmates could have risen to these serious, sky-regarding, unselfconscious heights? What remarkable self-possession!

'No, there's no trace of it here,' the doctor said again, after a moderately long silence.

'I thought it was only on my neck.'

Sir Ronald's lids were still lowered, Clare noticed, moving her own eyes somewhat gingerly from the great outdoors to the specialist's face. He gave the impression of being at least twice as clean as most ordinary men. Even so, interesting as it was to observe at close quarters a knight who shook hands in the social pages and was very clean—

Further reserves of equanimity had to be called up while an injection was prepared and jabbed in her

111

upper arm, a prescription written out, and general warnings uttered regarding allergy-producing plans and soaps. Clare would *not* feel at a disadvantage in this situation, so she received all, standing there in her white body with the demeanour of a sincere, spiritual and devoted nudist.

'Well,' said Sir Ronald, after another ticking silence. 'You can—ah—get dressed now, Miss Vaizey.'

For the first time since she had appeared from behind the curtain, his grey eyes raised themselves to hers. He looked briefly but deeply at Clare, and as she looked back it seemed that an invisible rocket sped between them, rocked the room, shocking and enlightening her to the very tips of her high-heeled shoes.

Oh! Behind the floral barricade she pulled on her clothes and combed her long hair hastily. For herself she was startled, but for Mrs. Robertson, who expected much of knights, she was indignant. So that was rank!

'Thank you, Sir Ronald.' They shook hands. 'Goodbye.'

On her knees Laura was digging weeds out of the lawn with a small garden-fork, her soft energetic arms working fiercely. Even from the gate Clare could see that something was wrong. The rueful laughing surprise she had been juggling in her head and chest all the way home, sank instantly to a sickening sense of apprehension.

'What?' she asked Laura.

Laura lifted her head, eyes fevered and abstracted, then bent again to the lawn. The back of her neck was slightly sunburnt between the pinned-up light-brown wavy hair and the collar of her pink-striped blouse. Damp cut grass stuck to the thin rubber soles of her shoes.

'Where's Felix?' Clare's eyes were everywhere; her voice was low. The garden might only seem to be deserted.

'Out,' Laura gasped, heaving at a deep-rooted weed.

'What's wrong?' Clare looked round at the cushiony lawn, and up at the clear thin blue of the late-afternoon sky. The air was cool and moist.

'He's just taken the factory books and stationery over to Peter Trotter's. It appears he sold him the business six weeks ago.' Laura thrust the fork into the garden-bed beside which she had been working and looked to gather her limbs up from the ground by an effort of will.

'*Sold* it?' Clare stared warily at the side of her sister's down-turned face as they walked towards the house.

'So we have to tighten our belts, he said. He's paid off the gardener.'

'Mr. Gilroy? That's why he hasn't turned up! But there's so much of it! Why didn't he tell you before?'

Laura shrugged, though Clare's astonishment, trepidation, and hurt on her behalf, woke her interest almost as if she had shares in her sister's emotions and was watching prices fluctuate. Starting to peel potatoes for dinner, she said bitterly, 'When he told me, he smiled!' And clearly, her innocent conviction of her value to him even in terms of mere usefulness had been felled in a second. Clare looked at her with dumb compassion and exasperation, and as she expanded with partisan bewilderment and outrage, Laura felt life become more bearable and even found excuses for Felix. Gradually, her necessity to remain in a state of frozen tension was revoked.

Felix was unusually late returning home, so Clare had dinner alone, relievedly, then shut herself in her room. In fifteen minutes or so she had polished off her shorthand homework. She next found herself brushing and brushing her hair, grey eyes fixed in warning on her looking-glass eyes. Noticing, she dropped the brush and lifted a book she had been reading with outrageous happiness—*Scarlet and Black*. In reality now, though, all she did was listen, breathing lightly through her parted lips, at every sound moving her eyes from printed page to bed to wall to door in time with the movement of her heart. Since *that* night, apprehension, caution, came like charms to ward off evil spirits.

Hers was a pretty, sterile room carpeted in pale green; its walls were white. The bed, the dressing-table with three mirrors, and a stool were made of rosewood. So was the small chair in which no one ever sat. The curtains and covers were of a quality that should have been unprocurable, but a man who had bought a used-car business from Felix years before and made a fortune, had produced all the lovely stuff in the house coupon-free.

The room's great disadvantage was that there was nowhere in particular to *be* in it. The centre light exposed every shadowless, polished and dust-free square inch of it. It was very silent. Clare's other library books and the few she owned were out of sight in a compartment of the built-in wardrobe for tidiness. Anyone or no one might have lived there: she made no impression on it at all. But then, she wasn't meant to.

'What are you sitting in here by yourself for?' Laura slipped softly into the room, smiling disingenuously.

'I'm reading.'

Felix was home now. He and Laura were together in the sitting-room, with his action and her reaction between them and not mentioned, and with their minds and eyes lighted and searching, so that the room was like an arena before a bull fight.

'I'm reading. I can't concentrate in there.'

'He'll wonder what's wrong if you don't come in.'

'Can't I just want to be by myself? When I do sit in there you only talk to each other about business.'

Laura glanced back at her from her inspection of the room—making the place untidy on a cushion on the floor, pretentiously reading a book.

'Why don't you sit on the chair, for goodness' sake? You look as if you're camping here. Come on,' she said with uncertain firmness. 'You can often cheer him up and put him in a good mood when he's like this.' If Clare was disobedient, if he did not have his way, he would not like it, and that would be unfortunate. If he did not like it, he might succumb to another of those freakish storms, or odd little moods. He might do—almost anything. Hadn't he hinted that some unspecified action of *hers* had caused him to sell the business at what amounted to a loss? 'Come on, Clare. Don't be silly.'

Yes, the trap was firmly settled about her. She shook the bars once to test it. 'I don't want to. Do I have to?'

'I've asked you!' From leaning against the wall in a rigid and uncharacteristic pose intended to suggest extreme ease, Laura went to the door. Her voice was tart. 'Please yourself!' She went out blowing her nose angrily.

Clare's heart shifted. Laura was frightened. It frightened her that Laura was frightened. 'Damn, bugger, blast! Damn, bugger, blast!' She clamped her teeth together till her gums pounded, drove her nails experimentally deep into her hands and arms, not knowing how to hurt herself enough.

116

But lately this happened all the time! Felix deliberately did or said something that mortified Laura to the bone. *She* witnessed it and felt, at the very least, upset, not happy. Then, without quite inciting her to brood and chafe helplessly when they were alone together, Laura was not discouraging, because she too was at least upset and not happy. Then there always came this marvellous turnabout. 'Come and make Felix laugh! Come and tease him! He likes it when you do. Concentrate on him, for my sake!'

Clare picked up her brush and applied it viciously to her scalp. In a sense, to be obliged to assume an attitude she did not feel was the worst thing that could happen to her. A thin line like an arrow advancing before her and vanishing into the future had to be kept sight of with a sort of fantastic precision. Yet from this essential tracking and waiting which was her most natural instinct, she was to be dragged again to counterfeit.

In a tumult of rebellion, she brushed her hair. Oh, she had resisted these appeals before. Oh, yes. Many times. She had kept her inner eye with passionate attachment on her way. Oh, sure. The only snag was that it was a little hard on Laura, who was allotted the role of Hostage Number One. If Felix cared to exert himself and use his power to dismay, they were vulnerable. Ruthlessness and hatred were dismaying. And, of course, he did care to, too.

'I won't do it,' she said through her teeth, rising and pulling her sweater neatly over her skirt. No one felt forced to say to *her*, 'What happened at the specialist's? Are you by any chance dying of a fatal, incurable allergy?' No one was so afraid of how *she* might react that they ever thought to ask, 'How was college?' or 'What are you reading?' Clearly, it mattered very much more that some people should not have their whims or feelings slighted than that others should not.

Why should *she* dance in there like some third-rate vaudeville act shedding tears of rage inwardly enough to drown herself, and at the same time hippety-hopping round the guest of honour and showing about forty-eight teeth in a smile? She did not *want* to.

Oh, of course. She was beginning to be afraid of Felix. He was not rational.

Hair thick and smooth to her shoulders, eyes dangerous but changeable, she pushed open the door of the silent sitting-room and the performance began.

PART TWO

Felix was weeding the lawn. He had been weeding the lawn from before breakfast-time till about five o'clock every evening for six weeks. At first Laura had felt there was something almost abnormal about such persistence (although persistence was a virtue), but she accepted it now.

'I'm just going up to the shops, Felix. Can I get you anything?' She leaned over the verandah railing at the front of the house and called down to him. There was a pause. She waited. In time, he lifted a bleak face till his eyes were level with her shoes; he looked at them with blind contempt and bent his back again like a slave.

Laura went away.

Just as Jack Roberts had disappeared and, according to hearsay, prospered fantastically, so Peter Trotter had vanished and prospered. Now, without interest or income, Felix was too morose to go further from the house than the garden. Although it was an experience he had undergone quite often, it surprised and aggrieved him that, having sold his business and gratified Peter, he should not still have a business and see Peter as regularly as before. He chose to act with bravado; he did not choose that there should be unpleasant consequences for him.

He had a prodigious memory for unrelated facts. He could add very large columns of figures involving

121

pounds, shillings and pence as fast as a comptometer. He had machine-like perseverance in the uprooting of weeds, or the pursuit of a discrepancy in the company's accounts, or in the packing of cartons. His powers of concentration went far beyond what any industrial psychologist would have described as superior. Given training, he would have excelled in a variety of careers of a scientific nature, turning miracles of attention on the puzzles and tricks set for solution. Yet what was obvious to him now, reduced to weeding this vast lawn, day in, day out, was that someone had plotted to bring this about. While his back was turned. While he was asleep. People—Of all things, they were the weirdest and most dangerous. Vengefully, he weeded.

Laura hurried back from her shopping, string bags suspended from every finger, and began to belabour the house, sighing often, as she did when she was alone. Looking surreptitiously through the floating curtains she saw her husband's crouched figure. Poor Felix!

His misery was infectious. Not that he said anything! In fact, he was very quiet. He barely looked at anyone. He never, never smiled. You would hardly expect him to, either, considering—He merely walked slowly into the house with this dark, aggrieved and bitter air that inspired a dreadful awe and feeling of guilt in her as she let him pass. Clare watched him sombrely.

'Where's the *Herald*?'

(He was speaking! Oh!)

Felix began to study the 'Businesses for Sale' column at breakfast, which thus became a very prolonged affair. Buttery fingerprints scalloped the edge of the paper.

'Come in here a minute. I want to dictate some letters.'

(This was another speech he sometimes made.)

After dinner and at weekends, he took his household out in the car to inspect many unique businesses which enterprising men hoped to dispose of (with the deepest regret) usually in a way diametrically opposite to that in which Felix had disposed of his, with all the benefits falling in quite another direction. The more fragile, the trickier and crankier the invention on which the purchaser's fortune was to depend, the more it captivated Felix.

'I'm intrigued,' he said to an incredulous seller. 'This's a fascinating kind of gadget. It's got *me* in. Why wouldn't it sell like hot cakes?' (The inventor did not see fit to tell him.) 'Calculated on a population basis, I reckon—'

Laura eyed the shaky devices of cork, tin and string—toys, window de-rattlers, glove driers—with trepidation. She found several grey hairs among the loose waves of her hair.

'Already?' Clare said, staring at them, surprised, remembering the time when Laura had been her own age, not long ago.

'After twenty-five,' advertisements said, 'nourish your skin nightly or tell-tale signs of age will mar your beauty.' Twenty-five! She had always smiled at that. They would say anything. That was still quite young. Signs of age! Yet see this now—Laura with grey hairs showing.

In the bathroom, he took a handkerchief from his dressing-gown pocket and wiped his eyes. Christmas always affected him like this. In the midst of untying a present from Laura, he had had to work up a fictitious cough and leave the room, flapping an arm to restrain anyone from following him.

'What's money for, anyway?' he said, and filled pillowcases with underwear, bathing costumes, chocolates and books.

In return he was given a shirt, a wallet, a pen, a pipe, some nuts, and a compass he had wanted for years. To save up, Laura had suffered over every sixpence of her housekeeping budget for months. Clare did some typing for Mrs. Robertson's customers after classes, and they both withdrew the balance from bank accounts that were now nonexistent. But how worthwhile it had turned out to be!

Giving and getting, spending money and receiving goods bought for real cash, were symbolic and significant, painful and rewarding beyond what was normal, to Felix. To the extent that he gave, he atoned and acquired new virtues, to the extent that he received, he was admired, loved and respected.

'After breakfast down to the beach, then home for Christmas dinner. How's that for a programme?' Marching back to the bedroom, arms swinging, he shouted cheerfully ahead.

As if Felix's smile had opened the gates of Utopia, Laura looked up at him from the bed where she was once again enveloped in visible affection wrapped in red and blue paper. Here was the real Felix at last! Not the gift-giver (she didn't mean that), but the kind-hearted man who was easily touched by a traditional occasion, the one who looked at her now and at Clare, in appeal, craving the goodwill they were relieved to the core to be asked for. Sacks of it, sacks of goodwill, he could have. From today it was quite evident to their eyes, hopes and spirits, that this would be the permanent Felix. Heavens, he was just like everyone else, only wanting pleasant days. Laura saw that he believed at last that she had no designs on his life, savings or pride, that she wanted what he wanted—everything good for Felix. Her fingers nervously pleated the edge of a sheet of blue starry paper.

Beyond the barbed-wire barricades set up to delay the Japanese invaders, the sand glared and squeaked dryly when their feet sank into it. The surf was strong and noisy, the beach crowded. Clare went into the water alone, leaving the others half under the striped

125

umbrella. Laura was browning her legs in the sun and Felix was exposing his back. The swell lifted her up and let her gently down. Her arms and legs rippled like seaweed. The water was glass-green. As she lay face down in it, it supported her so, she could have moaned with relief. What an illuminated day it was! Up, up and gently down, the ocean swelled. She lay on it, slowly moving her legs and fingers, dreaming, as though it were the trustiest mattress.

'I bought Reg Carroll's artificial-flower factory the other day,' Felix thought to say on Boxing Day.

Laura raised a hand to shade her eyes as she looked up at him where he stood, barefooted, untying a piece of string from the neck of the hose. 'Did you, dear? I'm glad you've found something you like.'

'You and young Clare are on the staff.'

'Are we? Did you hear that, Clare?'

Clare, a reluctant gardener, was on her haunches by a bed of petunias, extracting weeds. 'What doing?'

'Bit of office work, bit of factory work.' Felix untied the last knot and screwed the nozzle of the hose back and forth, looking down at his staff, rather enigmatic. 'He's got five girls there already. With you two as well it should run like clockwork. Oh, and by the way,' he gave an exaggerated start and it was not possible, quite, to hide his pride, 'Reg and his wife are coming for dinner tomorrow night, so you'd better throw a few extra spuds in the pot.'

Heavens, he was in a good mood, being funny and everything!

In summer the small, single-storeyed, backyard shed which was the factory was stupefyingly hot. In winter, it was to be found, it was leaky and draughty and smelled of the kerosene heater. The row of windows behind which the girls worked faced a dilapidated brick wall. It was rat-infested when the Shaws took over.

Felix and his family drove from Neutral Bay to industrial Concord every morning in time to start work at eight. Laura brought lunch from home and made tea on an old gas-ring at half past twelve. The girls went down to the shops on the corner to buy chips, pies, hamburgers and milk shakes. At five o'clock work stopped.

'And what do you do of an evening, love?' Elsie Trent asked, chewing gum with white teeth behind plum-coloured lips.

'Help Laura with the house. Read.' Clare pressed the base of some archetypal red flower firmly round the stem she had selected from the box which sat between them, and flashed a sideways glance at her neighbour.

'Oh!' Elsie, who was thirty-seven, eyed the girl with dull, not bad-natured, avidity. 'Haven't you got a boyfriend yet, then?'

'Not yet.'

Elsie felt her plump pompadour with one hand and took a stem with the other. 'Ah, well! Seventeen.

You've still got time. Money's not everything, love. You'll find that out.'

Clare turned to her to understand her, and seeing Elsie's brown eyes roll defiantly in the direction of 'the boss' and his wife, did.

'No, but I thought you might of had one,' Elsie pursued, licking her forefinger and thumb to separate some pink petals, 'because you been looking a bit peaky. I said to my hubby: either she's seeing too much of some young chap or not enough.'

Clare stared. Elsie had thought about her when she was not present! What a surprising thing! How kind of Elsie! This had never happened to Clare before. She was sure it hadn't. She felt a little the way she had when, as a very small child staring into a mirror, she realized for the first time that she was not of necessity observed by others full face, that she had these unknown sides to her face, that even when her eyes were not fixed on someone else's, they could look at her. It had made her feel oddly as if there was more of her and, also, as she grew older, that people in this way deceived and were deceived. People thought they could possess you when you were not looking and listening, and perhaps you thought the same.

Elsie scratched at her pompadour, using one of the stiff green stems to get through to her scalp. 'Not that you'd have any trouble getting a boy if you wanted one! They're getting worse! You only have to be looking in a shop window and they pop out of the awnings. "Surrender!" I say, "Listen, kids, I could be your mother." Does that bother them?' She laughed. 'Really, I've got a lot of time for the Yanks. I don't care what they say. Oh well, we'll soon have our own boys back.'

In the front seat Laura sat white and tense. Clare hurled herself into a new position in the back seat of the car, and with arms welded across her chest, stared out at the grey street, footpath and crowds with hopeless grinding anger.

'If we could only catch the ferry! But we sit here outside the hotel every afternoon of our lives for nearly two hours! Such a great favour leaving the factory early. I'd rather stay! Anything! Anything!'

'What've you got to complain about?' Felix would sneer at their silence. 'You're not working, are you? You're just sitting around in my car twiddling your thumbs, aren't you? Taking it easy like ladies? That's a joke!'

'Well, you can't catch the ferry.' Laura's voice was dead, yet she spoke with a terrible, feeble kind of force-fulness. It went without saying, really, that neither of them could move.

'And then,' Clare continued, low and bitter, 'by the time we do get home he's like a lunatic. He isn't sane. And we have to sit and be—'

With murderous deliberation his glass moved from table to mouth, his hand moved from glass to bottle, his eyes moved unwinking from one woman to the other, his whole face contorted.

Not having realised that Felix had been 'on the wagon', they did understand now that he was off it.

Clare shivered coldly and shook herself back to the moment. 'If you could just do something without having to think about him! If you could—But it's like a prison!' Her tone was desperate but abstracted because her mind was occupied at a deeper level, because unfinished conditional sentences had become a reflex. 'If I could live my own life!'

Over her shoulder Laura cast back a scornful look. Live her own life! How affected! What would she do with a life of her own? Who did she think she was?

'How didn't you know he was like this? All those years you worked for him!'

The double swing doors of the hotel were held almost permanently open by the increasing numbers of men who thronged from office, building site and shop, to find fulfilment with one foot on the rail and their own kind six deep behind them clamouring for numbness, unconsciousness.

Bleakly, Clare looked away.

'He never came near the place when he'd been drinking,' Laura began in a quiet, tight monotonous voice, and no more than she had attended to her sister

130

did the girl attend to her now. 'Evidently he had enough sense to go home and stay in bed. And he isn't like this all the time. He can give it up for months when he decides to.'

'Do you think he ever will again?'

'I don't know. When he begins to remember he could kill himself off with it he might.'

The bygone days when Felix had been merely unfathomable, irrational and frightening, merely unlike other people and unpredictable as an unexploded bomb, had begun to seem idyllic. If there could be a return to them now—

'He can't keep this up night after night. His health won't stand it.' Laura looked at but did not notice the traffic lights at the corner changing from red to green.

'*His* health! So you've been saying for months.'

There was another silence. Then the expressionless voices continued their separate monologues.

'I want to go away, Laura. I can't stand it.'

When the traffic lights had changed again, she repeated, 'I have to go away. I can't stand it. *I can't stand it.*'

'Where could you go? You haven't got a penny.'

'I'd work. I couldn't get less than I do now.'

Laura glanced back at her with speechless scepticism. They had only ever worked for Felix, and Felix had his little ways about money, but with all his faults you could not say he was mean. Look at the

Christmas presents, and how munificent he was to Reg Carroll when he bought this flower factory. And he only employed Clare as a kind of favour. He paid *her* nothing, of course, and Clare received pocket money. Also he had said enough these months of nights of abuse to convince Laura that it was hardly likely that any stranger would value their services, or even bother to try them. And he knew the business world and men.

'Anyway,' Laura said.

'Anyway,' echoed Clare's mind.

Anyway, the obstacles were unarguably too great. Who could break out? Who could do more than marvel dully at survival? Who had energy and initiative now to spare for what was merely reasonable? What promise had the world held out ever that there was anything to escape to? What was there to desire in this nightmare but the cessation of strain? On the other hand, what sensible kind-hearted citizen would not scoff at the suggestion that there could exist in a charming white colonial house in the suburbs a human situation slightly beyond the powers of commonsense to mend? Sydney was such a pretty, ordinary city! Women are notoriously neurotic, of course! What's the harm in a fellow having a few beers at the end of a day's work? If his women are gloomy, no wonder he drinks! Good luck to him!

'Why does he do it? (I feel I'm going mad. We keep saying the same things night after night.) But what makes him do it? Do you think he always has?' Clare looked at Laura's back with a sort of bright despair, as if she might really have some new information on the subject.

Laura shook her head again. 'For a long, long time he has. Since he was very young. As for *why*—He thinks as long as he can get up and go to work, no one should complain. He doesn't realise what he's *like*.'

'He realises,' Clare said implacably. 'He's like himself then, that's what frightens me. He hates us. He loathes everyone, everything.'

Desperately she looked out of the car window as if some merciful passer-by might stop and say, 'God bless you.'

Laura said nothing, looked at her watch, rubbed the fingers of her left hand across the line on her forehead which had only recently become permanent.

'It's almost as if he's in disguise when he's sober,' Clare muttered, plastering her hair flat against her skull with all the strength of her arms.

He seemed to regard drinking himself sodden nightly and terrorising his compulsory audience as a perfectly natural way to behave. It was inconceivably baffling! And the awareness that Felix was dark, mysterious and closed to himself was eerie in her mind; and, indeed, it was clear that he was not as much as mysterious to himself, for that would have implied consciousness of there being something unknown.

Clare knew this was so, but was most unwilling to believe it. She knew why she did everything. In the very vortex of anger or unreason or elation, had she been asked, 'How are you behaving, and why?' she would have answered at once with total accuracy and total calm. Surely, really, in spite of what could look like substantial evidence to the contrary, everyone was like that? Otherwise, if she had to believe that some people did not know what they were doing, it would make things slightly petrifying.

Clare had studied the works and case-histories of psychologists, but after much diligent and reflective reading, she began to think: *even so, even so.* Their works contained many stock solutions, but no awe; many classifications, but no respect; many judgements, but no love.

The presence or absence of a mother or father; being youngest, being eldest, being wealthy or poor, being alone or too much in company—any one such clue magnetised a sensible scientist according to the bias of his own mind, and sent him on his infallible way to solution ninety-four, since everyone knew that all neuroses sprang from the possession of large ears or, it could be, small fathers. In time Clare learned to predict with unfailing correctness the diagnosis which would inevitably follow each pathetic confession.

Gradually, disillusioned, she turned away. Who was qualified to finger souls with confidence? Who to receive the anguish of those he did not care for?

Oh, the strange and comfortless ones whose histories resembled each other so oddly were not as easily calculated as all that.

Shifting her position again, Clare looked at her watch. Outside, in another world, girls of her own age and young women of Laura's hurried past in groups, or came singly clinging to uniformed arms, laughing, faces powdered gold and eyes sparkling.

Laughing was something Clare felt she could be good at one day. But she looked at the lively faces as a soldier sitting in a ditch before a battle might look at a magazine's technicolour advertisements of glossy rooms and waxwork people posing as lovers and families, and which featured, for his benefit, Hollywood pin-ups and jokes. She stared at the faces.

Oh, people. Oh, someone. See us here. See us.

Laura looked at her watch. 'I don't know—He went to one of those boarding-schools in England for naval cadets. They were very cruel in those days. He wanted to stay at home and go to a day school, but his mother wasn't strong and he had to be sent away. Then he joined the Royal Navy and they seemed to be very brutal to young boys in those days.'

'Maybe that depended on what they were like.'

'He'd worked his way up to be paymaster when he caught that germ in the Persian Gulf and had to be invalided out. Hundreds of them died. If it hadn't been for that, he'd never have left the Navy. He loves the sea.'

'I wish to God he hadn't.'

Clare's muttered interjections scarcely touched Laura's mind. She went on, 'Then he took his accountancy exams here in Sydney, and he used to drive racing cars. It's a wonder he wasn't killed when you see those scars on his forehead. They were very bad accidents. Two of them quite close together. But I don't know—'

Even Laura, in whom circumstances had uncovered a protective tendency to wishful thinking, could not pretend to believe that the facts of Felix's life in any way revealed him to her.

'I know all this backwards!'

'He's been unlucky with some of his businesses, letting these men cheat him, but—'

Unseen in the back seat, Clare bit two bitten fingernails of her left hand down to the nail bed and they started to bleed. Better to do that than shriek aloud in the middle of the city. Better to do that than wreck the car, be carted off, rend—

Rocking painfully to and fro, clasping the torn fingers in her right hand, she lowered her face to the tangle of fists and pressed a cheek into it, eyes closed, teeth jammed together.

Laura looked at her watch. 'I hope he's not—' She looked at the brick-and-tile façade of the hotel. The double swing doors were flung out at this moment and Felix stood for an instant on the step and thus elevated cast smilingly contemptuous glances on all who passed in review. His face was a very dark red and unhealthily shiny. He stood, toes turned cockily out, coat unbuttoned, thumbs tucked somewhere into his waistcoat, growing paunch thrust forward and straining his expensive brown suit. His hat was tilted at an angle that brought Laura's arms out in goose-flesh.

Clearing his throat with some enjoyment, he pushed his way across to the car and fumbled in.

'Did I keep you waiting?' he enquired, sitting there as though he had arrived home. He looked from Laura across his shoulder to Clare with a slow red smile. 'I said—did I keep you waiting?—No answer! I should apologise. Mr. Shaw should go down on his knees, shouldn't he? You'd like that, wouldn't you?—Well, you know what you can do, don't you?' He raked the sewers of his vocabulary.

His normally so evasive eyes were now obscenely eager to make contact with other eyes, stalked them, sought them out with a strange and gloating pleasure, somehow smeared them with the filth of his own mind, gloating into them with a threatening and vile deliberation. He dared them to look away. He dared them to speak. Craven, in total submission, ruined, he wanted them to be.

Laura sat stiffly beside him on the green leather seat, every nerve at attention, her head thundering with pain. In the back seat, Clare had relaxed and now nursed her bleeding fingers in her lap, watching the two heads in front of her with almost a half-smile.

With finicky exactitude, Felix extracted tobacco and a paper from his leather pouch and began to roll a cigarette. 'So I kept them waiting, did I?' he asked at intervals. 'Hmmm? Well. That's too bad, isn't it? Yes. That's too bad.'

Months ago they had learned that there was no defence but silence, and that was no defence. He did so enjoy cajoling them into speech, but he had been known to be provoked to the very edge of violence by the sound of an answering voice. Not that he minded being brought to the edge of violence.

Fifteen minutes after he had returned to the car, Felix revved the engine noisily, then revved it again, then again, smiling broadly at Laura's pale profile and back into her sister's unwavering eyes. With a bound the car took off, passing a grey Chevrolet on the right. The driver shouted after them. As the traffic lights changed to red, Felix pushed on the accelerator and a convoy of cars with the right-of-way pressed forward.

Laura sat on the edge of the seat, looking now at Felix crouching over the wheel, and now at the lights, the dense traffic, the crossroads ahead, the bridge toll-gates. In the back, Clare sat utterly at ease, not quite smiling, her right hand stuck to her left with blood.

Felix guided the car in between two others, making them swerve dangerously. The drivers shouted.

Chuckling and darting gay looks at his passengers, he pretended to speed into the oncoming traffic on the bridge, then diverted himself by breaking the law and changing lanes. Men shouted. Leaving the bridge, he pressed his foot to the floorboards and the car hurtled up a narrow and almost vertical hill, passing every-thing, horn blaring.

In fear of death, her shoulders queerly hunched and not daring to speak, Laura watched the road, her husband, the descending cars that Felix, grunting to himself, avoided less and less carefully while he passed and edged in front of steady travellers to the peril and anger of all.

With apparent pleasure, and totally at ease, Clare watched the playful game. She was sufficiently indif-ferent to it, however, to notice and admire in the steep grounds of the old convent a row of dark pines stiffly pointing into the exquisite and prophetic evening sky. And from her soul, the while, she sent a still, intense and loving prayer: Crash us. Kill us. Crash us.

'What do you make of these atom bombs?' Elsie Trent asked the boss's wife, when the boss was outside talking confidentially to one of his suppliers.

Laura looked up from her typewriter, startled. 'I don't know, Elsie. It's the end of the war, of course, and that's wonderful, though it makes you think of all the poor boys—'

The day the war ended officially they would be officially and permanently dead, the boys who were not coming back. Till that day it would always seem that peace could resurrect them, fully fleshed.

'It will be a very sad day for a lot of people.'

'It will that,' Elsie agreed, regarding a blue flower of her own creation in a disparaging way. She took another stem from the box and cleaned under her nails with it. 'But what do you make of the new bombs?'

'Well—' Laura smoothed her fingers along the shiny keys of her machine. 'It might be *clever* to kill more people with fewer, and they say it means terrible things, but I can only think—if someone's killed, what would the brand of the bomb matter? But I'm probably wrong,' she added hastily, to forestall announcements that she certainly was.

'Well, you know what men are. Anything new gets them in. They like a big bang. They see these things different from us.' Completing her manicure with the poison-green stem, Elsie proceeded, daintily, to stick petals round it.

At the beginning, Elsie had been inclined to respect Mrs. Shaw: she was terrific when anyone was sick, and kind and capable and never fussed. She was a first-class worker; too. But something about the way the boss treated her tickled Elsie and the others. He was a pig to her, really, and she was nice and everything and gentle and ladylike, but you had to giggle. Without ever turning in their direction, or acknowledging their powers of hearing, he subtly gave them leave to take a poke at her. So they did, just for a bit of fun. Elsie found a new bantering tone to use on Mrs. Shaw, and the younger girls kidded her. She never let on, though.

'Are you goin' to watch the victory parade and everything?' Elsie asked, one afternoon a few weeks later.

'Oh, no!' Laura smiled a little patronisingly at the idea. 'We always think home's best on days like that. We don't like being out in crowds. It's very pleasant to have a quiet day at home. We've got a lot to do in the garden.'

In truth, she had suggested to Felix that they might go into town. 'It would be nice to be with all the other people. It's a historic occasion, after all. By yourself it doesn't seem so much of a celebration.'

'What've *I* got to celebrate?'

'I didn't mean celebration. Event.'

'The Taxation Department's going to sting me for the best part of what I've made this year!'

'A little break would do you good. You never get a change of scene.'

'And would you mind telling me where I'm going to find a place to park my car? I wouldn't take it into town on V.J. Day if you gave me a million quid.'

Elsie pushed her pointed chin deep into her neck, making little rolls of powdered flesh ripple out from it.

'Hoh!' she scoffed. 'You can stay home when you're an old lady. What do you want a quiet day for at your age? You need a bit of life! You're as white as anything.'

'Oh well—' Laura smiled with the sadder air of one who is wiser, and glanced down at her shorthand notes and back at her page. You could hardly explain to Elsie that people had different values.

Dr. Bell sat behind his desk—a busy, prosperous man of forty-five, with olive skin, close-cropped black hair and serious social aspirations.

Clare Vaizey sat with her left hand bandaged in her lap. Her sister, whom he had seen the night the girl was admitted to hospital, had come back for the last visit with her. She was watching him now—an ordinary, timid housewife, hard-working (he looked at her hands) and short of money (he looked at her clothes).

He turned to Clare. 'I suppose you know it's no thanks to you that you've still got two hands? If you'd deliberately set out to have that amputated, you couldn't have done better. Tetanus is no joke, is it?'

She gave him a steady look.

'You had a good chance of killing yourself right off. You know that, too, don't you? Yes, I think you've learned your lesson.'

She regarded him. This had all happened as he said, and with its happening a great stillness and silence had

142

fallen in her, as though she contained in herself and looked out on the windless fields of eternity.

'If you give yourself another infected hand I don't think you'll start gardening with it in such a hurry.' He looked at his notes. The sister had brought up a number of extraneous symptoms and troubles, wanting more than her money's worth in the usual way. 'Your sister tells me you still have nightmares about the war. But that's all over. It's pure imagination. Morbid. I'd advise *you*,' he turned to Laura with condescending facetiousness, 'to wear ear-plugs at night so that she doesn't wake you. And as for *you*,' he looked back at the younger girl, 'I'd advise you to give up all this reading your sister talks about. Where do you think that'll get you? I don't know what you people expect out of life. Get yourself a job with more variety. Go out and get yourself married and have a baby. You won't have time for books and gardening with poisoned hands then!'

Clare saw that there was no limit to what he felt he might say to her. He was quite fascinating in a way. But of course it was not fair to sit like silent Cassandras in the surgery of an up-and-coming doctor who only wanted to be very rich and associate with the right people.

Catching her eye, Dr. Bell allowed himself to hector her a little more because—well, it was not likely that anyone would stop him. An attractive girl, with those thin brown arms, grey eyes, and fair hair to her shoulders what did she mean by treating him as though he were—just anybody? At the door he repeated, 'I don't know what you people expect out of life,' and gave a short affected whinny. He was a handsome man with smooth olive skin.

'"You people!"' Clare said, unlatching the gate and walking out on to the footpath. 'What does he know?' She let her leather bag bump against her knees.

Laura looked at the suburban gardens lining the street, stark new rose bushes, straggly stock. 'I wish I knew as much,' she protested.

'You know more.'

Laura laughed and looked interested. 'You wouldn't like me to take out your appendix.'

'If you'd learned how to do it, you would do it better.'

Flattered, Laura laughed again and pictured herself, white-clad and competent, conducting an appendectomy.

'But you'll have to do what he says, Clare. You've been very sick. All these weeks in hospital. You're really very lucky to be alive. Felix has been terribly upset.'

'I know he has.'

'We've both been very worried.'

'Yes.' She allowed that. They had been genuinely startled, and had had something new to say to each other.

They walked along the quiet street. Clare said nothing. What did it matter what Laura said, or the doctor, or what she answered? The uselessness of having plans, taking action, was truly amazing to her. Tendrils of initiative were thrown out for no other purpose, it began to seem, than to be pruned back. She felt an amorphous, cold awareness of the existence of some force, and not a friendly one, powerful, invisible, voiceless, armed with shears and choppers, ranging the world for hope to kill.

Laura opened the door and two voices came from the front of the house—a lecturer's cultivated drawl and Felix's hoarse growl as he argued back at the wireless.

'*Who* says? You think so, do you? Bloody mug! Bloody professors! Christ, I'm hostile to you blokes!'

In the familiar way, Clare became conscious of her heart in her chest beating unevenly, fatigued, of her blood receding.

'Go to your room and if he remembers to ask what happened, I'll just tell him you've been ordered to get a different job and stop reading.'

'Wouldn't it be better if I did it?'

'No.'

'He didn't like you coming tonight. And he'd had a lot even before we left.'

'Lock the door.'

Abhorring her boredom and weariness and the ease with which Laura resumed her armour of apprehension, Clare gave a soundless groan and went to her room. Leaving the door ajar, she leaned against the wall listening, arms and legs crossed in a classic pose of idleness. Bandaged hand, fuschia-coloured carnations in a crystal vase, stool, chair, bed, curtains— the windows were black reflecting mirrors now. Night already. Again. Always night, always day, always waiting like this—

She was alive and could have been dead with all the slippery acquiescence of the world. She had not aimed as high as death, but she had been prepared to give her hand for her independence. *They* were not to damage her most. In her own way she would be free. In the only way she would outreach them. She would go so far in damaging herself that they could never hope to touch her.

The wireless was turned off. Glass clinked against glass.

'Her—that thing—what do I care if she goes? Good riddance! Rotten stinking women—fat, filthy— vomit—Don't you, you—'

Clare listened, without a change of expression, only unfolding her arms because she found it hard to breathe.

I see, I see, she thought, almost politely, as if someone was explaining a new and astounding fact to her. At the same time she wanted to drop to her knees with grief and mourning. And she attended, too, to an idea that emerged from the centre of her mind to stand brightly lighted: *he could kill.*

Words like poison continued to insert themselves in her ears, and she heard them with a faint smile of horror. Dangerous. Even at a distance, he was that. Because thoughts had power. He had the desire to torture and, perhaps, a talent for murder that he had not yet tapped. Carefully, she closed her door, saying softly, 'Don't think about it. Don't think about it.'

Half an hour later, when Laura came tiptoeing in, Clare had her clothes packed.

'I'm going, Laura. Don't try to stop me this time. Let me go without—*us*— having to thrash anything out. I just can't bear it!'

'No!' Laura said angrily, glaring at the two suit-cases. 'You're under age. I'm your guardian legally. Where could you go? You haven't got a shilling.'

'What does that matter?' she said savagely. 'A little sense of proportion, Laura! Where I'm going if I stay here is insane. I don't care where I go. I'll go to a police station. I'll sleep in a park. What does it matter?'

'They'd bring you straight back here. I'd ring them up. You haven't got a job if you leave the factory. You don't know a single soul to go to. He doesn't want you to leave, you know that. In many ways he takes more notice of you and what you say than of anyone, and he hates the house to be empty. That's what's caused half the trouble—you shut up in your room reading at night, or out walking, or going out with these silly little girls and boys. He wants you to—just—sit in with us at night and listen to him telling the politicians what to do with the world.'

'Don't I? It's all I do! I'm like a prisoner! We both are!' Tears, anger, sheer incredulity at the madness and stupidity of their lives choked her.

'I know we've heard it all before, but it doesn't hurt much. It isn't much to ask.'

Laura took a clean handkerchief from the pocket of her skirt and rubbed at the dressing-table, tremendously defiant.

'It does hurt. It is much to ask,' Clare cried passionately, watching her sister's actions automatically. 'What about us? What are we? I mean—are we both supposed to exist just as a sort of hobby for Felix? All these years! Maybe you don't want a life for yourself. I do. I'm a person, too. Not a wooden toy you pick up and put down. I'm a person. Why is my life so much less important than Felix's? How can you *let* him talk to you the way he does? Oh, Laura. The war's over. There's more—there's everything.'

Laura was watching her with a grim, almost amused, incomprehension.

'No, listen!' Clare pleaded, crying. 'Listen. There are people who are saints, and temples thousands of years old, Laura, and camel trains crossing the deserts. Cities are broken to pieces, and people are climbing mountains and making pilgrimages to Mecca. There's beauty and terror and so much more than we know. Nothing is this small.'

'You're hysterical,' Laura said contemptuously.

'No! *There is very much*—life doesn't have to be like this. I don't believe it. I *know* it doesn't.' Clare turned away, leaning into the corner by the windows.

'Stop crying,' Laura said unconvincingly. She was awkwardly embarrassed, as if an importunate stranger had walked in at the back door and made demands on her emotions. 'Anyone would think you were losing your mind if they heard you carrying on like this. You're hysterical. You're still nervy after being ill, that's what it is.' Laura rubbed again at a non-existent mark on the dressing-table, willing the dreadful sounds to stop.

'*Will you speak the truth*?' Venomous, piteous, Clare's voice rose to a scream as she turned from the wall, tears pouring from her eyes. 'You never, never can admit the truth. I want to be free! That's not unnatural! I do not want to make artificial flowers in a factory all my life. Why should I? You want me to abase myself before him the way you do. I won't do it! I hate him! I won't do it! I'm too—'

In a way, she was wonderful. She felt she was. She could do anything. There was something she had to do.

Laura said uncomfortably, 'I know he's been nasty tonight, and you've been very sick, but he didn't mean to be. Stop crying. You shouldn't have been listening. I told you not to. What would have happened to us, anyway, if it hadn't been for Felix?'

'For God's sake! Can't you be honest for one moment? What has? What has happened to us?'

'Lower your voice! And I won't have any of that language, Clare, if you don't mind. Look at this lovely room! Look at—At the very least he kept you till you started work. Our own mother didn't do that. Felix did.'

'*You* did. *He* didn't. You've worked harder even than you did before you married him, and still had to be under an obligation because of me. But anyway—'

She sat on the bed and wiped her face with her bandaged hand.

'Here.' Laura tossed a box of 'Kleenex' over to her impatiently, but it fell disregarded to the floor. Laura unknotted and knotted the green silk scarf at her throat. This abandoned display of emotion made her feel pestered and unclean, but not agitated, not sympathetic. The result of all this, the result, was what she cared about.

Clare gave a shuddering sigh. Head hanging, eyes closed, she sat in a dull trance, empty of everything but deep spasmodic sighs. With the need for air she raised her head at last, and Laura's shaking fingers fiddling with her scarf halted her listless eyes. Empty, salty, laid waste, not a person at all, Clare nevertheless kept her eyes focused on her sister and without thinking began to be aware of certain facts about her. Laura looked queerly mortal. Insubstantial. She was almost

150

innocently shifty and scheming—desperate. But underneath that she was supplicating. Clare's heart turned over with compassion.

'If I have kept you then,' Laura said, breaking away from Clare's pitiless observation, 'you might do this for me. Not worry me like this. Think of someone else for a change. How can I let you disappear into the city? If you went, I would never want to see you again, Clare. That's the truth. Felix would hate it, too. In his own funny way, he thinks the world of you. Even at the factory they've said to me that you could do anything with him if you handled him the right way.'

'Handled.' Clare moved her shoulders uneasily, beyond revulsion. They had said that, and more than that. They said it as if she should be flattered. If she would only pander to Felix, everyone would be happy. How could Laura exact this of her in the first place? And in the second, had she forgotten that he *was* pandered to? And what was the result?

Out of a deadly misery and extreme physical weakness, she began to cry again till it seemed inconceivable even to Laura that there should be no consolation for such unhappiness. But she watched with distaste and curiosity. Through the bedcover, through her ears, skin, fingers, alarm began to reach Clare. Heaving herself up she looked about and saw her staring sister and almost groaned with outrage and anger. 'Go *away*, go *away*. Leave me alone, for God's sake!'

Laura spoke hotly for two or three minutes, then went out. Clare took her hands from her ears, rose and locked the door and, switching off the light, went to the window and opened it wide. She knelt down and leaned out into the night, breathing the smell of darkness, grass, trees and sea. (There *was* consolation.) The sky was exceedingly dark, vast and high; without light. The moon had not risen. The stars were merest points.

Clare stared up into the cold blackness and heard the wind rising and felt its bombardment against her head and arms and chest. Blackness all about and above. The night existed, forbidding, unfeeling. Anything was bearable. The wind was clean and undemanding. Blotted out in the tremendous night, in the midst of it, she was at home. In a way, all she had was herself and the sky. If she looked down from it, there were asphalt streets, cement footpaths, tight little bungalows, ripe gardens, and scratchy ones, hovels, crowded reverberating streets in the city, advertising, dust, nothing wonderful, no work of genius, only the monotonous harbour, dead from being over-admired by its suburban landlords. But this wild and unconsoling view of the universe, with its everlasting indifference could do much—do much—

'Clare!' Laura's voice was a furtive half-whisper.

'What?' She unlocked the door.

'I told Felix you had your cases packed. He was very upset. Very upset. You see. You're too quick to jump to conclusions. He said those nasty things because I didn't explain properly when I said you'd have to change jobs. He didn't realise the doctor ordered you to. He thought you just decided to yourself, to get away from us, and naturally he was very hurt.'

'Was he?'

They exchanged amazed looks.

'*Yes*. He thinks the world of you.'

Clare smiled. Laura always did that. She had no artistic sense. If no one checked her, she exaggerated till her most credulous listener was obliged to grin.

'I think you should go in to him.' Laura widened her eyes as advisers do, and knotted her green silk scarf.

'Oh. Not tonight.' What gifts they had, these two, to make it seem, when it suited them, that only she could create discord or harmony. She was used and, in theory (if she had been someone else, for instance), she resented it.

'I think it would be the fair thing to do, after all this.'

Clare looked at her hard. If Laura wanted or needed or asked as much as this, why not? She had nothing else to do. No one else required her. And she felt nothing whatever.

'Yes. Okay. Okay. Okay.' She almost ran to the other room. 'Anything.'

'Well now, well now,' Felix said, pulling a jolly face like a butcher at a trade picnic. Clare was manoeuvred into a low chair. Felix rose and put his hand on her head, holding her head there below him, powerful, chuckling.

'What's it all about, eh? What's it all about?' His rough smiling voice had a note that was sadistic and obscene. He was pretending to comfort her! Pretending in a sentimental, sadistic, drunken way to console and forgive her!

That she permitted this, that she permitted his hand on her head, caused her to suffer greatly. Laura came in and the two continued to regard Clare with such false smiles of reprobation that she could not look at them. In their separation from what *was* they were infinitely alien. Clare felt a paralysing sense of sin, but smilingly conspired.

'Well, there's two thousand in cash,' Felix said to Gilbert Blaine, nodding at the stacks of folded notes on his desk. He dug into the pockets of his khaki shorts and crossed his feet, drawing close to himself and smiling at the younger man, pompous and wistful. 'Two thousand smackers!' he repeated, suddenly depressed.

Gil Blaine studied the money as if Felix were a sculptor of genius and this his controversial master-piece. His expression both reassured and hurt Felix, but he tried to cope with his mixed feelings by watching Gil, who was good to look at. He had youth, beautiful teeth, frank brown eyes, the face of a male mannequin.

From the divan his wife, Julie, a glamorous, bored-looking girl with upswept black hair, watched the two men and the money. With a minute movement of one foot in an elegant white shoe, she slid the canvas overnight bag towards her husband. He picked it up abstractedly and began to pack the money, flipping through each roll.

'You won't be sorry, Felix. In the long run it's going to look like *your* lucky break.'

Willing though he was to be comforted, Felix gave a painful smile at this, and his attention jumped again and again from Gilbert's soothing patter to his busy hands.

'I hope you're right, young fella. You'd better be, or I'll end up in Queer street.'

'I noticed a new Jag in your garage.' Julie Blaine drew her cheeks in and opened her eyes like the beauties in cigarette advertisements.

Felix's look was as cold and surprising to her as a slap in the face with a wet fish. He turned slowly back to the young man and Gilbert hurried to say, 'We'll get the beer-garden working in a month, Felix. The finance is all fixed up. We only needed this bit of ready cash to tide us over.'

'I hope so. I hope so.' He was a little sententious, but who had more right to be? 'All safely packed, eh?'

'Yep!' Gilbert let his charming teeth be seen. 'Only the receipt now to keep it all above board. Have you got a duty stamp on you?' He felt in his pockets. 'Blast! I meant to make sure—'

'Receipts!' Felix threw his arms about casually. 'Red tape! We're not a government department! Next time's soon enough.'

Young Blaine eyed him with deference and compunction, making Felix give a broad, indulgent smile.

'No, look,' Blaine protested after a moment, 'that's not good enough. I'll make out an interim thing—except that we still can't get round the duty stamp!'

'Forget it! Forget it! I can trust you.' Felix shook Gilbert's arm paternally, laughing. 'What about a spot of lunch? How'd that be? Lobster mayonnaise. How about that?'

'Ah—' The Blaines darted a look at each other. 'We couldn't manage that today, I'm afraid, Felix. We've got some cocktail thing on at Julie's mother's place tonight and we'll both be flat out one way and another—' He smoothed the back of his head with his right hand and grasped the bag with his left.

'Is that so?' A joylessness much more positive than the mere absence of joy overflowed in Felix and went out from him like a minor death ray. 'We'd better make it one day in town next week, then. It'd be easier to talk business alone, anyway.'

'Yes, or—I tell you what: I'll call at the factory one afternoon.'

Julie Blaine was opening the door of Felix's office, walking out into the shady flower-decked hall.

'Will you? Yes, that's the shot!' Felix stood still to adjust to this compromise which might turn out to be far far better than lunch today. He hurried after the young couple, then led the way through the garden, grateful now for anything he might be thrown. Like a child, with a plea, a sad smile in his eyes, he looked at Gil Blaine and clapped him on the shoulder, laughing unhappily.

The car leapt away from his side. Disconsolate, he sauntered back down the steps and past all the green swaying garden, hands in pockets.

'Isn't he staying, Felix?'

'I am not aware that he was invited.' There was a lofty pause. 'He had some stupid piece with him. I can't conduct a business discussion like that. We'll meet in private next week.'

'I see.'

Usually on Saturday the house was cleaned from chimney to cellar while Felix retired to the garden or the office. Very early on Sundays Laura did the week's washing and finished the house off in time to iron at night. This Saturday, for the first time since Ruth's visit long ago, the routine had been altered to include a luncheon party—'A luncheon party,' Laura said, 'for Felix's friend Mr. Blaine.'

'I see.' Laura changed colour, and her soft pale face

looked a little puffy. 'Will you have your lunch now, then, Felix?' Lobster mayonnaise.

'I'll have some bread and cheese later. I'll let you know when I'm ready. I have letters to attend to. And by the way,' he looked into her eyes, startling her, 'there's another overdraft now, so you'd better go a bit easy on the housekeeping.'

Laura breathed in through her nose, looking after him. Recently she had joined the sales staff, going about the city and suburbs on foot with a suitcase of samples. Selling was physically tiring and in other ways so against the grain of her nature that she shrank from waking to each day, but she *would* have Felix happy, his business a success.

'I thought we were doing quite well.'

He halted, shoulders drooping, seeming persecuted to death by the sound of her faint voice. 'It so happens,' he enunciated, not turning, 'that I have decided to go into partnership with Mr. Blaine. Today I gave him a certain sum for petty expenses. In order to raise sufficient capital I am negotiating with my bank. Are you satisfied?—Are you still curious?—Or am I permitted to get on with my work?'

Laura watched him go, half-suffocated by the press of anonymous emotions. She hated, hated (presumably), the people, things, that had done this to him, raised up his corrosive bitterness, antagonism of the bone. She used to try to rally him at first, refuting his grievances and coaxing him out of his tragic role. She persuaded Clare, who was better at it, to imitate some of his ludicrously gloomy poses to such effect that he had to roar with laughter to see himself so. He loved to be so concentrated on. Yet how quickly he wearied of being wooed from his blackness and gnashing of teeth! How almost resentful he appeared later at having been seduced to laughter and sense! Like a fretful child he allowed himself to be distracted briefly, and crowed and accepted the spotlight with fractious high spirits, only to hold a grudge against the author of those good spirits ten minutes later.

Laura wandered into the dining-room set with real silver, soft-looking silver, for the luncheon party. The walls and ceiling reflected the harbour's trembling surface. Today of all days, because Felix was so amiable before the Blaines came, she had plucked up the will to ask him for a new dress. She had dragged herself to the idea of this as easily as she might have urged herself to the rim of an active volcano: it was against nature.

But—it wasn't even that the shabbiness of her few clothes made her vulnerable to the snubs of the expense-account tycoons she had to bargain with daily. It was, rather, that she had to make a gesture from herself to herself, do something to assuage, make amends to—

Really, she was foolish. He had told her ages ago, 'Ask for anything you want.'

'Then—could I have some pocket-money every week? Not a lot. Only to save up with.'

'What? Isn't that like a woman? You go and spoil it straight away. What do you want *money* for? *I* know what to do with money. I said when you want some *thing*. Aren't you fed and driven about in a new car? The only thing women can do with money is spend it or put it in a savings bank. No. Come to me and say, "Felix, I want a—whatever it is—please." And if sales are looking up, we'll see what we can do.'

'It's me,' she said to Clare. 'I can't do it. I don't know why.'

And now the factory, that they had thought, breathed, spoken, eaten and slept since Felix bought it in its death-throes, was to be drained to pay off the overdraft supporting Gilbert Blaine's business. Whatever it was.

Head drooping, she stood at the side of the table.

She had sought out new materials for flowers, and searched a thousand fashion magazines and garden catalogues and gardens for the golden idea that would free Felix from his weird bondage to misery. If she could help to make him more than prosperous, so that he need never think of money, cash books, ledgers, overdrafts and mortgages at all, and never with fear, then—

At this point her thoughts always dispersed and darted off like a cloud of finches. But what she knew was: life could begin then.

Boxes, chocolates and artificial flowers were, really, nothing to her. Yet for years her life had been devoted to their production and sale as selflessly as it might have been devoted to music, or the care of the sick. Their names—box, chocolate and flower—were the words she had said and heard most often in these years. On the words with which they were coupled depended her peace of mind, almost, her safety.

She had concentrated on each one in turn with a fierce and dedicated will, since to go through the fire of dull box, chocolate and unreal flower was the only way out for Felix to the 'then' when life could begin.

Quite what it might be like then, she could scarcely imagine, but she visualised a Felix visited with ease, the wires that tormented and ham-strung him cut. That dense threatening blackness in him that rose for no reason, which was almost visible, making him seem physically bulkier, all shoulders, arms and head, would go. The towering gloom without object, seeking revenge for no particular hurt—all these would go. The Felix who must belittle her in front of strangers would alter, too. He would be—not some impossible paragon, only like anyone else, and only occasionally short-tempered and cruel. As it was, it was the sensation of deep malice, of bottomless glee, behind the derogatory remark that was so debilitating to her spirit.

But *then* with the factory working so well that they need not sit over its accounts nightly as though it were a feverish child, Felix would be light-hearted and gay. From Friday night to Monday morning they would never mention it! Felix would take back old Mr. Gilroy, the gardener. (The garden was not only large, but working in it as a pleasure had been ruled out for ever by the peculiarly punitive pressure under which they were made to labour there. It might have been fun, it might have been rewarding, except for the fact that it was not meant to be. Felix's all-too-obvious intention was not to create a beautiful place but to create another situation in which he could test his power. And in addition, Felix slogged beside his work-force, the pace-maker, the deeply-wronged foreman, no sound, only grunted instructions from time to time, and the harsher the weather the better.)

But *then*—at night and at weekends they would be free even to make friends. Why should they not? If it was not exactly obvious what Felix would do with a friend, it was only because neither he nor she had had much practice with them.

They would all sit in the garden, actually admiring it for a change, and having afternoon tea; or they would sit out on the terrace and watch the yachts racing.

Then, while Felix knew facts about the foreign countries he had visited, and could solve anagrams, and add brilliantly, and distinguish Scotch from local whisky, and might—if he chose—win fame as a genius on quiz sessions, *she* knew nothing about anything.

What time had there been since the day of her father's death to acquire any knowledge that was not utilitarian? There was never time even to read a paper. Occasionally she borrowed one of Clare's books, but she was usually so tired that her eyes slid over two pages and she was asleep. When had she had half an hour to sit and listen to music? Felix was always active, and you could hardly loll about while he was working! It was years since she had even seen a piano, much less touched one. And singing—Once upon a time she had loved to sing, she had loved to practise dance steps alone on the slippery kitchen floor. At school she liked French so much the girls accused her of speaking English with a foreign accent! And as a very young child she had picked out melodies on the piano by pure instinct! Her eyes grew round with the wonder of all she was telling herself. Then she sighed.

Felix had sometimes said, with a puzzled expression, 'If we did have a bit of time and money to spare, you wouldn't want to go to the races, or the dogs. You wouldn't go round to the Beach and Pines for some beers, or play poker.'

She had done all these things, but let it pass. Laura looked down and picked at a loose thread in her grey pleated skirt, found wanting. But since he was kindly this day, she said, 'There are other things though.'

'Are there? *Are* there?' Genuinely baffled, Felix rubbed his bristly chin, trying to think. 'What? You mean going to the Australia for champagne? Buying fur coats and dresses?'

He remembered other women and what had pleased them. The few barmaids he had known had seemed satisfied with cosy cheerful rooms, drinks, dresses and races. Wealthy women, he assumed, wanted more expensive versions of the same things. What Laura could mean or think she wanted, he was at a loss to guess. But slowly, as she explained and he began to comprehend what she was suggesting, his eyes withdrew from hers, without moving from them, to a series of inner visions: *Mr. Felix Shaw, well-known man-about-town, at the first night of—*

Since he took no action, however, and failed to become overnight a new Mr. Felix Shaw, the elevated pictures Laura had fooled him into believing turned out to have been a swindle. From standing staring, naïvely taken with this revelation of his possibilities, he turned, jaundiced, back to his ledgers, and when he and Laura had worked to a standstill at night, and had half an hour before going to bed in which to realise that they were bored to the edge of insanity by figures, artificial flowers and vacuum cleaners, he would complain peevishly of his isolation. She had driven away all his old pals. If she was like any other woman they would be out at the trots or the dogs, having a good time.

Still, still—*Then*, he would be more content than he could dream of now. He was only bored, only lonely (probably) just as she was. When their friends said, 'Felix, come fishing this weekend!' or if she could say, 'Look, two tickets for the Old Vic tonight!' Felix would thaw with delight. He only wanted to be thought for, entertained, coddled, treated kindly (probably). She wanted to do it. He wanted to be popular. She wanted him to be.

From what she could discern (Felix kept the books locked up), the factory was running well and sales were increasing, so any minute, she had thought, it would be (there was an automatic pause here for scaling down: the truth always seems excessive) possible and a good thing, very nice, if they could—decide to live. Much of that extra work was self-inflicted. Laura had felt her nerves straining, all but spent, for that instant when not Felix exactly but things, the omnipresent, terrible, invisible examiner, would call, 'Enough!'

Now—

She stared at the table, dully understanding that that absolutely vital relief was as far away as it had ever been. Instead there were to be new burdens, new strivings, new sets of books, new unreasonable reasons for silence and labour and putting her down with his eyes with that amazing look of arrogance.

'No!' she said aloud. 'No! she said to the waiting table. She felt a sudden tearing sensation as if half the contents of her head had been violently catapulted off from her. Like someone pushing through dense bush, she went to her bedroom, tugged on a coat and grabbed a handbag. No one was about. She went swiftly outside, and up the path to the street.

It was one of those magnificent days that people are inclined to think unique, perhaps the most exquisite they are ever destined to see, a day to wring superstitious vows from any who wander into it with untroubled eyes. They will remember this unearthly radiance for ever! (They forget the regularity of days fit for trumpets and angels.) On the ferry, Laura sat outside staring fixedly at nothing.

The city looked tawdry, dirty, flimsy as a fun-fair, grit falling from half-demolished buildings, deserted scaffolding rising above those still under construction. It was Saturday and the shops had all closed at twelve; the streets were emptying rapidly. Neon signs hung low overhead from low awnings and stretched into the diminishing distance—a printed roof of glowing signs in queer off-reds, pinks, yellows, blues and greens, misspelling lunatic messages with demented jocularity, letters jumping, flashing and changing, messages from things to no one, silently chattering over the blighted streets.

Laura walked down Pitt Street from the Quay to Central Station. She walked back down Elizabeth Street to Hunter Street, down Hunter Street to George Street, along that thoroughfare to Bathurst Street, up Bathurst to Castlereagh, along Castlereagh to King, down King to Pitt, along Pitt to Market, up Market and along Castlereagh to King, down King, along Pitt, up Market.

She could not make her feet stop walking. She yearned to stop. But if she ever did, how could she make it appear ordinary to other people? And what else was there to do in life? What alternative? If the other aimless strollers knew the screaming emptiness of her head, if she stood still forever on a corner, what would happen? If she lay down in the gutter, or broke things that did not belong to her, what would they do? Would anyone come?

She yearned to stop. She had walked for hours. But her feet bore her on past every terminus. Her thoughts and the impressions received by her senses were fragmentary and disordered.

Late in the afternoon, with the reflex of someone falling who snatches hopelessly at a dry branch growing from rock, she found herself halted and saved. A grey man in a bundle of clothes had sold her a newspaper, and stood waiting for his money. Laura fumbled in her bag, clamping the paper under one arm. Shaking, her legs giving under her, she dropped a few coins into the dirty outstretched hand of her saviour.

The clockwork spell dissolved. No longer driven, she crossed the street and taking a few steps into Hyde Park sank down onto the grass. Some of the wooden seats set further back in the park had single occupants, sexless derelicts slumped in the dying afternoon sun, unnoticeable as rocks.

On the cool grass, Laura opened her paper, and it was only now, when she began to look for work and a place to live, that she comprehended even obliquely what she had allowed to happen to herself. Little by little she had resigned away the trust she had been given to be herself—out of pity, from a desire for peace at any price, thinking nothing really lost, anyway, by her silent acquiescence, not noticing the contradiction since all was so unconscious, that believing herself invulnerable to change, she hoped for a change in Felix. Silence was the least harmful course she could take, she had decided: she could think her thoughts. Since she had reserved the right to do this—think her thoughts in silence, while offering no resistance outwardly to Felix's version of herself, life and the world—how could she be damaged?

She read advertisements. Her head began to feel hollow and deep and without boundaries, as if a pebble tossed in her mind would fall for ever. What did she know? What did she *know*? No box, chocolate or artificial flower factory wanted help. She had no references. She had no school certificates. A most tremendous inertia which sprang from the paralysis of a will too long suppressed shackled her. She could do nothing. The habit of living each day as it came, grateful, after it had passed, for any hours that gave even the appearance of concord, had rendered her incapable of forethought. She had achieved this state with much painless suffering, committing murder by proxy.

In truth, at the deepest level, she did not know what to do, and knew what she would do.

Meantime she reasoned in a rapid and flickering series of reflections that she could not apply for these jobs, anyway, till Monday morning. Nor could she rent a room with five shillings, which was all she had, and Elsie Trent at the factory said people bought the *Herald* at four o'clock in the morning in their efforts to find accommodation, so strenuous was the competition for living-space.

It was becoming clearer and clearer that circumstances made any action impossible. She had no choice but to resign herself to the unchangeableness of her existence. Yes, the more she understood this, the more she felt almost a grim satisfaction, a burning self-righteousness. Very well then! She had tried. A sort of anger that felt like strength flared briefly. Very well!

Felix and Clare sat at the kitchen table eating dinner.

'Oh, hullo. There you are.' Felix looked up mildly from his book. 'Are you going to have some food? There's some left, isn't there?' He turned to Clare.

'Yes.' She and Laura exchanged bleached glances.

'I had to get out of the house for a while. I don't

know what came over me. Just for a change. I only went to town.'

Felix's pleasant expression somehow affected her breathing. She hurried a few steps into his office, dropped her coat and bag on the divan and returned to sit down at the table.

'Ah.' Felix looked up mildly again, his dark-brown eyes faintly enquiring, his smile a little deaf-looking. 'How did you get on?'

'I only walked about.'

Having registered courteous astonishment, he turned back to his book, and the kitchen was so quiet that Laura could barely swallow for fear of being over-heard. She and Clare looked down, silent, sick, not daring not to eat. Felix chewed with his mouth open, sucked at his food, mused over his book.

Laying down his knife and fork finally he read on for a few moments and then lifted his head with signal innocence. 'Should I be waiting here for anything else?'

'Yes, yes. There's fruit salad and ice cream in the fridge.' Laura began to resume control of her kitchen.

Throughout this course, and while he ate biscuits and cheese and they all drank coffee, Felix read and no one spoke. No one ever did, of course, unless he did, granting an amnesty. ('It's hard to read when other people are gossiping just twelve inches away,' Laura sometimes said. 'He doesn't get much chance to look at his paper.')

170

While the dishes were washed Felix remained in the kitchen reading, and then all three moved together to the sitting-room where they sat till bedtime, reading. Felix spoke a few words about the factory, but he was supra-naturally mild and pleasant and easy. Laura and her sister avoided conversation entirely even during his single absence from the room. The china Bluebeard stood over the seated semicircle of three.

Later in the big double bed, Felix read till midnight then went straight to sleep having uttered no word of any particular significance and certainly none of reproach.

'Thank God! Thank God!' Laura muttered thanksgiving without ceasing all morning long on Sunday as she cleaned the house. Everything had blown over. No repercussions. Yet she felt so shriven and strange to herself that she might have come back from a long illness. 'But thank God, thank God!'

Clare helped about the house, washing floors and paint-work, and Saturday's jobs were gradually overtaken. Everything was going to be all right. Laura had finished hanging sheets and towels on the inconspicuous lines at the sides of the garden when some strangers stopped up in the street and stood, evidently admiring the house. One man appeared to be making a speech; the other man and woman paid attention.

Here was a scene Laura had often visualised: strangers ecstatic and envious staring at their lovely house with its unparalleled views and embroidered verandahs and low window-sills with flowers reaching up to them. She half-loved these people on the instant. How nice they were, and of what judgement!

The orator opened the gate and ushered his audience in; the three strolled down the steps.

Felix!—In her mind Laura was calling him to greet their visitors. Stirred and excited as she always was at the astonishing approach of other English-speaking natives, she hesitated a moment longer before running round to tell Felix. It could be a mistake, a public-opinion poll, anything. It always had been.

'Miss Shaw? You *are* the daughter of the house, I take it?' The leader had spotted her and now advanced with outstretched hand. His hair was black and shiny. He was tall and well-dressed and had the disarming manner of a born salesman.

'*Mrs*. Shaw.' Laura smiled apologetically, anxiously, half-whispered. Now she hoped to be rewarded with a cry of: 'Good news!'

'Of course, of course! Mrs. Shaw—' he gave the impression of a slight bow, 'may I introduce Mr. and Mrs. Terry. Remember,' he added, when she failed to respond, 'I told your husband about them yesterday afternoon.'

'Oh! How do you do.'

Mrs. Terry had a white flowery hat on; Mr. Terry was even taller than the other man, and very brown and thin. They were old enough to be Laura's parents. They looked kindly at her.

'We've come to see your lovely home.' Mrs. Terry smiled under her shady hat.

'Well, do you mind if we—start looking round, Mrs. Shaw? I think I've got you a couple of very interested buyers.'

There was a longish pause.

'I'll get my husband first, if you'll wait. He's in the front garden.'

'Oh, have they come?' Felix stuck the fork in the ground and rested his foot on it. He wiped his face with his forearm. 'Phew!—Well, I better put in an appearance, I guess. I thought,' he said amiably, 'that I'd just get someone to take the house off our hands. You don't think too much of it, do you? I mean, you don't care what happens to it, do you? Eh?'

Laura stared away past him to the harshly glittering harbour. She looked out at it from under her raised hand, and through narrowed eyes, for the sun was dazzling. There were a lot of boats about.

Everything looked black in all this sun.

Five days later Felix decided not to sell the house.

Oriel Carter-Wright said, 'And then the bomb fell. A minute or two later I saw that my brother was dead.' Oriel said, 'Paris.' She said, 'Oxford. History.' She said, 'I'll drive home from Singapore.'

Oriel said, 'I'll stand again at the next General Election, I trust, for another constituency.' And very often and warmly, Oriel laughed. She had travelled all over the world taking jobs of every description, at all levels. There could be no question of being in competition with so exotic and temporary a being, so although she was sometimes looked at shyly, and with defensive cynicism, she was generally considered a feature in this government office. Having been labelled 'different', Oriel might thereafter have spoken in Hindi for all the attention the actual matter of her conversation received. For it was 'different' conversation, hard to fathom, not to be taken seriously. This was what came of her having, one girl remarked sympathetically, a trained mind. But they did like to stare and stare at her white, flawless, flower-like complexion, at her dark-blue eyes and wavy dark-brown hair.

Clare listened to Oriel. She listened with a singular absorption, sifting her statements this way and that through all the meshes of her intuition. Methodically, like a jeweller whose passion was rubies, she laid out on black velvet with theoretical appreciation and yet with dissatisfaction the semi-precious stones and even the diamonds given off by Oriel Carter-Wright: wit, intelligence, vitality, education, experience of a severe and testing nature—of war and death, opinions based on fact, a developed political sense. These and other fabulous possessions Clare admired and laid aside while she continued to wait, weigh and sift.

At this moment she and Oriel stopped with their cups of morning tea at Janet Adams' desk. At thirty-seven, Janet was the oldest inhabitant of this all-female section of the Department, and carroty, freckled, irascible, unendingly berating the operations of Head Office.

'You'd never get this sort of inefficiency outside!' she exclaimed, flapping a handful of pink and yellow memoranda at her smiling friends. 'What are you grinning at?'

'You make it sound as if we were in gaol. Your innocent view of commerce,' Clare said, over her cup.

'You should have stayed in it when you had the chance,' Janet said darkly. 'These morons!'

'She's right, you don't belong here,' Oriel said, low-voiced to Clare, when Janet turned to answer her raucous telephone. 'Why don't you go? I don't mean into the brave world of commerce.'

Forbearing to ask what Oriel did mean, Clare went off to answer her own telephone.

Out in the corridor at the trolley, Oriel poured herself another cup of liver-coloured tea before return-ing to her post beside Janet. One of the junior girls punctiliously held the door open for Oriel to pass before her. Her ways were so courteous and thoughtful, her thanks for small services so warmly-phrased and unfailingly delivered at the right time, that everyone else felt hoydenish and uncultivated but, too, strangely expanded, for Oriel's straight look saw all the inherent graces each knew herself to possess. Oh, it was not surprising that the total of her differences rendered Oriel almost alluring. Even Janet Adams, who was harsh as a nutmeg grater, was softened by Oriel's flattering presence.

Putting down the receiver now, Janet brought out a long beige garment she was knitting, to boast a little, ironically, because she was an unhandy person and knew it. Clare returned to finish her tea.

'I've been admiring your freckles.' Oriel smiled down into Janet's eyes. 'They're amazing! I don't know how you do it. I've often thought how much I'd like some.' She said, 'I know. Who could produce a freckle in London? Alas, you're quite right. I'm full of envy.'

Left-over smiles stuck to Janet's face and Clare's, then as the words translated themselves and were understood, Janet turned a dreadful dusky red beneath freckles that were not cute at all, which had martyred her, caused her sharper suffering for decades of her life than many a lingering fatal-sounding disease would have done.

'Are you?' Janet's voice was dead and rasping. She bent low over her desk.

Even her hands had blushed, Clare saw, as she stood stupidly still, looking down at Janet's rather scraggy gingery head, the back of her dusky red neck, and her shapeless beige jersey dress.

Grasping a memorandum fiercely, even Janet's hands were red. And freckled. Clare knew what they had meant to her, had always known, had not had to use a geiger counter, or to be in her company for ten years to know.

For a split second, recovering from a painful body blow, Clare stood vague and muffled, yet at the same time with light, crystal light, pealing in all round her. From Janet's clenched hands she looked over to Oriel, who was turning away with one of her graceful movements. She gave Clare a bold, bored, defiant, whimsical look and walked away.

Back at her own desk, Clare started to draw squares, circles and other geometric shapes at a furious rate on a scribbler.

That look of Oriel's! My true colours! So what? it had clearly said. She bores me. I'm bored. What's Janet Adams? it said.

All the facts Oriel had at her command, her rich life and intelligence proved nothing whatever. Nothing at all. Her views had been so civilised, perceptive, fine-grained. In theory, her attitude to life and people was a model of rectitude and loving-kindness. It had seemed unreasonable in Clare, even to herself, that Oriel's fluent, witty and informed conversation should have had as draining an effect as any sample of Mrs. Robertson's famous social life. Oriel had described the world where everything that mattered happened, was actor and eyewitness, and yet, listening, Clare had often had to assume a vitality, engagement and interest far greater than she felt. She had been alarmed to have to admit to herself that even now, when subject and speaker should have enthralled, she was in reality still waiting at the forgotten bus stop, urgently, in a high wind, with a talkative stranger.

It was all as—it was all but tinkling bells and cymbals—Or sounding brass—Or whatever it was.

And now she knew why.

'Laura? I forgot to tell you this morning, I'm going to a play at the Independent tonight with Mike Rankin. I won't be home for dinner.' (It was mean, but it did avoid a long, long, mangled discussion, not to have said so this morning.)

'Oh? Very well.'

Clare waited at her end of the line, then said, 'You sound puffed. Have you just got home? Is Felix with you?'

'No. He's been at the hotel with Gil Blaine all day. He dropped me off at the factory this morning and went straight out there, so—'

'So,' she had no need to say, 'I'll just have to wait and see.'

Almost every night since Felix had bought an interest in Gilbert Blaine's hotel, she and Clare had done exactly that. And the sound of footsteps which was the end of waiting was the climax of the day: most often they were heard slowly lurching and stumbling down the steps and down the path, and the women prepared to wait it out as people wait out an air-raid, suspended, with existence itself a matter of either/or. When the footsteps were quick and heavy, however, there was a rapid unscrewing of nerves, a lighting of lights and playing of music, so that when Felix entered it was to find a peaceful and relaxed scene in which his wishes were all in all to everyone—all three.

'I hope it's—everything's fine tonight,' Clare said with a pang of guilt, wretchedly conscious that she was failing in her duty, and that her absence could increase the night's unpleasantness for Laura if the wind was blowing north, south, east or west.

'Have a good time,' Laura said bleakly, deliberately not asking, 'Who's Mike Rankin? What play are you seeing?' just as she would never ask in the morning, 'Was the play good? Did you enjoy yourself?'

'Yes. Okay,' Clare said with equal bleakness and resentment, feeling as if her lungs had been sucked empty of breath. She was aware of Laura's regret at not being able to refer her evening's outing with Mike to Felix, that Felix would no longer be able, anyway, with inimitable friendliness, like a smiling tiger, to refuse permission. By some blessed miracle, imperceptibly, she had become too old.

There had been a time, even after it became impossible to blackmail her into rejecting all invitations, when Laura and Felix invariably happened to be out in the car posting letters or getting a breath of air when the theatres emptied. 'You two young people' were kindly given a lift home, Clare's escort discarded, and Clare herself, in the back seat of the car, was enjoined to admire the view as they approached the white citadel once again. There were guns held to her head. 'Look at that moon over the water! It's pure gold tonight.'

Now she went out from time to time with Les from the office, or Keith, whom she had met on the ferry, or Mike, whose sister worked in the office and who had been introduced by Diane on Balmoral Beach one Sunday.

If she had taken to prostitution her family could hardly have given off more silent unhappiness. When it was convenient to him, Felix relied on her company. If he was busy, she took herself obligingly to her room, but when he had a rare idle hour and was sober, he did expect her to exert herself a little to divert him.

If she remained in town with another girl, the slight was not so hurtful. It was always aggravating to see someone treat the house like a hotel, and to feel that Laura's excellent and important dinners could be forgone, but it was chiefly the thought that Clare sometimes chose to spend her time with some unknown male, in preference to spending it with Felix (who was a man, too!) that made him smile sarcastically at her with dark, demanding offended eyes. Laura could understand this perfectly.

'Why you would want to go out with a man if you didn't have to—' she said to Clare.

'Oh, Laura. Give me strength! You are married to one.'

'That's different. You know what I mean. You don't want to marry any of *them*, do you?'

She did not. She was so much too old, so in excess of what they imagined her to be, that she went merely because it was a matter of survival to her not to react like a weathervane to every variation of pressure her family chose to impose on her. The independent action available was often not very preferable to what she abandoned at home and, in a sense, she knew it did not matter greatly what she did. Nevertheless, as some sort of principle, almost for Laura's sake and Felix's, she would not even appear submissive. So she went out now and then with these boys. They spoke to her because she was, in effect, the pair of ears, the mouth, the body that happened to be standing next to them at the bus stop. Anyone about her age and size would have done as well. Nothing about her entered into it. They were content to be with a young female who had straps to be pulled at, ears into which they could try to poke their tongues. They were children on a picnic. They kissed her as if she was something good to eat, and she did not object. But they made her lonely.

Not like any girl of the right age, shape and so on, after all, but like a woman leaden with experience, she turned away. Between two lies which were, on the one hand, going out with the boys and, on the other, seeming to submit to *their* combined wills in not doing so, she began to choose the latter. If she had cared, it could have rankled that they should think her docile and obedient in not deserting them and her square room, but at least alone pretence was unnecessary.

But see tonight how essential to patrol the boundaries and make use of the rights of the free!

Felix strode into the hotel and felt at once the heightening of power that a king might experience returning to his country from foreign parts. He was in the home of alcohol. The air was heavy with it. There came from all about the echoing hollow sounds of hotel life. Under his feet in the cellars there was alcohol enough to keep a Roman fountain tumbling for days. Through the swing doors to his right there were rows of superlative whiskies with renowned labels, each one of which he cherished. There were classic, and dimpled and square bottles. Advocaat, cherry brandy, crème de menthe, cointreau, all the liqueurs, spirits, sparkling and still wines with their beautiful inviolate corks and wires and tin-foil wrappings. There was no need to fear, in this harem of delights, that a scarifying thirst might descend and remain ungratified. Nothing could happen to him here. Safety was within arm's reach. Eloquence, great gestures, physical strength, magic, hypnotic powers, were in every thrice-blessed bottle. The contents of any one of them would let him out of his cage. He, Felix, Mr. Felix Shaw, was returned to himself and the world by these perfumed liquids. He could jump. He could growl. He could open his eyes wide and frighten everyone. He could impress them all, at any time he chose. He could emerge in his real majesty and glory—

Striding along the stony ringing corridors, on his way to do a job of stock-taking with Gilbert Blaine, he felt an almost religious satisfaction.

'Is Mr. Blaine anywhere about?'

The hotel 'useful', Nobby Clark, came down the passage with the addled fish eyes of one who has not been completely sober for years. He stopped when Felix addressed him for the second time.

'Is Mr. Blaine about?'

'Gil? 'aven't seen 'im.' Sluggishly indifferent to peremptory voices and efforts, however unconscious, to put him down, Nobby went his way to the bar.

'Ah.' Felix rattled the change in his pockets abstractedly, and stood alone in the corridor, ostentatiously thinking. As if to demonstrate that there is indeed a little justice left in the world, he was actually seen there.

'Hullo, Mr. Shaw! You look deep in thought!'

Felix gave a colossal start, quite frightening his discoverer, and then began to laugh. 'Oh! Oh! Yes. Hullo there, Josie. Where's Mr. Blaine?'

'He sent a message a while ago. He can't come in today. He said for you to go ahead and he'll talk to you later.' Josie was a tall bony woman with black hair rolled back from her forehead. She gestured with a large tin tea pot. 'He said you better start in there.'

Felix was like a fire abruptly deluged with water, snow, rocks and dirt. 'He did, eh?'

Young Gil was more often missing than not when you wanted him, but at least his absence proved his confidence in Felix. Felix supposed. When he did turn up he would quite likely say, 'Don't tell me you've finished already? They said it took three coves to do that last year, and then they buggered it up.'

To date, Felix had drawn no money from the hotel, though he had spent more time working here than at the factory, which did continue to provide him with an income. But one day this place would be a gold mine. Gradually he would extract more money from the factory and increase his holding here. He would double the refrigeration capacity. He would carry the biggest stock of liquor on the North Shore. He and young Gil might set themselves up as joint resident managers. *She* could keep the other place running.

Solitary, in a sealed-off section of the Bottle Department, Felix began a preliminary stock-taking. Tomorrow night, when the last customer was chucked out, the real job would begin. Meantime, he would demolish so much tonight that young Gil would be staggered by his ability to get things done.

He would reward himself before leaving with a special, extra-special, hoary old bottle of whisky. A whole bottle. All to himself. The thought made him solemn. Naturally he would pay the full retail price for it! What did they take him for? No one worth his salt would cheat a young publican of his just profits.

With his mind on nothing but the labour ahead, Felix took the cap off his fountain pen and began to work with the reverence of a backwoods scholar let loose in the Louvre.

'Why *should* Felix pay social service taxes? He lost everything during the depression, but he picked himself up again. Then these others who're too lazy to do the same expect to be spoon-fed by the State.'

'Oh, Laura! Isn't it possible to talk about anything without dragging Felix into it? Couldn't we some-times—'

Clare looked across the table at her sister. More and more Laura's nature was being overlaid by the shadow of Felix's. Almost wilfully she was retreating from herself.

It was Saturday afternoon. Felix was at the hotel. They sat polishing cutlery and plate. They had discussed their new neighbours, said to be called Parkes, but Felix had intruded there, so Clare began to maunder on about welfare states and the penal system and slum clearance programmes in the hope of shaking him off.

If she used these topics as a soporific to her nerves and Laura's and was disingenuous to this degree, it was not that her thoughts or feelings were the less genuine for that. Any subject not *Felix* was, to some extent, camouflage and dishonest. But she would not abandon everything in life, her own self, utterly. She would not be defeated as far as that, though she was frequently brought shamefully low as when, for instance, experience, prudence, Laura's lowered eyes all counselled silence while her spirit said only, 'Speak!'

'Come on now, Clare, I'm catching up to you. You've still got those forks to do.' Laura rubbed at a dessert spoon with a dull manic energy. 'For heaven's sake, Clare, are you going to finish the silver for me, or aren't you? I don't ask you to do very much! Here!' Laura grabbed the polishing cloth from her hand; Clare pulled it violently back. 'Well then, do it!'

'I don't even remember what we were talking about,' Laura said, after a silence, glancing up at her passionate and alarming sister. 'You're so argumentative and moody—' She almost bent a frail silver fork in an effort to make it gleam, or perhaps in the hope of moulding her sister into some more amenable girl. 'Yes! Why *should* Felix help people who won't help themselves?'

'Who knows?' Clare said flatly. 'Can't we just leave it?'

'I agree with him, too.' Laura's expression was defiant and venomous as Felix's was when he made some such coat-trailing remark.

'Oh!' Clare groaned, exhausted. 'Oh, you don't, Laura. Be natural. Be yourself,' she suddenly pleaded. 'Don't be afraid. If you would just say to *me* what you really think, sometimes. If we don't even speak the truth sometimes it makes me feel—I feel I'll go mad! Everything so false and deliberate! It's like living in an asylum. The air even seems demented.'

Laura drew herself together in prim disapproval, but was satisfied somewhere to have brought about this collision. 'Don't be ridiculous. You're too old to carry on like this now.'

Clare pushed her chair back and stood up. Haggardly, she looked about the pleasant lemon-and-white kitchen smelling of silver polish and bananas and pears, full of Saturday afternoon quiet and the meaningless and, it seemed as she noticed it suddenly, ghastly tossing of poplar leaves outside the window. Natural objects like trees and their sounds always signalled to and reproached her, reminding her of time, and her multitudinous obligations and wonders to perform before it was too late.

'For God's sake, at least agree that I should go away. Agree to let me go, Laura.'

'If you'd get a tea-towel and dry these things it'd be more to the point.' Laura dashed the silver into the sink and clashed it noisily through the hot foamy water.

'Without any fuss—without quarrels—if I could go without discussions.' If Laura would release her, say, 'Go with my blessing. I choose to stay, but I willingly release your mind and person. Be free.'

'The day you leave this house,' Laura said rigidly, rattling the silver out onto the rubber mat, 'will be the last day you'll ever set eyes on me, Clare. If you go, don't ever come back or try to get in touch with me for any reason, because I won't be here.'

Sombrely, Clare dried a handful of cutlery. 'Why? —Where would you be?'

'Somewhere far away. Far away.' With her eyes fixed on the rainbowed suds with their minute reflections of small square window-panes, and her hands rushing about of their own initiative performing tasks, Laura answered on a note that stated warnings to Clare's nerves.

She said, 'Probably everything that's wrong—it could all be my fault. You and Felix—I don't know how you can bear to be treated—it—to *see* it—to have to watch—But there'd be no extra reason for you to do anything because I did. They're quite separate.'

'Yes. All right. Do what you like. But remember. I've told you. You can choose. You think you know so much. You're not even married. When you marry, very well. Till then, as long as I have any say in it, we all stay together. With Mother in England hardly bothering to answer our letters, it leaves just the two of us and Felix. It's only a small family, but if I can't keep that together I'll know I really am a flop. I'll know I'm no good for anything. I might as well—'

Before she could finish, she turned immobile as marble and Clare did, too. With finger-tips, bones, nostrils, unmoving eyes, they listened to the approaching sound, the rasping sound of shoe leather grating over cement. Lurching and scraping, lurching and mumbling to himself, Felix came down the path to the house.

Breaking their poses like trees snapping branches, the women urgently regarded each other, cleared away all signs of work in an instant, examined their souls for defects, in a sense crossed themselves, and waited.

At the top of their pitch, but like gladiators who had been thrown unnumbered times into the arena, they eyed each other. Laura seemed to say: 'See! See how we're both needed here in this emergency?' and Clare was shame-faced as any deserter, suddenly recalled to duty and honour.

Felix came in, out for a little blood sport.

Dressing for a state ball, Blanche and Dick Parkes turned to regard each other with amused amazement.

'Sounds as if our neighbours are having a slight brawl,' Dick said, listening to the curious noises.

'There had to be some snags to a house like this. Plebs next door.'

'How do you know they're plebs?' Dick ran his eyes over his black-and-white reflection in the long looking-glass.

'They're everywhere. *Nouveau riche*.' Blanche, who had only recently acquired this phrase, said it extremely well, really. And so saying, she applied *Arpège* with grandiloquent scorn to several nooks and crannies of her person, and breathed it in with a sort of stern devotion. She was a very sumptuous woman and did take a natural pleasure in herself.

'Oh-oh, there it is again. Sounds like a bull with the D.T.s,' Dick muttered uneasily. 'Some crazy coot—Can you hear any other voices?'

Blanche rolled her gold rope necklace between her fingers and listened with a little lopsided twist to her lips. 'Yes,' she said. 'There's a woman's voice now.'

The extraordinary notes touched by the unknown voices in the distant house behind the poplars, made Dick Parkes feel queasy. 'As long as there isn't a murder.' He excused himself by adding, 'It'd send the value of this place down thousands in five minutes.'

'Sweetie. Do you want to go and rescue some lady pleb in distress? People don't murder each other.' Blanche smiled and spoke with loving raillery, stood in the ambience of it just long enough, then coaxed, sinking her voice to its charming chest notes, 'But do come on now, darling. It's getting late.'

A single plangent cry of protest reverberated suddenly from their neighbours' lighted house.

Dick looked as if he had toothache. His wife eyed him decisively. 'The car's waiting. That fellow of yours has been sitting out there waiting for us for half an hour. Come on, now. There's a good boy.'

Clare ran to the bathroom. Her hair streamed down in separate strands; her fingers were extended and separated, too, to avoid the touch even of one another.

'Laura! What's happened? Laura! Are you all right?' She pressed against the door, twisting the handle.

'Yes. Yes.' Laura's voice was controlled, but tight with pain. She unlocked the door and stood with her back to the blue-tiled bathroom, nursing her hands together clumsily.

'I heard a noise like someone falling—'

'Felix fell.'

'Is he—? What happened? Where is he?'

Laura moved her head. 'In there. In the sitting-room. Even his iron constitution won't stand this sort of abuse. He's sodden. He won't wake up tonight.' She was white, fierce, shocked, tearless.

They stared urgently into each other's eyes.

'What's wrong with your hands?'

'Nothing. My wrists. Don't shout. There's been enough noise for one night.'

'Was I?' Clare looked at the thick white towels and glinting nickel rails confusedly. 'I thought—'

'He's out of his mind. I thought I could manage him. He's never been as bad as this.'

'Did he just—collapse?'

'No, he tripped, and then he couldn't get up, and the next minute he was—dead asleep.'

'Your wrists! Are they sprained? Let me see.'

They both stared at Laura's thin bruised arms and reddened wrists.

'I'll get some bandages. Wait a moment.'

The excited chatter which was to each of them so much noise, like the rushing waves inside a shell, rushing in ears and mouths, gradually abated. They fell silent, standing with lowered eyes.

'Well!' Clare roused herself. 'Sit on the edge of the bath here and I'll tie them up—That too tight?'

Laura shook her head.

'Will that do, then? Would you like a cup of tea?'

Laura shook her head again. They exchanged hard-eyed glances full of hatred, bitterly accusing on Clare's part, guilty, baited, on Laura's.

Leaving her sitting there with her bound-up wrists, Clare wandered away, stopping, dawdling a further step or two, stopping, staring, seeing nothing. At the door of the sitting-room she hesitated, then with a series of small jerks turned her reluctant head to look for him. Easily found. Full length on the floor in one of his many dandyish brown suits. The master of the torture chamber unconscious on the floor. A trap? (She knew it wasn't.) A trap? A trap? Her feet cringed from the floor as from the ground where some atrocious crime had been played out. A little trap? Her legs ached with the effort of approaching him. With no surface feeling at all, she contemplated him where he lay, his dark-red face so bloated, bulbous and corrupted that it resembled the face of a monstrous gargoyle.

He was helpless now. Not physically strong now. Stretched deeply unconscious at her feet. Really, at her mercy.

I could kill you, she thought, and wondered almost idly what prevented her. Merely the fear of retribution? (Leaving aside the fact that she could not kill.) No, it seemed that there was more than that to restrain her among many factors, fear of contamination. She would not willingly have touched a box of matches belonging to him. So erratic, vicious and dangerous, so inaccessible to reason and human feeling had he demonstrated himself to be, and so bent on the spiritual destruction of those about him, that the very artifacts he handled seemed to sicken. His eyes, merely by looking, spread the contagion, so that the fabric and foundations of the house were diseased; the silver Jaguar that he drove as though it were a weapon of war was diseased. She herself. She herself. She shuddered. What wasn't? The wind? The sky?

Outside, in the dark garden, she walked over the quiet grass, under the trees.

Returning to the house, she passed the bathroom and through the open door saw Laura swallowing Veganin and drinking water with a feverish air of decision.

'Don't take any more of those things, Laura.'

'I've got a headache.'

'When haven't you?' she said unpleasantly. Though after all Laura's dreadful and incessant headaches were hardly her fault, and she never complained. Only the tablets, the whiteness, the silence, and the careful way she moved with her lids down, entranced with pain, gave her away.

'What are you going to do?' Clare's tone was conciliatory. She pulled a tiny ball of coral-coloured wool from her sweater.

'You'll see. You'll see.' Laura gave a sharp little nod. She wiped her lips over-precisely and Clare winced inwardly and had to look away while all her resolutions fell. No action of Laura's now, no word, ever lacked this air of having been chosen with discretion, after prolonged thought. Deliberation was anathema to Clare. In her experience it was synonymous with hypocrisy, equivocation, as if the *real* which was always at hand, and clear to see, spontaneously presenting itself for use, was always mechanically rejected in favour of

194

some cautious piece of strategy, some much-thumbed grubby piece of thought.

'What will I see?'

'A lot of changes. Everything's going to be different, I can promise you that.' Laura had a prophetic light in her eye, a fanatical look of purpose.

There was a pause.

Considering that Laura had made this statement on round about two hundred similar occasions, she was remarkably unselfconscious. She went on to the effect that every dog had his day, and that the worm had finally turned.

'Do you want to try to get him into bed?' Clare asked, averting another of those annihilating discussions.

'No. I don't want to wake him. Not that I think we could. I loosened his collar and tie. He won't choke.' With an ambivalent expression, she said, 'He'll live to be a thousand.'

The following afternoon as they walked from the building at five, Janet Adams said to Clare, 'A woman's waving at you from that silver Jag.'

'Oh. Yes.' Clare stood still. 'It's my sister.'

Janet rolled her eyes at the car. 'Whacko! I'll have to pay to speak to you after this. G'night.'

She wandered off along the crowded footpath in the direction of transport.

'Hullo, there!' Felix said jovially, when Clare went to the side of the car, and Laura explained quickly, 'We had to come to town this afternoon, so we thought we'd wait and give you a lift home.'

Clare stepped out of the world and into the car with the deadened responses of one whom nothing could surprise.

'Look what I've been given!' Laura said in a small coy voice, after adequate attention had been paid to Felix's feat of driving in the rush-hour. 'Look!' She half-turned and stretched out her right hand to Clare.

A diamond ring. A fierce cluster of diamonds. Clare looked at it and had no reaction at all. But these amazing people were waiting! 'It's beautiful.'

'It's lovely, isn't it?'

'It's lovely.'

Felix jerked his head round enthusiastically. 'I was darn lucky to get it. It came from some collection or other some rich old Hungarian brought over with him.'

'It was probably a family heirloom,' Laura said. Her hand was skeletal. The veins rose in blue welts from the milk-white skin. The heavy ring slipped on her finger and she straightened it guiltily, and pressed her fingers together. 'But see how the stones are set, Clare.'

'Yes, I see it.'

Felix said, 'You'd never get work like that nowadays.'

'The old man had it in the back of his warehouse, Clare, in his own private safe. He didn't want to sell it, do you think, Felix? (He really loves jewels, Clare. Not because of their value!) I don't think he'd have sold this to just anyone, do you? We were there for three hours. His nice girl brought us in a cup of tea and a little chocolate cake each.'

'Maybe not. Maybe not. Oh, I've known old Schultz for—twenty years.' Felix looked into their eyes as if they might not believe this.

'Really?' Laura did sound quite surprised, though he had in fact told her this incredible news several times today.

'Oh, yes!' he assured her. 'About twenty years— And so you think it's pretty good, young Clare?'

'It's beautiful.'

'So it ought to be!'

'Try it on,' Laura said generously, and Felix seconded her. 'Yeah—' He turned briefly to look at it on Clare's hand. 'How's that, eh?'

'It's lovely.'

'Be better if you didn't bite your nails,' he laughed.

'It still looks beautiful,' Laura said loyally.

What children were these who were killing her? Clare looked out of the windows as they drove across the bridge. Through a great mesh of grey girders and wire and piping she stared out and down at the incomprehensible harbour which, like all else, had deteriorated so, from being claimed, gloated over, by Felix. What children were these?

'Yes, we had to go along to see that Dr. What's-'is-name today,' Felix said in his exaggerated drawl. 'Your old sister hasn't been looking too good. We've got to fatten her up. Under seven stone! So we had a talk with old Thingummy and he reckons I'd better take her up north for a break.'

Clare looked at the familiar backs of their heads. There was a pause. She forced herself to say, 'And are you?'

'Yeah, I guess we will. Think we'll take a little trip up to the Barrier Reef for a few weeks. See if we can't put a bit of meat on her bones.'

'So isn't that lovely?' Laura asked, half-turning again in her seat to look at Clare.

'It is. Yes. It is.' She took a breath consciously, like an old woman. 'When are you going?'

'Tomorrow.' Felix gave a small-boy grin that showed his upper and lower teeth set together.

'You'll enjoy that.' She took another breath. 'This will be the first time you've been out of Sydney since you left school, Laura.'

'Never been out of New South Wales?' Felix marvelled. 'I'd been all over the world by the time I was your age.'

There was a thinking silence. Fortunately, they were almost home.

After dinner Felix wrote some letters and then he sauntered out to post them.

'He only went so that I could explain to you,' Laura said, folding away the ironing-board. 'Wasn't it lucky I had everything clean? All our clothes are ready to go away.'

'What?' Clare looked at her. Laura had called her from her room in an unaccustomed wheedling tone of voice. 'Explain what, then?' Clare repeated.

'We-ell—You've washed your hair!—Laura's eyes remained somewhat elusive in spite of her desire for frank communication. They touched on the white-painted cupboard doors, the Vent-Axia fan that disposed of cooking odours, the bowl of fruit on the formica bench, and gave the regrettable impression that her deeper consciousness was even now absorbed in the problems of housekeeping: 'Well, we had a long talk this morning—about last night and the whole situation. And at eleven o'clock we went over to see Dr. Hope. After we explained what the position was, that something had to be done, he rang up the new psychiatric clinic for an appointment and the doctor in charge agreed to see Felix right away.'

'Did he go? What happened? Did you go, too?'

'No, I came on home. I wanted to go, because you can imagine the act Felix puts on even if he's consulting an ordinary doctor about a cold in the head. As if he couldn't think what he's there for except to humour me! But they didn't want to see me.'

'Really? That seems odd. You'd think it would be fairly essential—' she stopped. 'Still. The main thing is—Felix went. How did he get on?'

Laura's eyelids fell; her brows rose. 'According to him, the psychiatrist said drinking never did anyone any harm.'

Clare fell back in her chair. Her expression faded. Then she laughed.

Wryly, Laura nodded, meeting her eyes. 'He said no one should be nagged for having a few drinks at night after work. Then they seemed to talk for several hours about some property he's selling at Newport. In the end he said there was nothing wrong with Felix, but if anyone over twenty-five was mentally ill or alcoholic it was impossible to cure them. Almost always.'

Clare had been sitting, her left elbow on the table, her left hand covering her mouth and chin. She moved this now to grimace her dismay. 'I hope he's been misquoted.'

Laura never shrugged; it was against her nature, but she did shrug now and shake her head. 'Anyway. Then he sent him back to Dr. Hope.'

'Does the psychiatrist want to see him again?'

'Evidently not.'

Clare felt the bone of her forehead meticulously as if her fingertips might discover something helpful there. She said, 'Why did he have to go back to Dr. Hope?'

'For a proper medical check-up. They rang me from the surgery to go back while he was there. When I saw him this second time, Dr. Hope agreed that Felix ought to give up drink for the sake of his health.'

'I see. Thank heavens! It doesn't *solve* whatever's wrong, but—What about its effect on *your* health?'

'He didn't seem to think it should have any. He really wasn't keen to ask him to stop it, you know. Still, he told us both to go away for a holiday, and he wrote out prescriptions—a tonic,' she laid a hand on her chest, 'and some new drug for Felix to help him—Then Felix took me to town and bought me this lovely ring, and made lots of arrangements for the trip. One of the representatives can stay in the factory while we're away and take phone calls and do the wages. But he's really turned over a new leaf, Clare. Everything's going to be different from now on.'

'That's good. I hope so.' Clare's voice was expressionless.

'I said to Felix,' Laura went on cautiously, 'that I thought you might be thinking of leaving the house after these last months, and he was horrified. He said what would be the use of trying to change if he'd broken the family up anyway.'

'*Please.*'

'What do you mean? Well, that's what he said.'

As if it mattered, Clare bent her head to feel the dripping ends of her combed wet hair. 'I looked at some rooms today at lunch-time. I took an extra hour off. I've rented one.'

Laura's small white face swelled. 'Clare! You didn't! You wouldn't spoil it all just when he's doing everything he can to show—I wasn't going to tell you this. I wasn't going to tell you because it's a surprise, but he's bought you a lovely gold bracelet and a big box of imported chocolates. He was going to give them to you in the morning before we went off. But if you're moving out, I don't suppose we'll be going, so it doesn't matter.'

A number of words came to Clare's mind. She said nothing. She felt a sort of haggardness of the soul.

'A beautiful gold bracelet. He took such a long time to choose it. He made poor old Mr. Schultz bring out every one in the shop. He is *trying*,' Laura said angrily. She could not stop performing unnecessary tasks—filling the electric jug, pulling fresh green leaves off the innocent ivy plant.

A row of pictures, secret photographs, maps, was exposed to Clare swiftly in such a way that each passing square was only partially visible. It was swiftly withdrawn. On a single breath she tried to remember its fading message: there was no end to pity. That was part of it. There was to be no end to the pity she must feel for Laura.

Her heart hardened. She hated pity. She hated Laura. She hated her febrile strength, her placating smiles, her tentative movements. She hated her nervous headaches, her obsessive nature, her selfishness, her self-sacrifice, her martyrdom and masochism. She hated her because she clearly willed to think that a gold bracelet might have the power to influence anyone, and had once known better. But above all she hated Laura for the contempt in which she held herself.

'If you stay,' Laura's voice was peculiar, 'I know he'll try to be different. Why shouldn't we all be happy and peaceful at last? Just when—Why should we all be separated as if we had no one to care about us? He only wants to do what's right now. Are you going to be temperamental and ruin everything?'

Clare sat at the table looking and listening, her raw fingertips spread on its lemon surface. 'Yes, I am,' she said tonelessly.

Laura turned to her with a tremendous embattled searching look.

'All right, then!' She gave a wild glance about the kitchen, saw and seized a pile of clean dinner plates and crashed them with all her strength onto the black-and-white tiled floor. She seized another pile and smashed them before Clare could jump from her chair.

'Laura!'

'Let go! You're hurting me!'

'What are you doing? Stop it!' She started to cry.

'What did you do that for? Why did you?' She let Laura tug her bandaged wrists and diamond ring away. 'Why did you break your dishes? That was horrible! That was mean!'

They were only abhorrent to her as sharing the general disease of the house, but Laura had cherished them. Now to punish her, Laura had broken them at her.

'Why did you?' she cried, her mind turning on itself with frustration. She felt heartbroken. The innocuous dishes were smashed. No one spoke the truth. No one in the world was natural. There was no length they would not go to to keep her.

'Well—' Laura waited to say, looking defiantly at her and the havoc about her feet. 'Well—' She slid the toe of her shoe amongst the broken chips and breathed in, shame-faced and aggrieved. 'I was—fed-up to think you were going to spoil it all.'

'What?' Clare screeched, catching her eye incredulously, brushing her own eyes and beginning to laugh. 'Fed-up? You were fed-up?'

The colossal inadequacy of the word dawned on Laura and she, too, started to laugh.

'It's awful. It's awful.' Clare laughed. 'It's so stupid, such a waste, so unnecessary!'

Laura laughed with a sycophantic eagerness, picking up the broken china, laughing and nodding agreement to Clare's every word.

'It is stupid,' she said with this same reasonable

eagerness, still smiling broadly. 'Of course it is!' She turned to watch her sister.

Clare threw her arms out, raising her brows, laughing and crying, addressing herself to some invisible comrade, not yet encountered in life but *there*, who knew what she meant. 'Why should it be like this? There's the whole world and millions of people. Galaxies. Much more than—' she indicated with one eloquent hand pity, fear, frustration, loathing and boredom. 'There must—it must—'

'Yes, everything's going to be very nice from now on,' Laura assured her with the lively non-comprehension of a salesman. 'You'll be a sensible girl, won't you? You won't go? You'd be kicking poor Felix when he's down. He only wants a chance. He thinks the world of you. You'd ruin everything.'

Listening to this intently, Clare's expression changed to what looked like wonder and delight. '*I* would?' she said softly, laying her damaged fingers on her chest to be sure there was no mistake. '*I* would ruin everything?' she asked hurriedly.

'What happens now depends on you,' Laura insisted, looking at her with the same animation and increasing confidence. Clare seemed to be crying again, but she was also half-smiling, so—'I can't stand any more unpleasantness, Clare. You won't be silly, will you? You've sometimes said how sorry you feel for Felix.'

'Yes,' she admitted.

'He'll be back in a minute. If you did this now, it would be the end of everything. It isn't as if there was anything to go for.'

'No,' Clare agreed, smiling thoughtfully while her eyes shed tears. By not a single word or gesture had the world shown any need of her. 'Except that I want to,' she added judiciously, as an afterthought.

'If you do—' Laura's voice cracked and she stared into Clare's eyes for some moments with an appeal so unabashed and calculating that Clare looked away for shame. 'All right,' she said, after a pause. 'What does it matter?'

It is a wonder of the world to notice how fundamentally people change from one second to the next when they are given their own way.

Monica Ewart caught Clare's arm as they pushed back along the narrow crowded footpath of Castlereagh Street to the office. 'Look! Everyone's staring at something.'

Wondering, the two were banked up against the stationary crowds. Often enough in the city streets at lunch-time or in the evening rush-hour, there was an impression that people had paused in a group to remark on some phenomenon just yards away. Almost as often the impression turned out to have been false. They had only stopped wistfully to look for something remarkable to look at. And in truth there was very little in the city's buildings to excite the eyes of a connoisseur of the beautiful, supposing one such to have been amongst the hopeful groups of gazers, and even less to arouse those others who were not even aware of what they missed or wanted.

'Oh, look! They've got him!' a woman cried.

And there emerged through the crowd on the opposite pavement two uniformed policemen holding a young man who seemed to be dead. With their arms deep under his, they were dragging his body across the street.

This half of the city block was silent as an open-air theatre, the road cleared of all traffic, the crowds motionless and leaning in towards this quiet, sunlit, significant spectacle like trees on a windswept headland.

No, he was alive, not dead, the young man! For now, instead of allowing his feet to drag helpless behind him and being entirely borne along by the policemen, he was stumbling in an effort to support his own weight. He could not lift his head, however, and he had an air of being mortally ill that reverberated pleasantly and horribly through the silent witnesses.

No, he was well, after all, not ill, the young man! Only struck down in some more than mortal manner, as if by a supernatural hammer, to find himself a captive thief in the real air, under the sun, surrounded by breathing faces.

Reaching the parked police car, he was dragged and thrust into the back seat between the two officers. The crowd watched. Anything could still happen! Ah, but slowly the car moved off, and the banked-up traffic was waved on. Reluctantly the crowd scattered.

Oh, God! Clare thought. *Cowed*. That's what it means. What a dreadful thing! Her heart contracted. Something no one should ever be.

Monica said, 'Look! This is the jeweller's shop I've been telling you about. Come and I'll show you a clock like the one I've got on lay-by.'

They peered into the small window full of trumpery rings, necklaces, brooches and tiaras. Monica pointed out a chaste-looking gold clock, and then went on to admire the display of large and expensive china ornaments: cats eating rats, dogs holding birds, insipid maidens palely smirking—

'Come on, kid, we'd better make tracks.' Monica was off.

They started to walk at the pace permitted by the lunch-hour armies, keeping to the left, Monica forcing her way across the right-hand stream now and then to dart her eyes over a display of shoes or dresses, joining Clare again and taking up her complaints against the man whose secretary she was exactly where she had left off.

Clare attended sincerely enough and would have noticed any deviation from this set-piece, but her nature, in which there were no offices or bosses, was experiencing pang after pang of deepest dismay.

Nimbly she and Monica began to overtake the walking back-views of people and hurry past. The faces approaching were vapid and low-powered. She glanced up at the buildings of from two to twelve storeys on the opposite side of the road, ranging from nondescript to hideous, with thousands of people filed away in them. She could have dropped in the street. But how exaggerated! What was there in the sight of a captive criminal, a china cat, faces and buildings, to cause such excessive horror?

(Where was the young man now? What had he done? Why?)

What was she looking for? What did she miss? And why did the world and the weirdness and significance of captives, cats, faces and buildings strike her with fresh surprise daily, as if she had arrived from another time and place, expecting the earth to be much different?

We could do anything, and we do this, what we do do. How lacking—How lacking in—

'I think he might be very clever,' Monica called over her shoulder in her quick voice, undeterred by all the wriggling in and out between bodies.

'Who?'

'Morris. The new man in Admin.'

'Oh. Yes. He's very bright.' But the world, poor world, was as over-burdened with cleverness as with stupidity, and in a sense (lacking this) did they not amount to the very same thing? Oh, he's clever, Clare thought, but who's *good*? Who's good? Who's good?

Like a lament the question sounded in her as she ran up the marble stairs with Monica, not waiting for the lift. Who's good? Who's good?

And it seemed that in finding the words for this question she had found them for all longing, and every question. For this meant everything.

I want to be in the presence of someone good.

Felix was squatting on the footpath outside the house with his back to the road, a pot of white paint beside him, when a car pulled up and tooted.

'Hullo there!'

Only very slowly, and in response to a second call from the lively, good-humoured voice, did Felix turn his head.

Gilbert Blaine leaned across from the wheel and wound down the window to let his face be seen, as though it were a gold pass entitling him to lifelong privileges from the community. Felix had seen it before, if not as often as he would have wished; it was still an even biscuit-coloured oval, with features so reassuringly regular, and smile from curving lips and perfect teeth to heavily-lashed brown eyes so frank, that it was no wonder he had always been extremely difficult to dislike. In some indefinable way, by instinct as it were, people knew that nothing disagreeable could ever be Gil's fault.

'I'm off on Wednesday, Felix. Just thought I'd say adios or what-have-you, since I was passing.'

'Eh? Be with you in a minute.' He turned to administer the last crucial brush-strokes to the gate-post.

In his red Cadillac Gilbert Blaine glanced along the Sunday street, stared down at his wrist-watch, took a cigarette from his case and waited, smiling a small smile.

'Well, that's just about it,' Felix grunted, slowly rising from his haunches and stooping again to dispose his paintbrush in a jam-jar half-full of turpentine. At last he remembered Gilbert Blaine.

Shirtless, shoeless, sweaty, and burned almost black with the sun, Felix was no sight for sore eyes, but aversion was an expression banned, in public, from Gil Blaine's charming face: he regarded Felix with an amiable smile.

'What about coming down for a bit of afternoon tea?' Felix leaned against the car and stared in a bitter, pessimistic way down the street.

'I'd really like to, Felix, but I should've been in Pymble an hour ago. You know what it's like going away—everyone wants to throw a party.'

'Yeah—' Rasping his fingernails over his unshaven cheek, Felix stared narrowly into the distance. 'Thought—' he cleared his throat, 'I thought I might've seen you one of these days to hear how it all worked out.'

'I did ring a few weeks back, but you were up at the Barrier Reef or somewhere. Oh, they were on to me like a pack of sharks. Just what you said.'

The mantle of blood through which he seemed to have to look, the corrosive necessity to appear to smile, in some way withdrew very slightly from Felix. And he jerked round with a sort of fantastic simplicity, putting both hands on the car door, to look at his ex-partner. 'After you, were they? I thought they would be.'

Gil jerked his head emphatically. 'I won't forget what you've done for me. If I make the pile I'm going to in South Africa, you're in on it. They say it's really lying around over there.' Still speaking, he slid back behind the wheel and fiddled with the ignition key.

'Yeah—' said Felix, noticing, speaking through his cup of gall. 'Still got this old bomb, I see.' He knocked his knuckles against the car's red duco and tried to laugh.

'No. Sold it to a fellow I knew at school. He's got pots of money and three other cars. Only took it as a favour to me. He's on the land. Gave me cash on the nail. I had to hand it all over to the legal mob. He's letting me run round in it till we sail.'

Felix rubbed the clenched fist of his left hand back and forth across his nose. 'And did you hear any more about Casey? Have they got on his track at all?'

'No, he's gone bush. They'll never get him now. He was always a bad risk. It was my fault for keeping so much cash in the place. Tough on you, too,' he added, as an afterthought, coming in strongly to say, 'Well, I'll have to push off, Felix. Say farewell to your—Mrs. Shaw—for me.' He gave a final, winning smile and revved the engine up.

A ludicrous change of expression—from strained interest and failing hope to stark myopic indifference—took place on Felix's face. 'Yeah,' he said, and walked back to the fence.

The red car started to cruise slowly away, its horn giving a mellow bleep.

For an instant before he turned the corner, Gilbert Blaine focused Felix in his rear-vision mirror, painting like a man on piece-work. He had looked up from his hot seat on the hot white footpath like a beggar full of dangerous misery at a Raja. Now, quite alone in the burning sun-stricken street, he was gnawed at, consumed by an overpowering wretchedness. His throat hurt, and he dug a thumb and a forefinger into each side, believing the pain to come from his bad tonsils.

'Afternoon tea's ready, dear,' Laura said quietly, appearing at his side. 'The fence looks better.'

'I can't come down till I've finished. I'll be about twenty minutes.'

He glanced up at her from his somehow deliberately cringing place on the ground, and she said gently, 'All right,' and went away.

Lower than the dust, she thought, as if Felix had transferred the words from his mind to hers. *Lower than the dust*.

'Poor Felix,' she whispered aloud, strangely anguished, and half-running through the empty house to her bedroom, shed sharp tears of pity for him.

'Hullo. You should have come for a swim, Felix. It wasn't crowded.' Clare trudged along the road towards him and called out from a distance of twenty yards or so.

'How was the water?' he asked, concentrating on the post, his head down.

'Oh, fine!—Terrific!' she said, oddly dismayed. Having approached Felix to reach the gate, which was propped open because of its wet paint, she went slowly, backwards, away from him down the path to the house.

'How was it?' In the cool sitting-room with the french doors open on to the verandah, lawns and harbour views, Laura was sewing buttons on a white shirt and listening to The Opera-Lovers' Hour.

'Fine. Mike's gone home to get on with building his car.' In her sun hat, blue sandals, shorts and shirt, Clare dawdled in the doorway swinging her canvas beach bag till the aria from *Manon* ended, pensive and shaken.

'What's wrong?' Laura looked up then down to thread her needle with beautiful absorption.

'Nothing.' Pulling her hat off she scratched at her hot head and felt her damp hair. 'Only—poor Felix!' she burst out, almost crying. 'What's the matter with him? He looks dreadful! He looks as if he could howl.'

'Clare!'

'No. I mean it. He seems to be—howling like a wolf. It's dreadful. You can feel it.'

Laura's needle slowed over the shirt. 'He'll be down for some tea in a minute. If you want to have a shower—*Manon's* lovely, isn't it?'

'Nasty news this morning,' said Mr. Robbins, the chemist. He liked to talk to Mrs. Shaw. He liked her gentle, worried, creamy face with dimples in it.

'Is there?' Laura started half-indignantly, looked large-eyed into the tall man's antiseptic chemist's countenance. 'I haven't seen a paper yet.'

'Only another crisis. It's hard to keep track of them all.' Mr. Robbins scooped the change from the till, checked the coins in the palm of his hand, then let them chink into Laura's. With a leisurely movement he tore a sheet of blue paper from the roller and spread it on the counter.

Laura cast her eyes about the pretty scented shop, its rows of gold lipstick cases, its glossy cards advertising patent drinks to make you strong and beautiful. Inhaling a great breath of sweet disinfected air, she returned to looking at Mr. Robbins's grey head, bent over his angular parcel.

'I do agree with you,' she said vehemently. (It was such a relief to think about world affairs! Like coming out of solitary confinement.) 'We've just acquired a new business—a clothing factory—after some months of looking about. We used to manufacture artificial flowers, but my husband—Anyway, one of our young machinists is an English girl, just out from London. She's got a room here in Neutral Bay not far from us. And do you know what she was telling us?'

'No,' Mr. Robbins said soothingly, his hands slowly wrapping the parcel, his mind aware of his two young assistants contending with other customers.

'Well, she was wakened up the other night by the sound of sirens—'

'Oh, yes, I remember.'

'—yes. She said the sound gave her a fright in her sleep, then she woke up and thought the noise must be ambulance sirens or fire engines, but it kept on for more than half an hour. Then she heard bells in the distance starting to ring an alarm.' Laura paused dramatically. 'Do you know what she thought it was?'

'No,' Mr. Robbins nobly assured her, following the shape of her blue eyes from inner to outer corner.

Laura leaned towards him. 'Nuclear war. The end of the world.'

'No!' Mr. Robbins backed away slightly.

Giving a series of tiny confirmatory nods, Laura went on, 'It was three in the morning. She thought the sirens and bells were trying to wake up the whole city. She thought we would all die any moment.'

Guardedly, the chemist rubbed his nose. 'She sounds a rather hysterical young woman.' His head turned automatically to the shelf where, in hygienically-sealed jars, the tonics for hysterical persons were to be found.

'No, she isn't, that's the thing! She said, "Mrs. Shaw, that awful din would've wakened any city in Europe."'

Rather moodily, but none the less dexterously, Mr. Robbins tied a knot in the string round the parcel and snapped it off the reel. 'What did she do then, if she thought the world was ending?'

Laura laughed. 'Grace said she didn't know anyone else in the house, and she hasn't got a phone or a wireless, so she ran across the street to the post office and rang the police. She said, "What are the sirens sounding for?" and the policeman, in a queer sort of voice, said he couldn't hear any sirens. Then she said, "There are bells ringing, too!" And he said he couldn't hear bells either.'

Mr. Robbins laughed, showing neat white false teeth, shaking his head and folding his arms. 'It was the fog on the harbour.' He kept laughing and saying, 'Ah, yes!' He felt wholly reassured, as if Mrs. Shaw's story of the little machinist had dealt with and disposed of the East–West crisis once and for all.

That night she went to the door of Clare's room to say, 'I could fill this house with people, you know! I make friends easily. People quite like me when I have a chance to meet them. All sorts of people. The people in shops. And not only them, either. I'm often paid nice little compliments by total strangers.'

They wandered through the devastated rooms as through a city abandoned after days and nights of bombing. From one room, from one chair, to another, they moved, not speaking, not noticing each other. Laura made a cup of tea and left it. Some hours later, Clare made one. They sat. They held their heads.

Felix stayed in bed and was invisible till late on Sunday afternoon when he strolled through the conquered countryside looking not dissatisfied, even sniggering a little, dressed formally in a suit as though in the uniform of a victorious general. A french door swinging lopsided, torn curtains, broken glass—a pretty satisfactory show one way and another!

Hearing him enter the room, and aware that Laura had shut herself away, sunk to the deepest level of silence, Clare roused herself to look up at Felix across the kitchen table.

'Felix. Felix—I don't know. Sit down and talk to me for a minute. No one can live like this. We're all exhausted. But—if you could—*say*, we might find out what we should do.'

She looked directly into his face as she spoke, and while she wondered at his nature, at the chaos he had so effortlessly and apparently without reason created, ill will was out of the question. She had no limitations left with which to feel the least animosity. Nothing so simple as that emotion was or ever had been called for in this situation. Felix himself could see that somehow his astonishing violence and roaring hatred had wiped the slate clean. He smiled.

'Talk? What's there to talk about? Everything's okay, isn't it? Nothing to talk about.'

He wore a look of peculiar elation, and Clare understood again from his intensely uneasy, somehow slippery, smile, the impossibility of their ever being able to talk, and she did experience, even through the coldness of her general anaesthesia, a faint feeling of surprise.

'Everything's jake, isn't it?' he insisted, with the same bluff, bright, slippery smile.

Obviously it mattered so little what she said that for a few seconds no words offered themselves. Then she said, 'But, anyway, I don't think there's much to be done about it.'

'Eh?' He gave her a smiling, deaf look. Then he pretended to think she was joking. Or perhaps he even did. Hearing him move, she glanced up and had the impression almost that he had slithered out of the room, so fundamental was his resistance to the very idea of reason.

Against all evidence to the contrary, Clare had once supposed that every person did carry about in some degree a knowledge of what was true and what was not, an awareness of the objective plane to which life-worn individuals could turn at last, casting off layer on layer of mistaken self-interest in bitter relief, crying, 'All right! Enough! I will be myself. Let us have the truth. However I have been before, I pine for it now.'

But Felix could never be startled or worn down to the point where any such decision presented itself to him. Some sort of bedrock that she had assumed to be present in all people was lacking then in Felix and, if in him, in the section of the community he resembled. For he could hardly be unique. She supposed.

The refrigerator began to throb. Clare glanced at it. Rising, she walked idly about the dreadful kitchen, touching its smooth surfaces that had received her eyes' conversation for so many years. Perhaps this was the greatest difference of all between people? It did seem to be a very great difference. How odd—all to look like one and yet to be, in a sense, two species.

This permanent awareness of what was *so*, regardless of her whims of the moment, regardless of what it would be pleasant to believe, or not pleasant, this solid bedrock was what she was, what she was about. What could there be in its place if you were differently constituted?

What use (the question came) had she ever made of this supposedly valuable possession? What use did she ever intend to make of it?

Oh, some. Some use, she promised. Because she could not die till that was done. And she sighed and frowned in abstraction, understanding what did not seem very understandable: that she was not yet good enough to die, could not afford it yet on any account. She walked through to her bedroom. Years ago she would have bitten her fingernails till the blood streamed, and all but cracked the bones of her face with grief. She would have banged her head against the wall. She sat on the bed, slipped her shoes off, let herself fall back flat on the pillows with a little thump. Stony and wordless and without feeling she stared at the white ceiling. Her recent promises of action sank away. Nothing would ever change now. All to be wasted. What a pity, she thought mildly. Her life was excessive. Really it was. It was inartistic.

The fingers of her left hand rested on her collar-bone. She breathed evenly and thought with a dangerous evenness and evenly felt the curious balance of her emotions—exactly poised between surprise and a dead lack of surprise. Oh, outside in the world there were people suffering tragedies she could barely imagine. There were people in prisons at this very instant, people in hospitals, streets and houses, enduring every searing degree of pain, anguish of spirit.

She noticed the direction of her thoughts and her lips half-smiled. Laura's influence. 'Think of the poor souls in concentration camps!' she would say with pious heat. 'How lucky we were in the war not to have been thrown into the gas ovens!' There were answers to be made to that, of course, and over the months and years they had been made.

Some suffering must be clean compared with this, she thought. There was collusion here. There was nothing not depraved, perverted. There was no feeling of sufficient grace to earn the august name of suffering.

And yet, she thought, I think we are probably very unhappy.

Luckily, though, the unhappiness, the thing, whatever it was, that was painlessly torturing her, had taken itself out of earshot, out of sight. She was aware of it, its dimensions and gravity, but as though it were a chronic disease, an idiot child, a physical handicap of most severe proportions, that she had learned to deal with objectively.

Her arm went out horizontally and switched on the small wireless set on the bedside table. Edith Piaf. *La Vie en Rose.* Clare listened attentively for a few seconds and sang a few words under her breath, then her arm reached out again and cut the sound abruptly.

'I caused a slight furore next door while you were away,' Blanche Parkes remarked to her husband while they relaxed over a pre-party drink.

'What did you get up to?' Dick Parkes watched her with loving indulgence. He was a pleasant, easy-going, ordinary-looking man of forty-five with more than half a million pounds distributed about the world.

'We had this Heart Week thing just after you went to New York and at the last minute, on the Saturday, two of the local church helpers had to back out. I rang Laura Shaw and asked her if she'd have a shot at it. It only meant doing a bit of catering in the church hall. What happened then—so I've deduced from the few things I've heard, you know me—was that she asked old lover-boy for permission and actually got it. Nice as pie. So she came along and did a good job. But meantime our hero was not as thrilled to see her acting off her own bat as he kidded. He climbed down off the wagon—where he'd been for a while—drank a bottle of Scotch, rang an estate agent, sold the house and its contents on the spot and sat and waited for her to come home to the good news.'

Blanche paused to drink, and Dick grimaced his incredulity. 'Rotten old bugger. Then what?'

'Cigarette, darling—' Blanche ate an olive, had her cigarette lighted and resumed. 'You know how I always put two and two together in my inimitable way? Well, I gather there was a shocking set-to and the next day when Clare was climbing into a taxi with her luggage and he was still on a bender, Laura came down with a large attack of rheumatic fever.'

Dick pulled another face. But he was very interested. He was a soft-hearted man, even squeamish, but he did love to gossip with Blanche about all the weird characters who were not Blanche and Dick Parkes. 'Thank God we're normal!' He smiled at his fair wife, who was dressed, made-up and bejewelled with the excruciating moderation of the astute new rich.

'The doctor said it was psychosomatic after he caught sight of Felix skulking about. I don't know about psychosomatic. She looks a helluva sick woman to me. Anyway, Felix sobered up long enough to try to cancel the sale. Not for her sake, but he'd given the place away. Naturally, the agent wouldn't hear of parting with it, but he offered them the Robertsons' place further along the street and he more or less had to take it. Clare helped him get enough furniture in for the time being, and now they're settling in.'

'She didn't leave, then?'

'I suppose someone's got to look after Laura.'

'Has he gone off the grog again?'

'Uh-uh. I had to call in to get her receipt book from Heart Week and when I passed the window I saw him haranguing her from the foot of the bed about the medical expenses and what he'd lost on the house, and how it was all her fault. She ought to be in hospital, but she knows he'd go through the roof if he had to pay any more out, so—'

'He must have a couple of pennies to rub together. What is it with them? He's a century older than her, but what is it, do you think? Incompatibility?'

Artlessly they eyed each other, breathing and sipping their whiskies. Blanche did not laugh or even think to. Her powers of analysis had always fascinated Dick. He liked to snuffle about amongst the bones of strangers' lives, but he was uncertain of his judgements: it was not *nothing*, however, to have carried off a sybil and married her.

Laura leaned over a card-table in the sitting-room, working out the factory wages. Felix was shut up in the office at the back of the house with Tom Mason, a good-looking English boy who had been a waiter and was now one of the Shaws' two pressers.

In this new place, Laura had risen from her long illness like someone who had undergone major surgery. She had been cut down. Home was only a word now. In many ways this house had charms and advantages the other one had lacked; the only thing was, she did not care so much about anything any more. She had been intimidated far beyond the place where she had imagined the limit to be. There was nothing to be relied on anywhere now except the presence of violence in Felix and his power to inflict punishments. Yet she was obliged to feel that he had been hurt into this shape and not created in it. Otherwise—

'Hullo!' Clare looked into the room. She had been to dinner with Alec Stevenson, an architect from Brisbane, who took her out when he came to Sydney. He was married and deeply wrapped in racing cars and high-spirited.

She sat now on the arm of Laura's chair. 'How did you get on with your visitor?'

'Oh, we had a lovely evening. It's such a long time since we had anyone to dinner. Tom's out with Felix in the office. Coming home tonight,' Laura confided with shy delight, 'Tom was telling us how he misses his mother and father in Nottingham, and he asked us if we'd mind if he called us Mum and Dad. Not in the factory! They'd think we were favouring him and it might cause trouble—but privately.'

Clare said nothing. She stood up. Then she said, 'Oh.'

'Wasn't that quite sweet? He's only young.'

'That's good.'

Laura began to pack her books and papers together and folded the card-table away. 'It's time for coffee. They'll probably want theirs out in the office.'

Clare dumped her coat and bag in her bedroom, and read a letter that had arrived that afternoon from a friend travelling in Canada. In the sitting-room Laura was setting cups on a low teak table. 'People are funny,' she said, not turning. 'Tom—that boy—was quite cheeky to me just now. I won't put up with that kind of thing. It's an imposition. He was really nasty. Felix only smiled. I don't think rudeness is funny.'

'What did he say?'

'Oh, nothing. But I won't put up with it.' She handed Clare a cup. 'Tomorrow I'll say—I'll tell that boy—and Felix—' Pressing her small chin nervously into her throat she stammered out preposterous threats that no one but Clare would ever hear.

In the background an A.B.C. announcer was reading the world news. Clare tried to listen to it for the sake of her sanity. A guerilla band exterminated. Warships ready to move in. Laura kept talking. Clare said, 'Never mind. Never mind. Forget about them. Maybe there's a programme you'd like to listen to.'

'Felix's even given him a rise! We pay above award wages as it is.' She simmered. 'Sometimes I think he should have *married* one of his dear boys. He seems to worry much more about their feelings and opinions than he ever does—'

Clare was combing her hair with her fingers, eyelids lowered. She said, 'You've spilled some coffee in your saucer, Laura. Don't let it drip on your dress.'

'Oh, so I have.' Rapidly, she padded off to the kitchen. When she returned Clare was listening to some programme so fixedly that Laura did not like to interrupt her.

At the wharf, in the shop that sold everything, the little English soul whose past occupation—drink-waiter aboard various passenger liners on the Australia run—had fired him permanently in its mould, leapt about, his expression gay, nervous, sycophantic.

This ramshackle weatherboard dump hanging over the harbour was destined to be his El Dorado or his tomb. It had become a kind of symbol to English ships' stewards everywhere. In Calcutta and Hong Kong and Southampton there was talk of the little mixed business at that suburban wharf in Sydney, Australia, where if you could stick it for two years, seven days a week, early morning till early morning, you could make a fortune and set yourself up in something less strenuous. Every two years it passed from the enriched exhausted hands of one steward to another, usually without event. Last time, though, the owner committed suicide, by drowning, in the harbour. If populations were more settled he might have been a local legend now, but hardly anyone remembered already—

Out of the corner of his eye he saw Clare Vaizey come in. Roy ran nimbly round his three counters, serving out a *Herald*, a packet of cigarettes, an early-morning malted, smiling largely all the while above his blue bow tie, bowing, chatting, slicking back his long hair when the bending and stretching disarranged it.

He kept Clare waiting since she seemed disinclined to come forward into the crowd of her fellow ferry-travellers. If she waited, they might talk. He would like that.

'The general public—' he sometimes said to her, close to tears. 'They come in here, throw their dry-cleaning at you: "See it's ready tonight!" Never a smile or the time of day! You're not a human being!' These days his hands were always shaking. He often felt thoroughly broken-up.

'I know,' she sometimes answered, and he felt she really did. He realised that he was not, after all, upset by these people. 'But they've all got their worries,' he jumped in eagerly. 'It's not deliberate, really. You don't ignore anyone on purpose.'

'Of course not.'

Outside, the ferry bell rang and the crowds pressed out of the shop's corner doorway, clutching newspapers, and raced along the old wooden jetty, yapped at by stray dogs, looked at mechanically by seated passengers still more than half asleep, hoarsely exhorted and chivvied by the weatherbeaten admiral whose job it was to yank the gangplanks on and off the boats. Down they clattered. Pandemonium!

Clare looked after the stampeding legs and caught the routine clamour of the seven-fifty-five's departure. She had turned to follow and was stopped, all her weight on the toes and ball of one foot, by Roy's unctuous, 'And now what can I do for you? I didn't serve you before. I knew you were early. I knew you wouldn't be wanting to get this one like the others.'

Did he? Didn't she? Early? Oh!

229

From staring at him through her dark glasses, over her shoulder, behind his counter, Clare relaxed suddenly and went to the glass-topped case, giving Roy and his near-visible stewards' paraphernalia of bottles and siphons a sudden smile. She even saw what she wanted, and indicated the tube of toothpaste to Roy, not speaking, but continuing to lean and smile in a way that gave the impression of speech. Raking in her old coach-hide handbag she produced some money, took the packet into her fist, and sauntered from the empty shop, not having spoken. Roy watched the peacock-blue back, fair hair, tanned legs. Then the eight-ten types started surging in.

She was alone for the moment on the floating pontoon wharf. The piles creaked under the stress of the tide. The harbour glittered all about in the sun with an eye-straining brilliance. She leaned against one of the new wooden piles that still looked like a tree, and had bark on it, and was splintered. Her mouth curved as she stared out over the harbour's white fiery surface, examining and greeting the day. It looked portentous. The very air seemed to shine, and the leaves on the trees, and the inside of the old jetty ceiling did, too.

Downstairs on the ferry and outside, just feet from the water, she sat jammed between two heavy men, each generously extending half a page of newspaper in front of her face. She remembered Gerald Harding, out from London for six months with the Department.

At lunchtime, over sandwiches and a carton of coffee, they used to talk: they shared an office.

'Your newspapers,' he said. He was bored. He was not pleased about this temporary transfer away from his real life. His salary troubled him deeply. So he told Clare Vaizey what was wrong with the daily news as it was available to her in Australia, in detail, and even went to the bother of bringing her over a period of weeks his airmail editions of the best English papers. She studied them.

When he was leaving he asked, 'What's the verdict?'

She said, 'Oh, you won.'

And he told himself that hers no longer gave her the innocent distraction, the innocent illusion of feeling well-informed, that they had done before. 'Alas!' he said, in his affected way. 'I have sophisticated a native.' He promised, 'I'll send you some of ours when I get back.'

'Thank you. But don't bother. It doesn't matter. It makes no difference.'

He said uncomfortably, 'You have virtues of your own out here, you know.'

'Thank you.'

'You get a bad press in London.'

'Do we? Never mind.'

Abruptly she extricated herself from the company of the human bolsters on either side and edging past the rows of knees and polished shoes went to stand in the open doorway of the ferry while blocks of flimsy home-units, and swimming-pools and anchored yachts, and rubbish dumps all rusted tin, and lawns and gardens slowly passed. The light was so dazzling on this sunny side of the boat that everyone without dark glasses sheltered under hat brims or else lifted forearms and blinked wet eyes at the mesmeric scene.

Suddenly bells rang and the ferry shook to a stop. A white ship, one of the big passenger liners, loomed ahead. *Arcadia*—The ferry travellers rolled their eyes up, and a few ship's passengers looked down at the small red-and-yellow boat, then over beyond its tiny funnel to the bridge, the cloud-reflecting buildings of glass at the Quay, the curving green of the Botanic Gardens.

The ship completed its turn and the ferry's engine quivered shakily again, agitating dozing hearts with its noise. Soon the two vessels berthed. The well-dressed, prosperous crowds pushed off the ferry, slipped coins in the ancient turnstiles and clanged through, out into the concourse of the Quay.

Even as early as this, the small shops were busy—the bread kiosks, milk-bars, dry-cleaners and delicatessens. And *he* was at his usual post. He recognised her as she went towards him. Every week he looked smaller in his loose navy-blue uniform, and frailer and dustier; every week she thought he would be missing.

The morning breeze that lifted her hair and flapped the old man's uniform was seaweedy and salty. Traffic rumbled. People ran. Clare stood before the old man and let some shillings fall into his box. The small Salvation Army soldier watched her and she watched his lips and weak blue eyes, waiting, determined. (Yet she might be rebuffed.)

'God bless you,' he said simply, looking at her like a child.

Oh!—Clare relaxed. 'Thank you,' she murmured. She was blessed, who was most in need of blessing. Blessed.

Having received what she had paid for, she moved on.

PART THREE

Felix cursed when he saw that there was no parking space vacant near the factory. 'Who do they all belong to, anyway? Silly damn stupid women shoppers, I suppose. Look out! Was that a place there?'

'Where?'

He laughed bitterly. 'It's too late now.' He speeded up a little. 'I'm past it now. You've got to look out for a space if it's not too much trouble. I can't take my eyes off the road.'

'I am looking, Felix, but the thing is—' Laura swivelled about in her seat, striving as she perpetually was impelled to for omniscience. 'We're not usually looking for anywhere in town at this time in the afternoon.'

'I am aware of that,' he enunciated with awful distinctness. 'But thank you for telling me.'

Returning to Sydney after a week in Melbourne, they had collected the car from Bill Willis's factory near the airport, and Felix and Bill (whose factory supplied the labour for the Shaws' excess orders) had stood swaying on the edge of the gutter, smoking, reflectively uttering great truths about the state of the rag trade.

Laura was fidgety, and wanted to push on to the factory and home. Felix knew. But she had been too useful in Melbourne. People had complimented him on his wife! He stood and stood, then pretended to lose his way in the streets behind Bill's factory, and only after he had silenced her completely, sped towards the city.

Now, alternately gliding and darting along the road in search of a parking place, he began to feel resentful again: he wanted to drop Laura off at the factory so that she could surprise the staff, but he wanted to keep her in the car so that if he should be forced to tramp miles back from whatever spot he eventually found, she would have to tramp, too.

'Look, Felix, there's a place just ahead where that man's pulling out.'

'Where?'

'On this side. Look! The blue Ford.'

Accelerating slightly, he passed the vacant stretch. 'Where do you mean? I can't see it.'

Laura tried to sound sympathetic and cheerful. 'Oh, what a shame! You just missed it.'

'What? *That*?' Felix turned to stare at her despite the convoys of dusty, multi-coloured cars menacing the road from end to end.

'Why?' Laura contracted under his eyes.

'Blue Ford! Blue Ford! That, my dear woman, was a Chevrolet. Had I known that that was the car you meant, I could easily have got in. As it is, we're so close to Elizabeth Street we might just as well go down to the parking lot and get a bus back up.'

Laura stared at the veined hands folded loosely on her lap.

The news went through from the cutting- and finishing-room to the factory proper: 'Old Shaw's back!' Twenty heads were lowered. Twenty machines roared.

Felix stood in the doorway, smiling a closed smile. He loved this about the factory. Even when no one looked at him, not daring to, everyone noticed him. The machines were thundering. He smiled, tolerating the bent backs of girls over whom he had power, who joked with him sometimes in hoarse voices, admitting that he was indeed their lord and master.

'He's got another new suit and hat on,' Marj Curtis advised her sister Doreen in a cracked whisper. 'God, you wouldn't read about it!'

Felix was conscious of his new clothes, too. His suit had been tailored by a man from Savile Row. (Imagine!) And Laura had described its colour as 'a subtle muted brown', tickling him with the words as if they were so many feathers. And the hat! Laura had trudged the city to find one that matched; but it had to tone perfectly, of course, or the whole thing would have been pointless.

She came up to him now and touched his beautiful sleeve, enormous-eyed. 'Something's happened.'

'Guess what?' Felix greeted Clare that night.

'What?'

'We've got a visitor.'

'Have we?—Where?'

Felix grinned, tipping himself backwards and forwards like a rocking-horse. Clare looked at Laura. Laura looked at Felix and they spoke to each other across Clare, as they often did, with faces slightly uptilted, in a public way, the better to catch double meanings.

'Oh, tell her, Felix. Don't tease.'

He was suddenly serious and confiding, taking his hands out of his pockets. 'It's young Bernard, then.'

'Bernard?'

Laura nodded, coaxing and prompting further revelations from Felix.

'Which Bernard?'

'There's only one. Young Bernard, the presser. The second presser. The kid we got to replace that English Tom What's-'is-name, the thieving hound. The one with the Dutch father we had out to dinner the other month.'

'Oh, that one.' An unlikely addition to Felix's merry band. Still, by the law of averages, Clare had to concede, Felix was bound to strike someone not actually an aspiring criminal once every twenty years.

'Where is he?'

'In the spare room,' Felix said, tantalising, enjoying himself.

'Well, tell me!' Clare protested, smiling. 'Don't make me drag out every word.'

'You tell her,' Felix capitulated to Laura all at once. 'I'll go and have a squizz at him.'

'How did you get on in Melbourne?' Clare called after him.

'I think we did very well.' Drawing her red silk scarf from her throat, Laura glanced at Felix, who had returned to the doorway.

'So-so,' he admitted grudgingly. 'Don't forget the week's expenses.'

'What about Heath's order?'

It was Felix's way, however, to regard financial good news as extremely relative, and bad news as quite absolute, so he could not be cheered or reassured by the pointing out of any ostensibly heartening facts. Genuinely alarmed in case it should strike them that he was making money, Felix gave a knowing laugh and moved off across the hall, still laughing.

Listening, Clare took off her coat. Listening, Laura had a drink of water. When it was safe to speak, her look signalled to Clare, who felt obliged to ask, 'How's everything?' (She did not want to know.)

'Oh, Felix had some trouble parking the car in town tonight.'

'Really?'

'He was good in Melbourne, though, almost all the time.'

Clare lifted the lid of the casserole and looked in. After a pause she managed to say, 'Was he?'

'But you know what he's like in the car.'

Clare dug her teeth into the flesh of her closed lips and nodded again, her back to Laura.

'Once he—'

'Is this all right? I fixed it last night.'

'It's delicious, Clare. I meant to say. I've tasted it.—Once he—'

'I still haven't heard about the visitor.' Clare spun round. 'What's he doing in the spare room? Is he sick or something?'

'As a matter of fact he is.' Laura was solemn. 'Oh, Clare. The poor boy. I was sitting in the office just thinking about coming home and I heard a commotion out in the pressing room, and when I ran through there was Bernard on the floor with all the girls around him.'

'What happened to him?' Clare yawned and added in parenthesis, 'My holiday starts on Monday.' She caught Laura's eye and repeated, 'What was wrong?'

'Malnutrition for one thing.' Laura was deliberately stark.

'Goodness! How can that be? He's quite well paid, isn't he?'

'Of course. But he's been sending it all to his family. And Joy spoke to his landlady on the phone tonight and, Clare, he's had a terrible time.'

'Oh?' Clare looked at her watch 'Shouldn't we put the casserole in the oven?'

'I was letting it heat up. Yes, it can go in now.'

'I remember he said that night,' Clare slid the dish on to the wire oven rack, 'something optimistic about saving up so that he can take ten degrees in biology. Or botany.'

'Yes, he wants to study. (Although he's doing very well with us and I think Felix would let him train to do the accounts and office work, if—) But he came out here six months ago with his father, and his father, Clare, used to be a pianist before the war but he couldn't go back to it afterwards, and he came out here as a builder. And they left Bernard's mother and sister and grand-mother back in Holland till they had a place for them. Bernard took this job with us the first week he arrived, and Joy just heard today that he worked five nights a week cleaning offices. He and his father were sending money back and trying to save. Then just a week or so after Bernard came here for dinner his father was killed in an accident. A fall, the landlady said. Imagine, and we didn't know a thing about it. And since then this boy's been supporting his family back in Holland and trying to save for this whatever he wants to do, and starving himself to death.'

None of this seemed very real to Clare. While she did not disbelieve the story, she did feel scepti-cal. It was rather pathetic, of course. If it was true. But why had he come here in the first place? Why had his father allowed himself to be killed? Why did his

243

family need to depend on the earnings of an eighteen-year-old boy? And why had he chosen to want a career that was clearly not open to him? It was unrealistic. All so hopeless. That night when he had come to dinner she had thought even then, hearing a fraction of all this, that he was unrealistic and that it was hopeless.

'But what's he doing here? I mean here, tonight?'

'I know.' Laura could hardly account for it herself. 'You see—' she extended her hands, palms upward, 'we had to revive him. And it was closing time. So Felix and I thought we'd at least have to take him home in the car. And when we saw the place, Clare! We couldn't leave him. An awful little alley off Taylor Square.'

She looked at Clare for understanding: Clare raised her eyebrows. She felt a perverse inclination to distrust the boy, his story, awful little alley, and Laura's impression of him. After all, Laura's judgement had never proved so sound in the past! Any greedy, small-minded fraud, so long as he was smooth and smiling, had won sympathy and similar recommendations from her gullible sister.

'But what are you going to do with him? Are you going to keep him here?'

'For a little while, I think. He's a nice boy, Clare. Felix likes him. He's a good worker, Dr. Bell came round and we explained the situation, and he said Bernard would have to go to hospital if we couldn't keep him, but that he felt to be looked after in an ordinary household would be much more satisfactory.'

'Well, it might be more satisfactory for him, but what about you? It's all very well for Dr. Bell to say keep him. He's a total stranger. Why should you?' Clare's indignation was as spurious as her suspicion had been. She said, 'I wonder why they came here in the first place?'

Laura noticed Clare's tendency to want to blame Bernard for his misfortunes and it strengthened her own desire to flutter about him, tending him. She had touched his forehead, taken his pulse. She loved it when people were sick and she could look after them strictly. 'Well, Clare,' she said a trifle reproachfully, 'they were there all through the war. And one of his sisters was killed—'

'Oh, no! You're making this up. And, anyway, everyone in Europe today over the age of six must have a war story of sorts. And none of them would be gay.'

'I'm only telling you that Bernard's twin sister was killed queuing for food in the snow. Machine-gunned. His father was taken prisoner. Afterwards, I suppose they wanted a new life away from their terrible memories. If they did, it's no wonder.'

After a slight pause, Clare said, 'Speaking of wonder, I wonder how our dinner's getting on? Since I made it, I can't help taking a deeper interest in it than usual. But, really, Laura,' she said, on a less disagreeable note, 'how will you manage? He'll be left alone all day while you go to work, and that won't be very stimulating for him, or quite what Dr. Bell had in mind. And I don't see Felix agreeing to let you stay home from the office.'

'No.' Laura lowered hostile eyes from her sister's face. How Clare had ever got to be such a hard-hearted girl—

'What then?'

Laura touched her face nervously, thinking. 'But what I thought was—if we could manage—Felix would love his company in the evenings. He gets bored. Bernard would divert him.'

Fee, fie, fo, fum—Clare repressed an urge to mention that Bernard might have some other, more vital, function in life than dispelling Felix's ennui, but the thought went out from her savagely and Laura gave a little false exclamation. 'I haven't changed out of my good suit yet. I'll just do that, and then serve dinner.'

Clare picked up her coat and went to her room, passing Felix on his way back to the kitchen. Having heard his approach, Laura waited where she was, and Felix looked at her significantly, letting his head somehow rear up on his neck as if he were making a very special point of meeting her eyes. He was teasing. He had a secret. It might or might not be a pleasant one.

Laura hovered. 'Is everything all right, dear?'

'As far as I know,' he said grandly. 'I am going to squeeze some orange juice for Bernard.'

'Oh!—Of course. Did he say he would like some?' In an instant Laura had assembled on the formica work-bench oranges, sharp knife, squeezer and glass.

'It occurred to me that he might, conceivably.' Felix eyed the equipment for the operation. Laura eyed him and it anxiously. Felix had never so much as put a kettle on to boil.

'Would you like me to do it? I'm more used to it.'

Ignoring her, Felix ponderously selected a small wooden tray from the rack in the corner and laid it on the table. He left the room, looking neither right nor left, and returned with a white laundered cloth delicately embroidered by some Indian hand. He brought the tray and the cloth together—a scientist combining two hitherto unknown elements. He approached the bench and lifted the knife. Laura was bemused by his ability to do these difficult things, by his purposefulness, the terrible importance of it all.

'By the way,' he drawled, not turning, 'you'd better give me that five pounds I paid the quack for his visit and the injections out of your housekeeping. I want to keep my account square for the interest.'

'Oh? Yes. Of course.' Distracted, Laura went to her handbag and counted the money from her wallet. She counted the balance. She put a hand to her forehead, though in fact the headache that was beginning to burgeon was at the base of her skull.

'I am inviting the boy to stay for a while,' Felix said, when dinner was almost over, as he helped himself to a chunk of Gorgonzola cheese. 'He can board. He's due to get sick-pay. When that runs out we'll see about the rest.' He crunched a hard biscuit while the women considered the best way to react. It was unwise to press him, but equally unwise to seem uninterested.

'You saw the hovel he's been in. If he isn't crazy, he'll stay, and I don't think he is. We can take him for runs in the car. He hasn't seen anything.'

'You haven't asked him yet?' Clare held her coffee cup out to Laura, who had raised eyebrows and pot at her.

'No, he's asleep. Old Bell gave him some sedative or other.' To have to admit to the possibility of rejection! Supra-casual, he lifted his face, on which tomorrow's beard of black and grey was already beginning to sprout. His eyes looked out nervously from the loose dark-brown skin of his face, from under thick untidy eyebrows all askew. His hands shook over his plate.

'He's in no condition to go anywhere, poor boy. He's sure to want to stay,' Laura said stoutly, deeply uncertain of the wisdom of this, its practicability, her own preferences.

They both looked at Clare, on whom they relied in singular situations to interpret the dangerous world and people to them. Since she was valued now in that external place by strangers (surprising promotions, salary increases, unknown people ringing her, asking her out) they had begun to notice her, as if avaricious prospectors had tried to lay claim to a small goldmine in their very own backyard.

'Why wouldn't he be?' she said lightly.

Felix beamed and sat back. He waved an inspired finger at them both. 'I'm going to get that crystal chandelier off Dave O'Brien. Been talking about it long enough.'

'Oh!' Laura clasped her hands and made great circles of eyes and mouth, like a Victorian miss promised a sugar plum.

'Let's make some plans, why don't we?' Felix cried. 'Let's get organised and line up a few outings.'

Clare stood up and began to collect the dishes together. 'You two can work things out while I wash up.'

Felix stopped laughing. They all exchanged looks. Laura said hastily, 'No, no, you have to help arrange things, too.'

Did she? Yes, on second thoughts, quite definitely, she did.

'Right,' she said firmly, sitting down again.

'Wait! I'll get paper and pens.' Laura was out of the room and back before there was time to speak, distributing scribblers and ballpoint pens. 'Now then—' She broke off to say, in a wondering voice, 'Do you know—Bernard's the first visitor we've had to sleep in all these years.'

Later, Laura and Felix disappeared into the invalid's room, combed and polished and on tiptoe. Clare refused their cordial invitations to join the company, saying mildly, 'Have a heart. The boy's not well.'

'Oh, we won't stay long,' Laura assured her, as they slipped in for an hour's conversation.

Strolling through to the front of the house, Clare went on to the balcony. A big liner, lighted all over, was moving noiselessly across the dark harbour in the direction of the Heads. Emptily, she watched it, breathed the moist air, stared at the level plain of sombre cloud. The ship passed out of sight.

It was Sunday morning. Clare was looking through the contents of her wardrobe. Laura sat perched on the edge of the dressing-table stool balancing words in her mind.

'Felix's writing some business letters.'

'Uh-huh?' Clare paused over a green skirt. 'Is that too old to take?'

'No—Clare. You wouldn't go in and talk to Bernard for a few minutes, would you? You haven't spoken to him since he came. He'll think it's funny if you don't talk to him. You're nearer his age, too.'

'I'm five years older than he is. How will he think it's funny? He doesn't even know me.'

'Yes, he does. He met you at dinner. We've mentioned you. He knows you live here.'

Clare draped a pair of slacks over her arm, saying soothingly, inattentively, 'Honestly, he doesn't want a strange woman drifting in to talk to him.'

'Please, Clare. Just for a few minutes. He seems to get nervous if he's by himself.'

'Nervous?—When has he had a chance to discover that? You two have been with him all the time. How is he going to get on tomorrow when you both go to work?'

Laura looked down. 'I haven't discussed it with Felix yet.'

Folding her clothes on the bed, Clare pointed out, 'I am trying to get ready for a holiday, Laura. A whole month!' With a whoop, she dropped to the floor and turned a somersault. '*Yes*, I'll talk to Bernard.'

Laura said harshly, 'Well, comb your hair first.'

Any display of light-heartedness in this house had a way of seeming indecent.

'I was told to bring your tonic and some fruit juice,' Clare said, going slowly in after knocking. 'We met a few months ago when you came to dinner.'

'Yes, I remember.'

Impressions reached her of illness, pallor, slanted hazel eyes, noticeable cheekbones, dark-brown tousled hair. Illness. She was chastened. She had glibly derided Laura and written the boy off as a plausible young tough. Well, he was young—

While she stood in the middle of the floor and they talked about the doctor's diagnosis and the view, Clare was recalling the night he had come to dinner. The cuffs of his sleeves were frayed. This made them unique in her experience. Though her mind offered no comment on the sight, she kept noticing them. Then she and Bernard had shaken hands. His palm was hard and calloused. He regarded Laura and Felix steadily, in a way that Clare had resented. At one point she had seen him in profile, and in the patience and severity of its lines she had recognised experience and respected it. He had a Dutch father, an English mother; he was bilingual, and meant to be a biologist. Or a botanist. He played the violin. He appeared to have many interests. Clare had been impressed, and thought timidly, yet beyond envy: *we don't know very much*. And the next day she forgot him.

Now, out of a deep lack of interest, she had asked him a conventional question and he was going on and on, not only unreservedly and willingly, but passionately, glancing out of his large, strangely-angled hazel eyes as though he were in some quite other place and company. Clare was a little affronted by the unexpectedness of it. But she began to watch him coolly, with cool compassion, cool attention, inside herself like someone in a rocking-chair on another planet.

'We had to come,' he declared. 'My father's hands were ruined. Better not to be reminded of what his life was before. There was nothing good to remember—my sister being killed, being imprisoned himself. He was told to go to a warmer climate and work in the open air. So we came here.'

Still he continued his mournful story his—grandmother, his mother, his young sister, Birgitte. With a wonderful lack of perspicacity, it now seemed, Clare had thought that other night that this boy was self-contained!

His voice stopped suddenly and Clare looked up, wondering what to expect. Bernard said, taking in his surroundings with something like chagrin, 'I've told you my life story.'

'Well, that's all right,' Clare said seriously. He was only young. And what stories could she not bear to hear? It was a long time since she had shed a tear. 'I was interested. I did ask you questions.' And she moved slightly on the chair, sliding forward to stand and go, but the sick boy looked at her for a moment and then started to speak again, and she saw that he believed whatever she politely said, and believed that she meant more and not less than she said. After the slightest hesitation, she sat back again in her chair because, in a way, what he thought was true.

'My mother still wants to come when I can arrange it. She asks me all the time what I've done about the university. She must think it's free, and that I'm free to go! It's only that she wishes she could help me. She knows how important it is that I should start soon.'

'Is it? Why?' Clare could not help asking, shaking her head slightly. He looked wild, excited, not safe. 'Biology.'

'Botany. Because it's what I would know how to do best.'

'Oh.' There was a pause during which Clare did not think. She heard herself ask then, 'How did you ever—choose that?'

'My English grandfather was a botanist. He came here to Australia once. My mother used to tell me stories about him when I was young. I've always known that I wanted to do this.'

'I see.'

'But it doesn't matter. I know that now. Nothing will ever be the same again. Whatever happens. All we ever do is pass the time.' His voice was unemphatic. He lay propped up against Laura's professional arrangement of pillows, staring with alarming stillness at the eiderdown.

Clare felt distracted. (*Nothing will ever be the same again.*) What were they doing with a person like this in the house? In addition to everything else. It had begun to dawn on her, in some disused area of her consciousness, that this boy might be trying to make claims on her, that he might be asking for help. *Her* help. Through a mixture of incredulity, sadness and amusement, she realised that he had mistaken her for a different person, a person helpful to people. And she felt flattered and yet untouched by this mistake which was so far-fetched, as if he had thought her someone of merit, impossibly famous.

Bernard turned towards the windows. Yes, Clare was certain that something was expected of her. She gave the averted head a wary look and stood up decisively. 'You're getting tired.'

Bernard turned back to her without lifting his eyes. 'You are all very kind to me.'

How terrible something was! Clare glanced at the pale, sick face with its lowered eyelids. 'I must finish my packing. My holidays start tomorrow. I'm going up the north coast.'

There was a silence.

'Oh, are you?' He actually changed colour.

'Yes,' Clare insisted enthusiastically, half-aware of the voiceless demands and expectations, half-inclined to pass her intuitions off as imagination, a little surprised that he did not share her sense of anticipation. 'I'll see you before I go,' she said, leaving the room.

'How about young Clare playing nurse for a week?' Felix suggested, looking at Laura blandly.

Without force, she protested, 'Oh, but she's all ready to go off in the morning on her holiday.'

Clare nodded inwardly. She had seen this coming a mile off, a mile off. She said nothing. If they liked to pretend she was not present, she could pretend, too.

255

Leaning on the verandah rail, they all stared at the rocks on the point straight ahead while the chameleon colours of the day yielded to the breeze before their eyes.

'You can't stay home after being in Melbourne, and I can't,' Felix argued, ultra-reasonable.

Laura agreed. 'Of course it isn't that he needs a lot of attention, only that he shouldn't be left alone in the house all day.'

It did seem to be insoluble.

Clare admired the bulk, majesty and glow of a tremendous armada of clouds passing slowly over the city.

'He's very intelligent. And he has nice manners. And he's read more books than I have.' Laura straightened her diamond ring. 'He's a little bit secretive, though,' she admitted. 'I mean, if Joy in the factory hadn't heard about his father from his gossipy old landlady we just wouldn't know about it.'

'Well, I guess he'll just have to look after himself,' Felix said philosophically.

'I suppose so,' Laura agreed, looking round-eyed at Clare.

Clare nodded, equally round-eyed, as if she supposed so, too. Her job was exacting. She was tired. Her head, eyes, ears and teeth shared a general neuralgic ache. Putting a hand over her right ear, she wondered what Laura could mean by 'secretive'. Not what *she* did. *She* had heard Bernard's life history in half an hour flat. And very like most war films of occupied Europe she had ever seen, it was. Very like any newspaper feature, any short story about immigrants she had ever read—hackneyed, in slightly poor taste, strained.

'He can play chess,' Felix said.

'You can hold great tournaments when he's a bit better.'

'He could work more overtime in our place. No need to clean office buildings.'

Clare listened to their talk, without attending to it. She was twenty-three and life was a game she had rejected utterly. Nothing about her own situation or anyone else's moved her in the least. A spectator distant from all turmoil and emotion, she took a theoretical interest in the play and in a sort of aside to herself registered very faintly the feeling that would have been natural to each situation had she and her fellows been real and alive and the universe of any import.

Still. She so wanted everyone to receive justice. And this boy might be an impostor like all the others. Poor Laura and Felix! (He had mentioned Felix's generosity in paying the doctor's fee. Her heart had fallen.) Then again, if he were not any sort of confidence trickster, but simply what he appeared to be—a sick, harrowed boy who knew more than she did—think of the coils and toils and tentacles all ready to strangle him.

'It's practically spring,' she said, with a glance at the retreating armada.

'It's midwinter. You're mad to take your holidays now.' Felix's dark, dark eyes watched her.

'Oh, well—'

'If you're going inside, Clare, I wonder if you'd mind taking Bernard's tablet in to him. It's just due. The green one.'

'Right.'

'You can't really expect her to put her holiday off,' Laura said, brushing the shoulder of Felix's jacket with her hand and smoothing it down.

But Felix had been ruminating; his eyes quite twinkled. 'He'll be all right. Better than in that old dump or some lousy hospital. You can leave his lunch on the hot-plate. I guess he'll be a bit bored by five o'clock, but we'll be home then. We'll cheer him up.' He gave Laura what her mother would have called an old-fashioned look.

'Your tablet, Bernard, and a glass of water,' Clare said firmly. 'I hope I didn't wake you up.'

'I wasn't sleeping.'

From her remote eyrie Clare noted that he looked at her over-intently, appearing to find significance in her least word and movement. 'There you are, then. The tablet's in the saucer. Would you like something to read?'

'No. I can't read.' The curtains flew out like wings from the open windows. The silence lengthened. From lying inert, lids lowered, Bernard suddenly heaved round in the bed and turned to the wall.

Surprised and repelled, Clare stared at his back. 'Oh, Bernard—' She looked about in the hope of finding that someone had materialised who was more interested in him, who would allow her to disappear. 'Bernard,' she said again gingerly, leaning forward but taking no steps towards the bed. Really, she had not misled him by pretending any great concern! Yet no one would act like this without confidence in his witness. 'Bernard—What's the matter?'

There was a long silence. Clare grimaced and looked about for help. The curtains billowed.

'I'm sorry I talked so much. I told you things I don't want to remember.'

Had he? She could hardly say she didn't care when he so obviously thought she did, and blamed himself for his frankness so disproportionately.

'People have to—talk to each other,' she said, awkwardly, staring at his brown hair, at the seams of Felix's pale-blue pyjama jacket. 'Everything will be—better soon.' In his expectation of her interest and kindness, in his apparent sorrow, alleged illness, in his breath, flesh, foreignness, intensity, he was ever so slightly repulsive to her.

'I wanted you to know.'

'Oh.' Wanted her to know what? That any of this mattered so was astounding. No doubt she was brutal and heartless, but she felt a faint internal recession of sympathy, and her respect for that look of experience worn by a boy who knew more than she did, was ousted by a faint contempt for this sticky display of emotion, the ludicrous esteem in which he had decided to hold her. Several sentences framed themselves in her mind. She said, 'Well. I won't tell anyone else,' and Bernard looked at her at last with an expression that made her shrink again with caution and disdain. She eyed him dubiously, saying, 'There's your tablet.'

'I'm sorry you have to go away.'

Clare looked at him, half-indignant. 'I *want* to go. It's not a matter of being obliged to.' She gave him an impatient smile, though it seemed unreasonable to dislike him so because he had decided to think she was better than she was. He made unfair statements. But he was desperate. But that was repellent.

Mentally, Clare turned about in a last effort to locate some more reliable and buoyant piece of driftwood than herself for the boy to cling to. He ought to see she was the feeblest creature, incapable of action as a stone, dangerously indifferent to his troubles. No one else had ever made this peculiar mistake, insisting so blatantly on her presence and assistance. It occurred to her then, however, that the worst that ever happened to Laura's and Felix's acquaintances was a temporary shortage of capital for investment, a loss at the races or a hangover; among her own acquaintances suffering tended to be on a smaller scale—girls quarrelled with their boyfriends, and never owned enough dresses; they caught colds, and their skin peeled after the first harsh dose of summer sun; the men would have liked more money and promotion, but no extra work; they brooded about their cars' performances and their own liquor-holding capacities.

Even as these reflections were filtering through her mind, Clare was saying, 'I can easily stay. Yes. I'll stay.'

Bernard was not surprised. Clare was. She felt as though someone else had made use of her voice. Her sense of her own identity diminished increasingly, and more attention, more concentration than she had ever known she possessed, focused, as though directed, on the boy.

It was almost inconceivable to her that mere persistence had been able to penetrate the sunless calm she lived in. Yet she felt extraordinarily light-hearted—like a scientist at the very moment of discovery. Of course she couldn't leave him. She looked at him in surprise to think she could ever have intended to. It seemed self-evident that the attention had to focus on the boy.

She and Bernard had traversed the same extreme country. Because the details of his life were so removed from hers she had judged him with airy contempt as excessive, bogus, as if he had invented a life spiked with tortuous incidents to win favours and interest and pity, when all the time—The complacency with which she had been able to accept his hard situation as his 'destiny' smote her. This was how she and Laura had been judged by Blanche Parkes and her kind: *Well, well, poor things. It's their own fault, of course. Nothing like that ever happens to me.* Yet fellow-feeling had nothing to do with the decision to stay.

Five minutes ago she could have sprinkled petals on his grave, her heart and eyes as cold as cement. Now she saw him with deep amazement and wonder. No, she thought, slightly shaking her head. Heavens. He had to be—all right. Let someone of such value sink from sight? What had the world been thinking of?

She marvelled somehow. Her nature surged with life. Like everyone, she was quite innocent in a way. She would do anything, spend all her untampered wealth of action, longing and virtue. It never occurred to her that what she offered might not be enough. The attention that had claimed her was in touch with the cause of things, and she did believe that it would be able to intervene.

Clare had needed help always, craved understanding and, above all, had longed to appreciate. When it was manifest that she was not to receive these blessings, her resolution to survive was adamant. She would *not* be disposed of. However, she had to remain a person whose entire strength was required to maintain her own equilibrium. She stood upright without support; in the circumstances, it was the best she could do. She did apprehend other people and feel them with clarity and depth, receiving information about them involuntarily from her intuition. She had never known what this gratuitous news was for. She wished her fellows well, but it had never entered her head that she—pusillanimous, vicious, sustained only by a peculiar sort of pride and insurmountable determination—could be useful to anyone. If it had been suggested, it would have seemed the cruellest joke. Interest and sympathy she had given easily, but acts had always, obviously, been impossible. She had no authority.

Now everything was reversed. Simply. Suddenly. As if a river diverted for decades by man-made dams and channels had violently returned to its own course in the space of a single storm and raced on its way with an energy and power not to be overborne.

There was the attention. There was a torrent of strength. There was a fine edge of life on which to tread, a sensation of fitness and certainty, of force bounteously and somehow justly given by the universe. There was a boundless vitality of the spirit, a thoughtfulness beyond words. She could encourage someone to stay alive. And this was what she was for.

'What? Has your nurse run off and left you ' Felix said critically from the doorway. 'All alone, are you?'

'She's gone to the university again.'

'Still trying to lose us our presser, is she? She won't do any good, you know. They're not going to take you in for free.'

'I know.'

'Why doesn't she stop wearing out her shoe-leather, then? She's supposed to be home keeping you company. She's just about haunted that place these last two weeks. And even if they're mug enough to listen to her, they're not going to keep your whole family. How does she think you're going to get round that?'

Bernard rubbed one eye severely to escape from Mr. Shaw's persistent gaze. 'She won't take any notice.'

'Huh!' Felix gave a short laugh. 'We'll soon have you back on the job. That's what you need. Bit of pressing. The work's piling up for you. What's the old sawbones say? When's he going to let you start?'

'He wouldn't tell me, but I could go back now. Tomorrow.' Bernard threw back the bedclothes and began to climb out of bed.

Laura rushed in. 'Bernard. Get back to bed. Felix. Fancy letting him do that. Dear, dear, dear.' Intimidating as any matron, she shepherded Felix out of the way and tucked her patient in.

Felix blustered, 'It's all right. He might be coming back to work in the morning.'

'Who said so? What an idea! He certainly is not. Really, Felix! He's only joking, Bernard. He knows perfectly well that Dr. Bell wants you to do nothing but concentrate on getting better. You're still a sick boy for all that you can stand up now without collapsing.'

Embarrassed, Bernard looked away from the over-hanging faces—Mrs. Shaw worried and kind, her curly hair standing up excitedly, Mr. Shaw dark, enigmatic and still. He said, 'But I should move back to my own room.'

Laura turned to Felix in consternation.

'Now, whoa there, young fella. You're staying right here. No arguments. Besides, we've given your room up.'

'What would Clare say when she comes home if we told her you were leaving? Heavens, she'd never forgive us.'

'What's it got to do with her?' Felix asked smoothly.

'Nothing!—Except that she's chief nurse. Anyway, she's left dinner ready for us, so if you want to wash or change, Felix—And I'll just fix these pillows, Bernard, then I'll have your's in in a jiffy.'

Left alone, Bernard rolled about in the bed groaning; he pulled a pillow over his face.

'Oh!' Laura whispered reproachfully. 'You made him feel like a—a malingerer, Felix.'

They went side by side down the hall.

'What's eating her, rushing out every afternoon to see the Lord Chief Justice about him?'

'She only wants to see if there are any scholarships.

If he's eligible for any. But you evidently have to make appointments with a lot of different people to find these things out.'

'Bunch of red-tape artists. He's all right with us. They're not going to keep his whole clan, anyway. *He* doesn't give a damn about his bloody old botany. Might as well be a gardener! He knows there's no scholarship. Didn't he check with these characters himself?'

'With two jobs? Look at all the time Clare's spent on it—writing letters and ringing up to see these men. It's a fulltime occupation. It's only because she's on holiday that she's been able to do it.'

'Yeah. Well. What's she taking such an interest for?'

They stood facing each other in the soft apricot lamplight at the end of the hall, and Felix's quizzical smile with closed lips was very set.

'We wanted her to stay home and look after Bernard.'

'She didn't have to go the whole hog, did she?'

'What do you mean?' If he would only blink, or at least say what he meant.

'She doesn't need to spend her savings on fancy food and presents, does she? She doesn't need to sit at his bedside *reading* to him.'

It did sound obscene. Laura could have torn her hair out by the roots. She said pacifically, 'That doesn't do any harm. Bernard likes it. It passes the time for him. And I don't think she's spent much money. She's only enjoying cooking nice meals for him during the day. The company's done him good. Dr. Bell said so.'

'Do you reckon?' Felix reflected into her eyes. 'He probably thinks he's on a good wicket. Her running after him.'

'I'm sure he thinks nothing of the kind. Though being the sort of boy he is he no doubt appreciates—' A look of immensely diffused and triumphant scorn on Felix's face truncated Laura's thought. For he seemed to know something deadly that would controvert for all time not merely her tenuous *belief* in the existence of grace, but in some more fundamental way its very existence. His anarchic eyes had watched the murder.

Felix began to chuckle, looking at her, and chuckled for a long time. Finally he managed to gasp through his merriment, 'I've left my cigarettes in the car.'

'There might be some in the sitting-room.'

He went off humming. Laura surged into the kitchen muttering fervently, 'Some day, some day, I will go to Alaska and never come back.'

'Hullo, Felix. Hullo, Bernard.'

Felix looked round. Bernard had already seen her. He breathed and gave the impression that he had been holding his breath since she left.

'So the professors chucked you out, did they?' Felix grinned so that it seemed his face must surely ache.

'Not really. He was very interested. Everyone's been full of useful suggestions. There must be fifty letters floating about Sydney this minute on Bernard's behalf. I have to ring this man next Tuesday.'

She and Bernard smiled at each other as if they were speaking.

To his own surprise, Felix remarked, 'You look radioactive in that dress.'

Clare looked down at it. 'Don't you like it?'

'Oh, I wouldn't say that. I wouldn't say that.'

But she was electric, electrifying, like a fiery avenger or angel, like someone alive twice over, and it had nothing to do with the colour of her dress.

Felix swept his hands over his thick hair. 'Laura's around somewhere—'

'I'll find her.' Clare started off amiably.

'Get her to tell you about the little obstacle you've overlooked,' Felix called cheerily after her.

'I'll do that.'

'It's insuperable,' Laura said grimly, watching her sister chop parsley for an omelette. 'You'd forgotten all about his poor family.'

Clare tossed the parsley over her omelette with a carefree hand. 'Nothing's insuperable. We'll think of something.' Picking up a fork from the table, she began to eat.

'At least sit down to have your dinner!'

'Oh?' She slid into a chair, continuing to eat and think rapidly.

Laura liked to eat with exceeding slowness. She liked to see other people eat the same way. She put aside the desire to mention these facts while she wiped the stove, the work bench and that part of the kitchen table not covered by Clare's plate. 'What do these people think when you go to see them?'

'Think? I suppose they think: what can we do for this—' she breathed and looked back at her dinner, '—nice, intelligent boy we've been hearing about.'

'Mustn't they think it's funny? You taking all this trouble?'

Clare raised her eyebrows very high and looked about the kitchen. 'No-o,' she said, somehow stalwartly, on two notes. In its impression of renouncing stupefaction where stupefaction might well have been called for, the effect was extraordinarily reassuring. But she wanted Laura to expect the best, the very best behaviour from everyone, since she had discovered that this was exactly what everyone required. Doors opened. Walls were symbols merely, ready to fall when expected. People were harmless, diffident, sweet-natured, earnest, with energy and deeds banked up and ready for use. People said *yes*. None of this seemed surprising.

'You didn't even like him at first.' Laura tipped water into the earth round her ivy plant and replaced the pot on the wide window-sill. Clare said nothing.

'Now you rush to the other extreme. You'd think poor Felix was the worst in the world because he spends the evenings in there with him.'

'No. They're all right,' she said carefully. (There was nothing to be done about it.)

'You said he found too much conversation trying.'

'Ah, well—' Clare stood up and poured herself some coffee. It was not that Laura and Felix wanted to destroy him, only that they wanted to survive, themselves.

'I only meant—you know how you feel when you have one of those rotten headaches. If anyone even looks at you you feel you're going to die.'

With a shiver of dread, Laura touched wood. 'Bring your coffee through to the sitting-room. Write your letters there. It's chilly out here. But Felix thinks your behaviour's quite odd, Clare,' she added in a low warning voice. She switched off the light. 'You mustn't let your enthusiasm run away with you.'

'No.'

They stood for a moment in the dark before moving.

'It's only because he's Dutch you think he's unusual.'

'I wouldn't say that exactly,' Clare said cautiously. She paused. As though assigned to describe to a blind person the features of a landscape over which poets had pondered, she hesitated. Minutely she considered.

Then as she might have said in simple helplessness, 'Hawthorn grows by the road. There is a river,' she said, 'He speaks well of people. He has a generous disposition.'

'You'll be back in the office on Monday.' Laura and her sister strolled round the garden together desultorily snipping a flower here and there. And a very excellent thing that would be, too, she thought privately. Bernard was supposed to be *Felix's* friend. 'You've had a sort of a rest, anyway, even if you didn't get away for a change,' she went on cheerlessly. A drop of rain fell on the crown of her head. She looked up at the sky through the Imperial plane tree under which they stood.

Clare raised a hand and brought down a bare branch. 'No, I'm not going back.' The yielding branch sprang up as she released it, and swayed.

Laura said many words. Underfoot the grass was spongy after a week of heavy storms. Clare walked over it, feeling herself sink slightly with every step. Laura followed her, saying words.

'No, I've resigned,' she said, when Laura stopped speaking. 'Yesterday. There hasn't been a chance to tell you.' An impossible act turned out to have been inevitable but of no importance. She had not even made a decision. It had just come about because it was necessary to stay with Bernard till he was well.

Laura stared at her sister's half-averted face, examining the curve of her hair, her full-lidded grey eyes and painted mouth. 'You haven't really resigned?'

'Yes. It was never an ideal occupation.'

'Ideal! Ideal!' Laura felt she had never been so angry in her life. Since Clare had become so inhuman as to be impervious, though, to terseness, temper, sarcasm, Laura decided it might be best to pretend the entire conversation had never taken place. 'How are you going to live?'

Clare smiled faintly. 'That's a question.'

Oh! This infantile obsession with Bernard. Well, no amount of torture on the rack would persuade her to ask Clare one single question. Heaven forbid that she should appear curious! If Clare chose to tell her her plans (which were only in her imagination, anyway) she would listen noncommittally. She strained to see, as though through a dense fog, the berries and leaves in the shallow basket slung over her arm. 'That should do for two vases.' And Clare saw there was nothing Laura was willing to hear.

'She's off her rocker. She's crazy. What? So she can keep an eye on young Bernie?'

'And keep chasing around to get him in somewhere for this famous course of his.'

'Oh, she is, eh? I think she must be up the wall. Well, well, well, well, well, well, well.'

To Laura's surprise, Felix began to look almost pleased as he stared at the traffic ahead and guided the silver Jaguar past all the peasants in tin cans who thought they could share the road with him. Since he could only find pleasure in tearing people's wings off, Laura's clenched mind considered the possibilities. Her thumbs tucked themselves under cover and did not emerge till she reached the factory.

At Bulli Lookout, forty-four miles south of Sydney, Felix drew the car up and there was a moment's stock-taking silence.

'Whew!' He turned to Bernard, searching his eyes. 'It's no easy thing holding a car like this in, I can tell you. Takes a lot of practice.'

'It's a beauty.' Bernard ducked down suddenly to feel the loose sole of one of his brown suède boots.

Giving his rusty laugh, Felix climbed out of the car and led the way across to the platform high above the ocean. Bernard waited for Laura who had sat alone in the back, insisting that she preferred it.

The day was magnificent. There was a small exhilarating wind, and there rose up before the bright rough blue of the sea a fabulous haze. Voices faded and ceased. Miniature waves far away shuddered and crumbled in slow motion, giving tiny belated roars. Invisible wheeling birds cried out spasmodically. Over all, the whole world, was a blue and legendary haze.

'Well, does this beat the Mediterranean hollow or doesn't it? Leaves Capri for dead, I'd say.'

The Shaws were fascinated suddenly to notice that Bernard was taking in the landscape with so much interest that Felix's remarks had passed unheard.

'Shh!' they mouthed at each other, gazing at him with delight.

'You'd never want to leave this country once you hit it, if you were in your right mind,' Felix sounded him, speaking louder.

Bernard had jerked round to stare at an undistinguished patch of scrub with that same thrilling concentration.

Laura and Felix exchanged glances and moved closer to him as though his returning vitality had been a fire they might grow warm at.

'A pity Clare didn't come,' Laura said experiment-ally, in her soft voice, raising her eyes to the angular young face.

'Yes.' Bernard pushed his fists into his pockets and turned to smile at her. 'But she was busy.'

'Of course we've stopped here often. Since she was a schoolgirl, really.' Laura sighed silently.

Felix looked about enviously. Even with the sleeve of his coat brushing Bernard's, he could not feel enthu-siastic as the boy felt enthusiastic. What was he seeing, looking over the Pacific? What was there to see? Except water and bush. 'How's about a cup of something?' he asked, stamping restively on the uneven rocks.

'He was happy as Larry today in the car with us,' Laura remarked to her sister in the evening, after the day's outing.

Yesterday, rather selfishly, Bernard and Clare had gone for a walk in the afternoon, leaving Felix all alone and at a loose end. It turned out that they had only sat in the little park at the end of the street, sunning themselves. And poor Felix had skulked round looking for odd jobs till he settled to weeding the lawn. 'It's nice for Felix to have a man's company,' she continued now, 'because he never sees a soul to talk to. When we're at the factory he's shut up in his little office and then all weekend here there's only us. Literally, he sees no one to exchange a word with but the man in the garage when he gets his petrol.'

Clare said nothing. Laura had called her in to the dining-room where she was on her knees washing the paintwork.

'I can see Felix is to blame for this himself, in a way,' she went on argumentatively. 'I know he's always put business before people. But you've got to do that if you want to get anywhere, Clare.'

'Well, then!'

'Yes. So he's just taken Bernard out to the office to go through the factory's books. He might take him in to the office. At the factory, I mean. He's even hinted that he might like to adopt him.'

'What?'

'Yes.' Laura was too busy, suddenly, to meet Clare's eyes. 'Then in due course he might make him a partner. Why?' She looked up from her job, her face glimmering with malice. 'You'd like it if he lived here all the time, wouldn't you?'

Clare took a deep breath and shifted restlessly, her movement expressing the extreme irrelevance of her liking to the probable and/or desirable outcome of the proposition. 'It couldn't happen. It couldn't happen.' She stopped abruptly. 'You don't want that, do you?'

'We'll see.' Laura's arms rubbed away fiercely at the spotless white paint of the skirting-board as if to set an example in these matters to all the world.

'Do you have to do that? It's so clean already.'

'It has to be done, Clare. It won't do itself, you know!—You've got your coat on.' She sat back on her legs and allowed her rubber-gloved hands to droop over the edge of the bucket.

'I'm going for a walk. Bernard and I are.'

Laura searched about in the water for the sponge and finding it wrung it out severely. 'Very fond of walking all of a sudden. You went for a walk yesterday. He's talking to Felix.'

'When they've finished,' she said patiently.

Laura's small person bulged with unspoken reproof and criticism. Her blue-grey eyes looked as unyielding as solid glass balls.

276

Clare turned away and walked down the hall, head bent in thought, scuffing the carpet as though it were turf.

'Hi there, young Clare! Where's your sister? News for you all.' Felix had his arm about Bernard's waist.

Laura came out into the hall where the three had met, and drew off her rubber gloves apprehensively. Her nose was shiny.

'Well. The big news.' Felix looked round at each of them separately, and he gave his down-turned gangster's smile, and his eyes laughed and jumped with a sort of unholy animation.

Looking into the intense darkness of Felix's gaze was not like looking into the eyes of an insane person, though the internal resistance was similar; yet it in no way resembled the experience of looking into the eyes of another nominally rational human being. His eyes were rather peep-holes through which a force could be glimpsed, primitive, chilling, subterranean beyond definition.

'What *is* the news, then?' Laura asked, moving her mouth stiffly.

'Only that I,' Felix proclaimed, banging Bernard on the back, 'am going to see this fella through his course. Pay his fees, feed him, get him a few rags to wear. What's he have to bother with scholarships for? You can forget all that,' he said to Clare. 'Let 'em keep their charity, huh? You don't have to be beholden to strangers while you've got old Uncle Felix, do you, Bernie? So all your letters and your important appointments with your mighty professors were a waste of time, weren't they?' He smiled at Clare again.

She shrugged easily, looking down at her shoes, hands in the pockets of her coat. 'Maybe. It looks like it. It was fun, though.'

There was a slight silence. Bernard watched Clare. She and Laura flashed a glance at each other.

Felix said, 'Well, you haven't got a lot to say for yourselves. You don't seem very interested.'

'It's you. You cut the ground from under a person's feet, springing surprises, that's all,' Laura said, working herself up into nervous high spirits. 'But it's—'

'—surprising,' Clare finished for her. She had an unfunny sensation of having to haul her eyes up to Bernard's face by a series of detours. 'What do you think of it, Bernard?'

They looked at each other with strained interest. 'Oh, I'm—very surprised, too. Mr. Shaw mentioned this to me three minutes ago. I said I couldn't take so much, but he—'

'Yes, yes, you must accept,' Laura cried recklessly, noticing that Felix looked hugely amused and gratified to have caused such a hullabuloo. (If only you could trust him!) 'And we'll celebrate. Tomorrow night I'll cook a very special dinner for Bernard's celebration.'

'You've got your coat on,' Felix said to Clare.

'Yes. We'd thought of going for a walk.'

'You two?'

'But it's getting dark. It's too cool. It wasn't a good idea. Why don't we all—go and sit down somewhere instead of standing in the hall?' Clare disappeared into her room, letting her coat slide off.

'You should go to bed, Bernard. The doctor only let you up on sufferance. Please. I'll bring your dinner in. You'll worry me if you stay up.' Laura gave his arm a little pat and hurried away to collect her plastic bucket from the dining-room before she set about preparing dinner. She realised that Felix was standing still, behind her; she remembered instantly the friendliness of her words to Bernard; she lurched into a black pit and began to clamber slowly up its familiar sides.

'What's me pal been sent to bed for? We were all set for a yarn. Everyone's gone and left me,' Felix complained, pretending to sob.

Laura rushed back, her legs liquid with relief, to console him, and Bernard and Clare appeared in their separate doorways. Felix was coughing and spluttering with laughter.

'After dinner we'll play chess,' Bernard said, and Laura agreed, 'Yes, you can adjourn to your boyfriend's room the minute you've eaten. Clare, would you put a match to the fire, please?'

The log-fire in the sitting-room was meticulously set ready to crackle, and Clare was shortly backing away to watch its flames.

'In a trance?' Felix sauntered in. 'That's some blaze!'

With difficulty, Clare looked away from its gorgeous face and silent conversation. 'Yes—Felix. That was generous of you to help Bernard like this. You'll be proud of him. And proud of yourself, too.'

They were quite close together. Felix examined Clare's light-grey eyes, and whether he was more inclined to devour her or strike her felt a very moot point.

'You think, eh? You think?'

'Well,' Laura said, when he had retired to play chess with Bernard and she and Clare were alone by the fire, 'he might have done something like this for *you* years ago instead of—' If steel spikes were stuck through her, Laura would not mention her own deprivations, past or present.

'I don't know. If he means it—It could be a fine thing all round. For Bernard and for Felix, too. I suppose.'

Laura rummaged through her button box, found a pearl button of the required size and proceeded to sew it onto the blue cotton blouse on her lap. She said in a hard level voice, 'But he doesn't like anyone to know any more than he does. He'd rather spend hundreds— throw it away on these—At least this time it might be doing a bit of good to someone. But it's surprising.'

They frowned at each other, the two women. Because it *was* hard to reconcile this gesture with what they knew of Felix. Bernard would learn what he wanted to know, would expand, grow beyond his benefactor, would be—in a word no one uttered—free.

'Just as,' Laura continued, looking down again, 'he would buy you a present for ten pounds, but make you ask for ten shillings in cash.'

Pushing her chair further back from the fire, Clare said neutrally, 'Well. It's nice for Bernard.'

'And it doesn't look as if *you* can help him get into his course.' Her hands occupied with needle and blouse, Laura bit sharply at the thread of cotton, snapping it with her pretty white teeth.

Back to the fire, balancing his coffee cup unevenly in its saucer, Felix laughed down at them. 'Licked him twice, gave him his knock-out drops, and you couldn't wake him with a brick. In three weeks he'll be fighting fit and flat out in the factory office making up for lost time.'

'What do you mean?'

'What do I mean? Chorus!' Perplexed, he stared down at his wife and her sister. 'Oh! Oh! You're thinking of his grand career? When he gets his family off the bread-line he can take up my offer. But that'll take him a few years, you know, and by that time he'll know he's not too badly off just sticking with old Mr. Shaw.'

Clare turned pale. Almost, it seemed intrusive to look at Felix's dreaming face. She said, 'I see—But Felix—what about—couldn't he work at the office during the day and go to classes at night? If he has to?'

Felix threw his head back and gulped down the last of his coffee. Without looking at Laura, he held out his cup and she refilled it from the shining percolator on which the flames were reflected while he said in wise, soothing tones, 'No, no, no, no, no! Do it properly or not at all. You don't want to be half-baked about things. He agrees with me. Everything's jake. Nothing for you to worry about. Except finding yourself a new job!' he added, stirring his fresh cup of coffee, then stretching out a hand for a slice of toast.

'Clare. Please come and talk to me.'

Bernard stood on the verandah. She started to walk up the steps. 'I thought you were still asleep. I was raking up the leaves. Laura and Felix left for work ages ago.'

'I don't know what to say. I don't know what you're thinking. Are you disappointed?' He shoved the hair up from his forehead with both hands and stared down at his battered suede boots.

'Nothing's changed,' Clare said lightly. 'Felix has only proved what he said the other day: you can't take up any offers or scholarships till we've found some way of taking care of your family. All I'm thinking is that we have three weeks before you're allowed to work in which to think of ways and means.'

'Would you feel the same about it if a government department had given it to me?'

'Yes. I don't feel anything in particular about it.' Her hands had the bright idea of rolling up the big collar of her blue sweater so that only her eyes and the top of her head were visible over it.

Gold-flecked hazel eyes and grey eyes stared.

'That isn't true,' Bernard declared, after a considerable silence.

'It is.' As she pulled the collar down, a crumpled tobacco-coloured leaf fell out of her hair. She gave him a straight look. 'Except that in that case you wouldn't have been—'

'—Felix's protégé.'

'You're not that,' she said brusquely, walking away to stand against the verandah rail, staring unfocused at the pile of leaves on the grass below, at the rake and the wheelbarrow. 'I meant—under an obligation to any particular person. Independent. Independence. I suppose that's all I was thinking about.'

'I know what you mean.' He tried not to think about it. He said, 'Felix is increasing my salary. I can save more, and at night I'll take another job. We have to be realistic, Clare.'

Incredulously she looked at his face. 'Is that what you call it? Nothing different? Exactly as you were?'

283

'I can wait,' he said stubbornly. 'Felix thinks I'll forget my plans, and he's wrong. But I can wait.'

'For how long? Why aim so low? Those egg custards I've been forcing on you were not meant to give you the strength to feel resigned! Work in that place with Felix for four or five years before you see daylight?'

'No,' he insisted. 'Everything's different. When I came here to stay I thought I was dying, and I wanted to die.'

Clare nodded, her face expressionless. He had told her this before, but she had known anyway. In the midst of her high certainty, he had transmitted this intention to her, to amaze and appal her.

'Dr. Bell talks about youth's natural resilience. He's pleased with his injections and drugs. So I don't tell him what made me survive.' Bernard picked up the leaf that had fallen from her hair.

'Good food and sleep,' Clare said quickly. 'Never underestimate my cooking. Not that you're a tremendous credit to it yet. Come and have breakfast.'

Bernard looked at her, eager but imploring. 'Though nothing appears different, nothing feels hopeless now. I can work and send money home till Birgitte leaves school and my grandmother is better. As long as necessary. And when I'm free, Felix and I will come to our arrangement and I'll repay him when I'm employed at the end of my course. I can live on very little. It wouldn't take so long.'

He leaned both hands on the railing and stared very hard at the harbour over the flowering hedge and the declining tiers of tree-tops and roof-tops, everything about him defiant, pleading with her not to disagree.

Clare realised her own cruelty in wanting to stir, agitate, discontent him. He was a boy who had known true things torn from life raw and still smoking with blood. For the moment he wanted to be safe, not to know, not to attract the attention of fate, circumstances, the mover of things.

'No, it wouldn't either,' she said tonelessly, out of her thoughts. She smiled at him with all of her attention. 'Wait in the sun here and I'll bring your breakfast out.'

The angularity went from his bones. He leaned heavily against the verandah post and smiled back at her through eyes narrowed against the light of such a day as must have heralded the morning of the world. And he felt overjoyed to be here and alive, with a person who knew more than he did, who would make everything all right.

'I'm sorry,' Bernard said, and there was a short, not natural, silence at the other end of the line. 'You see,' he started to go through his apologies again, 'I met them on my way to the clinic with Clare. They're sailing tonight, so when they asked me to have dinner, I felt—' He was confounded to realise how much it mattered to her.

'No, no,' Laura said, on the terrible high note of strain that women who never cry sometimes have to speak in. 'It doesn't matter. Have a good time with your friends. Is Clare going with you?'

'No, she wouldn't come.' Hardly knowing how to console her for his offence, but suddenly aware that he was now in the act of drawing a sword from Laura's breast, Bernard explained a trifle desperately, 'They're Americans, Laura. My father and I met them on the way out.' He spoke jerkily, his attention coming and going between the sense of his words and Laura's mystifying reaction. 'Josh's done quite a bit of exploring in South America.'

'Uh-huh,' said Laura, who did not believe in explorers or South America, and Bernard felt her painful smile of endurance, felt that she was physically deaf with the suffering he had caused her, but that she would stand smiling in obedience to the laws of ladylike behaviour and saying, 'Uh-huh', if he talked for a week.

'I won't be late. I'll be in time for a game of chess with Felix.'

'Uh-huh,' she said again, with that almost visible twisted smile of pain. As if Felix would play on these terms, having been shelved for American friends of longer standing! 'And Clare's not going?' She would salvage something.

'No,' he assured her, saying goodbye.

Starting across the hotel foyer, in the direction of the restaurant where he was to meet his friends, Bernard felt physically enmeshed, coerced by—he could hardly have said what: the Shaws' fondness, and kindness, and attention. Inflexions, silences, looks. Implications and inferences. Something monstrous, monstrous, seemed to pursue him from that telephone.

A few bull-necked young men wearing Roman haircuts and suits as expensive as small cars stood about. Bernard was looked at as he passed in his informal clothes.

'That you, Felix? Working in the dark?' Clare's heels made a steel clink on the cement steps down to the courtyard. There was an equivocal grunt from the shape bending over the garden-bed.

'It's been a lovely day,' she said encouragingly, to encourage him, herself, anyone who might happen to be listening.

'Has it? I'm afraid I've been too busy to notice.' The tone dead, sour, meant to puncture.

'Oh—what a pity!'

Bernard had had the effrontery to stay out tonight. On his own initiative. How shocking! Inwardly Clare gave a grim smile at the predictability of Felix's reaction. 'You'll pay for this, my hearties!' Et cetera, et cetera—My, he was unselfconscious. He felt no shame at all trotting out old Method Thirty-Two for crushing people. She often felt ashamed for him, as if it was a pity that he wasn't more original, and more successful at it, since this was the direction in which his talents seemed to lie. Clare sighed. And catching the end of this deeply indrawn breath as it left her, she smiled again. Misplaced compassion! His simple well-worn methods worked.

'You're late,' Laura said critically, coming in from the dining-room. 'I thought you'd decided to stay out with Bernard and his American friends. Did you bring the cheesecake?'

Clare tapped the box she had laid on the table. 'I missed the ferry,' she half-apologised, for she did want to appease Laura. Not that she would accept any excuse. What was more important than arriving in time for meals? It was all very well to pretend to be indifferent to food the way Clare did, but Laura would just have liked to see her trying to survive without it! And she had told her so, too. Many times.

'I thought Bernard might have invited us to meet his friends,' she lied antagonistically, cutting the string on the cake box. She blamed Clare for precipitating his meeting with these tourists, or whatever they were, when she *knew* how Felix felt about the boy's company.

'He suggested it. He didn't want to go, himself. But they're only here for one evening. I thought it might be a change for him not to be surrounded by—'

Laura's pallor and relentlessness were borne in on Clare in a long look, and what she endured silently, and what she could say if she would.

'Laura, I've thought of something terrific—marvellous—that might take care of Bernard's family almost right away.' Tentatively she approached Laura, standing in front of her, beseeching Laura for her own sake to be interested, enlivened, glad. 'Can I tell you? I haven't even mentioned it to Bernard yet, in case—'

'You're standing right in my way, Clare. I want to put these plates in to heat. If there's one thing I cannot abide it's hot food served on cold plates.'

'Well.' Clare made to leave the room.

'And what are *you* doing tonight?'

'I'm going to see Max and Alison Heckler. You've heard me mention Alison. She used to be in the office. Her husband's a solicitor.'

Laura's eyes were blank. 'So you're going to be out, too.'

Some conciliatory explanations occurred to Clare but in the end she only said, 'Yes.'

Exchanging another look, they both remembered: this is what it was like without Bernard.

Now that she was safely home, her hand on the cold iron of the gate, Clare could begin to attend to the night's conversation as someone descending from a tightrope slung over Niagara Falls might retrospectively appreciate the view. Away from Bernard, who was her responsibility, she was in peril. Near at hand, where she could hear if he called, she was as incontrovertibly indestructible. She had been catapulted back tonight, frantic with foreboding. Now at the gate the fear simply evaporated and, half-smiling with relief she started to run down the steps to the house. Then her heart lurched. She halted in mid-flight. Light came from every window of the house. And Felix's voice.

She tilted her head back for a moment. It was a vast black sky tonight, most pure and marvellously starry. Since she had spent more time in her life looking up at it than most people who were not professional astronomers, her eyes were at home there. Terrible as its spaces were, it calmed and comforted her always. Looking down, she breathed again and descended the steps slowly. And there was Felix's predictable voice.

'You wonder why he cleared out tonight, do you? Do you? I'll tell you why. I can tell you. You don't know, do you? You don't know—Do you? No, that's right. But Mr. Shaw does. Mr. Shaw knows. He's out tonight so he can be amongst men. *Men.* That's why. Yes. That's why. You didn't know that, did you? You didn't know he'd had a bellyfull of the sight of you, did you? You're too—stupid—to know he's sick in his guts of being in a house full of women. Christ! They're not fit—they're not fit for me to vomit on. That's why. You're just—things.'

Her handbag dangling, Clare stood in the shadow of the dark courtyard, peculiarly immobile, her mind thinly covered with ice, and bored, bored, bored. Yet it

290

was amazing to stand within yards of a human being so charged with loathing.

'Mr. Trotter and Mr. Blaine and—all the others—all my friends. Why don't you ever see them here any more? Because they couldn't put up with the sight of you whining about the place. You're just filth to them. Do you hear that? Say it! Say it after me! Go on—Yeah. That's right. That's what you are. As long as you know it. My friends—Mr. Shaw's friends think you're—'

He became more eloquent still and the customary obscenities assaulted the ears of his listeners.

Half-yawning, Clare went to lean against the rough wall of the house. The voice filled her calm head. She looked at the sky. (Hail, sky.) It was a cause for perplexity, she thought, that sounds like those still pouring from Felix could fail to poison the heart's blood or make the heart itself shrivel and crack. What a noble organ it evidently was! (Her mind paused, then rattled off:

> *Ah, Sun-flower! weary of time,*
> *Who countest the steps of the Sun,*
> *Seeking after that sweet golden clime*
> *Where the traveller's journey is done —)*

Feeling nothing, shivering impersonally, she sought out the planets for something to do, and the Southern Cross.

Felix continued.

Her mind paused. '*In India,*' it quoted a passage she knew very well,

'*in old times, whole communities used the method of passive resistance to redress a grievance. The technique was to sit motionless in a public place, without food and exposed to the weather, until the ruler agreed to the people's demands. Sometimes, when he was particularly tyrannical, his subjects would desert the land, leaving the ruler to live in loneliness and mend his ways. In ancient India it was considered the duty of a wise man to abandon the kingdom when all methods of weaning a king from bad ways had failed.*'

Eminently, eminently wise men.

'Felix!' Laura's voice, which had been inaudible this immeasurable time, rose to a high warning quaver. '*Felix—*'

Clare jumped with fright. She sprinted along the side of the house to the hall window and paused, listening with every nerve, heart and head beating *the knife, the knife, the knife, the knife—*

There was a long curved knife in the kitchen. What was it but a sly consciousness that his smiling-eyed unspoken threats of blood and death were felt in the marrow by his wife, that led Felix late in the night to perform his last grisly scenes in the kitchen, with its dangerous armoury of sharp pointed steel?

In that instant Clare recalled the scores of identical moments reaching back to her childhood, when the idea of murder was in the air, when Felix's mind toyed audibly, almost visibly, with the possibility. And it was always just like this: about to happen. There had never been a friend to call—only ever the night sky, darkened houses where strangers slept, darkened houses that were empty, lighted houses full of strangers who would carefully take no notice of neighbours who might ask, appeal, expose—unpleasant things. Only ever the indifferent papery sound of wind in the trees, and distant traffic, winking planets.

Like never having belonged to the human race, she thought. Never to have been known And she experienced a sense of isolation that was—bearable now, and even almost joyful in its rightness and inevitability since all had changed, whereas in the past it had sometimes seemed unendurable. It no longer mattered. It was only natural, only the way things were. And in some sense she went out to embrace and accept this fact while the knife hung in the air and Laura's voice quavered in panic.

A car pulled up. Its doors opened and slammed. In the kitchen there was instant silence, then furtive scrambling sounds of a scurried tidying-up, of chairs being scraped over the floor, and bottles and glasses being stacked. Then the lights went out. In Clare the tension fell as suddenly. She felt a little sick. All clear. False alarm.

Trailing round to her bedroom window, she lifted it and slipped over the low sill into the room. They had thought it was Bernard coming home; it was only some neighbour along the street. Felix's discretion in not wanting to be seen was fantastically out of character. A thorough-going nightmare with witnesses, during which he masochistically despoiled his unblemished image before the stranger to whom he still seemed like anyone else, was the normal ending to these ideal relationships. Another long night's scene. And because, in a way, they had no idea what was wrong, they would rise unpurged, inflexible and sombre all the mornings of their lives. In her mind she did not so much salute as take cognisance of their plight; but nevertheless, she thought, nevertheless. The level of her spirits was not to be assailed.

The room trembled. The noise was so great that the very furniture seemed to sway. Straight from an uneasy sleep, Laura was on her feet and running to close the windows. Felix raised himself on one elbow and looked about sharply.

It was very early, only just daylight, and a sudden extraordinary wind was making the solid house shake on its rocky foundation.

At the windows Laura cried, 'Oh, Felix! Come here!' and he was out of bed at once, shocked wide awake by the moving house, the turning world, the ghastly noise.

Standing with bare feet and rumpled hair, they searched each other's eyes with no difficulty for the first time for years, hardly noticing the boundary they had crossed in doing so, the minor miracle that allowed them to talk spontaneously without thought of profit or loss or hidden meaning. For out there in the grey of water, sky and land, there were dreadful clouds, a mad wind and hideous noises. They stood watching, sides pressed together, their faces distorted with apprehension.

'What do you think it is, Felix?'

He moved his head very slightly from side to side. 'I've never seen anything like it.'

They stared out at the strange water of the harbour and the stranger light in the sky.

'What do you think those clouds are?'

Felix looked into her eyes again, then back at the sky, which changed second by second, assuming cloud-shapes such as he wished he had never seen. 'What do *you*?' he prevaricated.

'I don't know.' Laura's body shivered with fear.

Felix rubbed his lips. 'It isn't a hurricane, either.'

But that was not what they were afraid of. They were not afraid of anything natural.

'It doesn't look too good, does it?' he said, and they stood silent together, looking out, for a long time.

'Should we wake the others?' Laura murmured. Her head reeled. She was afraid of fainting.

They looked at each other, deciding that that would be to admit too much, to acquiesce, perhaps, and alter some fine balance disastrously.

'Oh—I guess they're either awake or—if not, they're pretty sound asleep.'

'We'll leave them. It might be best. I've never been so cold.'

Chilled, silent, they watched from the window and listened. At length Felix said, 'Oh, well. We can't stand here all night. There's nothing we can do, anyway. Maybe it's all right. I don't know.' The house shook. 'Might as well go back to bed, eh? I am.'

Imperceptibly, then more swiftly falling back on themselves, they both began to remember: if by any chance this was not the end of the world, they were Laura and Felix Shaw. They had grudges, positions to protect, angles to work out.

Laura followed him, slipping between the sheets and stuffing her feet to the bottom of the bed where vestiges of warmth had remained.

They could still see the grey surrealist sky and feel the uneasiness of the house under the bombardment. Not talking, they put out all their senses to apprehend this peculiar dawn, breathing carefully so as not to impair their understanding of it.

Several countries were exploding bombs. There was another crisis. There were new weapons that killed people without damaging things.

Behind closed eyelids Laura read yesterday's head-lines. Could it be? Could it be? That they meant to kill her, to kill them? Never even having seen them? 'What do you think then?' She dared to turn her head although she did fear that the least movement might bring down the holocaust.

'Uh?' Felix's forehead was clearing, though it still felt possible that they were in danger, and the wind was hammering and howling all about. 'Oh—I suppose it's all right.' It always had been before. He had never been exterminated yet. What could he do, anyway? And, in a way, if the worst came to the worst, since he was older than the others and would die first, would it be such a bad thing?

Laura allowed herself to be lowered slowly, by degrees, back into her horizontal body on the bed. Immediately, her face set in the old way, and her mouth and eyes began to endure again, while on his far side of the bed, Felix let his teeth clash together in his suddenly splitting head, remembering who he was, and that he had to live and be this person now that this was evidently just a freakish morning. (Worse luck? Worse luck?) And now, more confident that they would live a while, they were peculiarly more miserable than they had been before. They were captured again, put back in their cages. They were quickly compressed again to this size that was not comfortable. They were known, filed, had records.

Known! Who had the effrontery to imagine so?

Ah, well! The world was in a bad way, but still spinning. So here they were—no holidays from themselves forthcoming—as they had been for years.

'Who asked your opinion?' Felix smiled. 'Who asked your opinion?' he said again, loudly, to Clare.

Tapping one small foot in quick march-time, Laura dissociated herself from them and stared at the cover of a women's magazine with an excited frown.

'No one. I gave it.'

'Then would you mind keeping your big mouth quiet, please?' He smiled at Clare, and through her black lashes she gave him back a closed and strangely glittering smile.

'Here's some peanut brittle, Felix!' Laura had remembered the white paper bag of sweets at her side and jumped up with it.

He took a chunk and stuffed it into his still-smiling mouth, not looking away from Clare.

Laura hesitated, then pronounced her sister's name on a discreetly low note, 'Clare?—'

Clare shook her head. Laura sat down on the sofa with a little bump, and lit a cigarette. She noticed then that she had one, newly lighted, in the ashtray.

'Oh! Bernie! Hi there, young fella!' Felix cracked the hard toffee with his teeth alarmingly and gave a disingenuous grin. 'Come on in, come in. What you doing out there in the cold, eh?'

'Am I interrupting you?'

'What? Oh, sparring with old Clare here? This harem of mine. Got to keep 'em in order somehow, or a man'd never get a look in. Come in. Or why not let's you and me have a game out in the office? How's about getting licked at chess?'

Bernard grinned. 'I don't even have to try—but do you mind if I see Clare for five minutes first?' He looked at her. 'I wanted to show you a letter I'm working out.'

Abruptly, and as if they were quite alone, Felix turned to Laura. 'You'll have to go through those accounts with me.'

'Now?' She put aside the magazine, and stubbed out her cigarette.

'I don't mean next week.' He strode past Bernard and Clare as if they were pieces of furniture, and Laura followed him, raising her eyebrows at them hopelessly.

Left alone, the other two wandered outside, not speaking. In the sheltered courtyard the sun was hot and the sky was almost colourless in its height, transparency and clearness. A ti-tree six feet high stood as if in radiant surprise to find itself so very young and ornamental, alight with tiny flowers, a wondrous pink. (Behold!)

Looking at it, Bernard asked, 'What was that about?'

'In there? Oh, nothing. I've forgotten.' Clare looked at the ti-tree. 'What letter were you going to show me?'

'Only an answer to that Department of Education letter. It's inside.' He said, 'I couldn't take any money from Felix.'

'No.'

'I'll have to find a room soon.'

'Yes.'

'What will you do when I go?'

Clare shrugged and they frowned at each other in the sun. 'I haven't given it any thought.'

'Why have you stayed so long in the house with them?'

Turning from the little shrub they walked over to the lawn at the side of the house. 'I didn't know I could go,' Clare said vaguely.

Bernard could not believe this, but knew it might be true. They dropped to the grass. After a pause he said, 'Laura's very nice. She's been very kind to me.'

'She is nice. She would brand you with hot pokers, of course, if Felix asked her to. Or hammer nails into you, apologising for the inconvenience, if she thought it would please him.'

Bernard looked pained. This cynicism, this disloyalty to her sister, had no place in his ideal picture of Clare. 'What are you saying?' He looked at her almost sulkily.

'I'm saying remember that you, and I, and people, only exist for Laura in relation to Felix.'

Bernard rolled over on the grass and sat up and stared about at the white walls of the house and the green garden. 'It looks charming. But I know you're right. From what I've seen and heard. What he's said to me. Nothing he does is ordinary; everything has extra meanings in his mind. Even playing chess. What does he want?'

Slowly Clare shook her head. 'I don't know. Anything obvious you can think of, he's had. And it's never been the right thing. Sometimes I think he wants to make us like himself, strangle our minds. To have us see everything as he sees it. He'd like that.'

'Poor Felix. I wouldn't.'

'No. And what enrages him so much, I think, is that he sometimes realises now that you can constrain people physically up to the limit without being able to get within miles of their minds. You can't change their thinking—leaving brain-washing and drugs aside.'

'He makes the atmosphere very odd. Tormenting you and Laura. He smiles at me as if I should admire this. I don't. When he speaks it's a voice from on high—meek attention. When he's silent—tremble silently. His assumptions make me feel as if I'd walked off the end of a gangplank.'

Clare nodded. 'Any sign of aspiration, affection, any gaiety or open-heartedness has to be axed to the ground. If you say a word in favour of the Buddha, it's a reflection on him. And how much more so if the favoured one is only a mortal still caught on the wheel of existence.' She raised her eyebrows at him and smiled faintly.

'What happens?'

'What happens? Oh, there's a first-class scene. Or he starts drinking again, if he isn't drinking. Or he'll even go to the trouble of getting involved in some new business, some extra, very worrying, slightly illegal, speculation. Nothing's too much trouble if it will drive—hope, I suppose—out of someone's head. The idea that life might be worth living. As if he was a deity set up to ensure that nothing and nobody should ever be appreciated.'

'But what would Laura think of his actions? She would see through them.'

'Yes. But she would be frantic with worry and fear. And then, she's adept in self-deception. For years she has thought: he isn't himself or he wouldn't be like this. That people can be themselves (not psychologically disturbed) and dangerous, and wicked, is something she will never agree to realise.'

'Can she respect him?'

'She thinks he represents security. She thinks he might change and be kind to her. She pities him; that enslaves her.'

Leaning forward over his knees, Bernard clasped his head in his hands. 'I wonder if—I wonder if—'

302

'Don't! Forget it! Laura's always saying, "I wonder what's at the back of his mind?" Which is just how he likes her to occupy herself. Well, I think it's sad about Felix: he's a miserable man. But I think the back of his mind should be *forgotten*. There's only death at the back of his mind. He's jealous of anything living. Death's all he wants to spread. Now show me your letter.'

'We're just leaving for home. You've just caught us,' Laura spoke into the telephone receiver to Clare and glanced at Felix waiting at the door. 'What's the matter?'

'Nothing. In fact everything's sensationally fine. We couldn't wait to tell you. You can tell Felix. Bernard's here just outside the booth. We went with Max—the solicitor, you know—to see the solicitors representing the building company Bernard's father worked for. They've admitted liability. They're going to settle out of court. They've agreed to pay Bernard's mother a—quite a lot of money. The figure's not settled yet but a scale was fixed. So this means—Well? Isn't it a wonderful day?'

There was a slight pause. Laura said in a niggling tone, 'It's rather hard on the company. He only worked for them for three months.'

A variety of strong emotions opened Clare's eyes and mouth and as suddenly closed them. 'Oh, Laura,' she said faintly, rejecting the twenty-four most natural responses that sprang to mind.

'Well! From being a very unlucky boy, Bernard's turned overnight into a very fortunate one, with a scholarship offered in the post this morning, and now this.' Laura's tone was brittle and joyless. 'Are you coming straight home?'

Felix said, 'Where are they?'

'Felix says where are you? He might be able to pick you up on the way through town if you like. It depends where you are.'

'No, thank you, Laura. Thank Felix. We're at the Quay. We'll be home about the same time as you.'

'Very well then. Goodbye. I'll tell Felix.'

He closed the office door and sat down on the brown leather chair reserved for clients. He pulled at his nose thoughtfully, then extended his right arm behind him on the glass-topped desk. Laura stood four feet away by the telephone table, her eyes moving above the level of his head, her pigskin-gloved hands readjusting the silk scarf at the neck of her overcoat.

'So all his troubles are over, are they? What do you know?' He mused. 'He's done pretty well for a stranger in a strange land, young Bernard.'

Going home in the car Felix was very quiet and for almost the first time that Laura could remember passed no abusive remarks about pedestrians or other people's driving. When they reached the house, Clare and Bernard, who had arrived first, flew out to meet them at the sound of slamming car doors.

'Oh, there you are,' Felix said abstractedly, not smiling, not appearing to notice that he had almost been knocked to the ground by the force of their excitement.

They were in the courtyard. Traces of a cold, crystal, piercing sunset were still visible in the west, but all of the vast remainder of the sky was totally dark.

'Coming home in the car I was thinking,' Felix turned to Laura, wiping Bernard and Clare out of existence. 'I think I'll get rid of the whole shebang. Sell the joint. It's all very well for you at your age, but I'm getting on a bit. So I'm going to take things easy, even if it means cutting down on the rations.'

All the words in Laura's head broke to pieces. She felt like someone suffering from delusions. She wanted to shake her head violently in the hope of shaking his words into some more expected pattern.

'What will you do if you sell the factory?' Clare managed to ask.

'Retire! Like all you blokes.' A real throwing-down of the gauntlet. He swung round at her. 'Do a bit of gardening. Take it easy. Got a bit of cement-work that needs attending to. And the soil needs building up. And I've got these weeds to get under control.'

Even yet his listeners could not believe their ears. They made feeble sounds of interest and assent. His expression was that of a man who had been hammering in colossal insults and threats, and had in some way justly triumphed.

'So I have a lot to occupy me. All you people go ahead with your dinner. I'll have mine later in my office.' He turned to Bernard as he walked past him into the house, 'So it's just as well you're not counting on me for a job, isn't it?'

Left outside in the darkness, Bernard, Clare and Laura surveyed each other.

Bernard felt his arms sailing out of their own accord to look for distracting things to do. He folded them. 'I'm afraid he's angry.'

'Has this been hinted at before?' Clare asked. 'Selling the business?'

'Never. No,' Laura said.

'Didn't you—did you tell him about Bernard?'

'Yes, of course. He was in the room when you rang.'

'Oh.'

Laura said, 'Well, it's getting cold. Let's go inside and get some dinner on.'

But Clare put a hand out to detain her and looked into her sister's eyes with unnatural intentness. 'But *you're* pleased about Bernard's news, aren't you, Laura?'

'Yes, yes. It's wonderful, Bernard. Sad for your mother. But it's only right that she should receive—'

Felix sold the factory just six days after his decision to do so. Because the business was superbly organised and profitable, and the terms invoked by Felix in his desire to be fair to unknown young men involved much paper but little cash and low interest, the first caller—seeing that his fleet had come in with his fortune—fervently claimed it.

'Well, no business to go to on Monday morning!' Laura came out on to the balcony where Clare was leaning against the railing. 'And Bernard going away soon. And you with no office. It's hard to get used to all these changes.'

Clare nodded and looked at her sister thoughtfully. 'What do you think you'll do? You're too young to retire from the world.'

'I don't know. I hope Felix doesn't get too bored.' In the dense sunlight, Laura shaded her eyes. She sighed and felt in her pocket for her cigarettes. 'We'll feel marooned in a way. When you've got a business there's no time to make friends or have interests. For some reason.'

Down in the curve of the suburban bay lined with weedy parks named after councillors, red-brick apartment buildings, gracious and dilapidated private dwellings, a yacht strung with flags was being christened.

'I wonder what you could do? Heavens, you're not thirty-one yet.' Clare glanced at the yacht. 'Classes of some sort. Social work. You could take children from orphanages out in the car and give them picnics.'

307

'Felix might like that. Playing Santa Claus,' Laura conceded, 'if I could persuade him to do it. Or you could. But—'

They exchanged a look that acknowledged the traps in this suggestion and automatically rejected it.

Laura went on, 'Some social work could be depressing, though. I don't know if it would be such a good idea. Besides, I'm tired of working.'

'Anyway—And every kind of club is out.'

'Drink. No. They're impossible.'

A rusty oil-tanker made its way toward the Heads.

Laura said, 'Really, it's just as well to stay home. I'd just as soon. And so would he.'

Clare nodded again, then said, 'It's being launched.' Indifferently enough the boat slid into the water. Among the small crowd assembled for the ceremony a band began to play *Auld Lang Syne*.

'It isn't only drink in clubs,' Laura went on, and Clare knew what she meant: strangers, Felix taken in, taken down. 'But with people—even if drink was no problem at all, even when he hasn't touched any for months—it's never worked out. I can get on with them, but he—We're much better to keep to our own little routine. Heavens!' Laura stood back from the rail and looked about at the blinding, myriad-faceted glitter of the water, at the tall towers of the city, at the world-famous bridge with its battalions of cars, buses and trains, at the great radiant exclamatory morning sky that started in eternity and came down to her very fingertips. 'Heavens!' she said again, exhibiting these wonders and the awe-inspiring colours of the trembling garden. 'We're lucky. We're really very lucky.'

'Yes.'

Laura's eyes faltered. She had thought the circumstances of her life as rigid as a steel foundry. Then suddenly everything shifted. Now an earthquake, a slow, prolonged and invisible earthquake was collapsing everything.

She said, somehow narrowly, 'And Bernard deserting you after all you've done for him. Leaving yourself with not even a job to go to.'

'What?' Clare turned from the view to look at Laura's face. 'I'm glad he's going.'

When Bernard had prepared to leave and declared his plans, Laura had pleaded with him to stay for a few more days. Felix, she said, was coming round, accepting all these changes, but it would hurt him if Bernard rushed away and he felt afterwards that they had parted bad friends. When Bernard consulted Clare, she agreed that it would be considerate and politic if he could delay—no more than a week—till the change could come about without disturbing Felix's balance. 'Only for Laura's sake,' she added. 'She has to live with the repercussions.'

Now, the facts of Bernard's scholarship and the

compensation due to his mother could be openly mentioned in front of Felix. And he smiled. And he took a sort of interest. His eyes had not recovered from looking offended and giving significant looks, but he was, Laura assured Bernard, coming round.

'I didn't think you'd be *glad*,' she persisted now, feigning absorption in the shipping on the harbour, and smoking with concentration. 'I got the impression that you had a great crush on him.' It sickened her to say this, as if her bare hand had been forced to touch something abominable. Emotion nauseated her.

'What?' Clare said again, but faintly this time. She told herself that she was not surprised that Laura had misinterpreted her actions. It was never surprising to be misinterpreted and, indeed, it had been obvious from the beginning that Laura and Felix both assumed that only a juvenile passion could account for her concern.

'No,' she said now. 'No, not really, Laura.' In love with Bernard? She felt as if heavy irons had been cast about her. 'Break it down,' she protested feebly, thinking hard. They both—she and Bernard—had so much to do! Everything was waiting. Everything. Something in her wilted in surprise and despair at the thought that they were in any way tied to each other. Not free?

Slowly, drawing her reflections slowly after her, she began to extricate herself from the hypothetical strait-jacket Laura had imposed on her. 'No, it isn't like that,

Laura. I only—' She only loved him, only knew him well. 'He's young. He just needed a little—kindness. And I—don't know very much.'

Suspecting mockery, Laura looked at her coldly, impatiently. She could not follow the workings of Clare's mind: Clare was pretentious. Laura warned her, 'I hear Bernard coming now.'

Inside the house, slouching back to his room from the prolonged contemplation of his face in the bathroom mirror, Felix heard laughter outside on the verandah and scowled. He stood by the bed cleaning his nails with a little steel file, idle, with nothing to do. The sharp little file scraped under each nail again. Felix breathed. Outside they all laughed. Felix gave his surroundings—the brocade of bedcover and curtains, the flawless wood of the furniture—a ravenous look. There was her diamond ring on the cut-glass tray. Diamonds—Felix was caught, stood, half-smiled, moved his head infinitesimally to be struck by shafts of topaz light, of scarlet light, of raging greens, sapphires. He looked, and was impressed. Then he was displeased. He put the ring into his pocket.

He had another idea. Out in the office there were letters written this morning waiting to be posted. Exchanging an intense private look with himself in the long mirror, he took his new suede jacket from the wardrobe, slid his arms into it and sauntered out.

Laura had begun to hang washing on the line at the side of the house. 'It's a glorious morning, Felix. I thought—on Monday—I know you don't like the traffic at weekends—but on Monday, how would it be if we all went off to the mountains for the day? We'd see all the spring blossom. It's Bernard's last week with us. And we've got no old factory waiting.'

Felix rubbed his chin, lids downcast. 'Oh, I don't know. We're pretty comfortable here. We don't have to drive a hundred miles for a view. And besides, it all costs money. Don't forget we haven't got any cheques coming in now.'

'Oh—He and Clare might have a day out, then.'

'Mmm?' Felix gave her a deaf look.

She tried again. 'Felix, what do you think might be wrong with this little pine tree? See—it's going brown at the edges.'

But Felix was like a doctor visiting a *malade imaginaire*, his own mind on some thrilling assignation just five minutes away. 'Yeah—' He crumbled the dead brown foliage between his fingers. 'Well, I'm off.'

They stared at each other, he smirking a little and full of mischief, Laura frowning appeals and smiling doubts, trying to decode his eyes' garbled messages.

'Might you be home for lunch?'

'Mmm?' A high sweet note of enquiry, another deaf look.

'Nothing. It's all right.'

312

Felix remarked, not censoriously, 'You're not wearing your ring.'

'My ring?—Oh! Neither I am. I'm all out of routine. It must be—it's in the bedroom. Isn't that funny? I always take it off to have my shower and then put it on at once.'

But Felix was walking away, slowly mounting the steps. Laura watched him, blinking, the thumb of her right hand pressed like a tourniquet against the ringless fingers of her left.

A few minutes later she was wandering distraught through the house. Clare and Bernard sat in the sunroom compiling the shopping list, having volunteered to collect the weekend food. They both rose when they saw her, prepared instantly for calamitous news. She looked like someone who had just received tidings of death.

'Have you seen my ring?' she called in a high voice.

'What? Your ring? What ring? What's the matter?'

'My ring. I've lost my ring. My diamond ring. I've lost it. I've looked everywhere.'

'Oh.' Her listeners adjusted to this serious but less than grievous intelligence. No one was dead. But Laura was suffering from shock, her movements were vague and uncoordinated as if she had been struck blind.

'We'll find it. We'll find it,' Clare promised, grasping one of Laura's helpless hands. 'When were you wearing it last?'

313

'This morning. I was sure it was in the bedroom.'

Bernard was already on his knees, cheek pressed to the floor, looking under the chest, acutely relieved that this was all the tragedy. He jumped up. 'That's one place it isn't. We'll start at the front and work through. We'll sift the garbage. It's too big to have fallen through the grate in the sink.' He looked at his watch. 'We'll find it before Felix comes back.'

No sign of the ring. No Felix. Every square inch of carpet and polished board stared at with eyes beginning to burn. Everything movable moved and the candid horizontal exposed.

'Unless it's fallen into something it isn't in the house.' Bernard looked up from the salad that had been no more than disarranged by their pretence of eating lunch.

Clare shoved back her chair and left the table unceremoniously. 'We haven't done the laundry.'

'It can't be there,' Laura called after her without energy. She had a feverish pallor and appeared to have lost weight in the course of the morning. She watched Clare's back-view cross the courtyard.

'Clare can make certain. I'll help you take the dishes inside, if you've finished.'

Tasting her cold tea as if under instruction, Laura put the cup down and rose. 'No, it doesn't take two. Thank you all the same. Just you go ahead with whatever you want to do, and I'll—'

Warded off, Bernard backed away three steps and turned and walked from the flagstones on to the grass, and turned and looked again at Laura, who, with an entirely uncharacteristic clumsiness, was attempting to gather together on the tray all the substantial remains of their meal. His memory stirred unpleasantly. Laura had forgotten him, was unaware of his eyes on her, was so far removed from the light movement of the air, the scent of freesias, the shimmering of leaves, that she suddenly seemed to Bernard, who had seen many victims, to represent them all. She was unapproachable as the condemned are unapproachable and he was responsible as the free always are.

Clare came towards him from the laundry. She shook her head. Between them, Laura pushed the cast iron chairs, painted white, with blue cushions, precisely under the table.

In the street above the level of house and garden, a car turned the corner and ground with a whine into Felix's garage. Laura flinched to life. The crumbs she had been collecting fell at her side. Fright exploded in her, and her flesh fell from her bones. She gave a single shiver. As metallic slams sounded from the garage above, Clare and Bernard on the right and left flanks moved up. Clare stooped to adjust the cushion on the chair behind which she stood. Disingenuously they sought each other's eyes. A tiny sparrow, round as a ping-pong ball, hopped between their feet.

The door in the side of the garage opened and Felix was heard to step out on to the path, was heard to stumble, heard to curse. And this was all to be expected. What else had his unscheduled absences ever meant?

Bernard had seen Felix sober but piqued, sober and not amused, he had seen Felix affected by three glasses of beer. He was aware of Laura beside him, breathing through her slightly parted lips, of Clare, concentrated, unknowable. And all at once the bright day, his new good fortune, plans for the future, collapsed like flimsy toys the wind had blown on. And he was conscious of having returned to a familiar place—*reality*, where human beings had to contend with what they had to be.

'A reception committee. Very nice. Very nice.' Felix emerged round the curve of the ramp from a jungle of leaves and stood, swaying ever so slightly, looking down with an expression of maniacal self-satisfaction and contempt on the three raised faces below. And his own conception of himself, in addition to his extraordinary appearance, made him impressive, even uncanny, to his alert but mesmerised audience, upward gazing.

'Thank you for waiting to have lunch with me. It shows your good manners. Waiting to have lunch with Mr. Shaw in his own house. Thank you so much. So kind of you.' His pronunciation no less than his manner was elaborately sarcastic. He towered over his subjects, his wide lips, his broad nose, his entire face drawn down in a sneer of fantastic hauteur.

'It's three o'clock,' Laura said, smouldering. 'You wouldn't say if you were coming home. Your lunch is here.'

His dark eyes flashed joyfully. 'The scraps? I am to be allowed to eat the scraps you leave? How gracious!' His manner changed. His face jerked forward, chin extended on his short neck, as if the life in his eyes was a panther on a leash. He rapped out, 'But Mr. Shaw doesn't care to eat the garbage while you stuff your bellies with food he's worked for. Not at all. He doesn't like that. Eating the scraps. Working while you play ladies and gentlemen and wait for him to provide you with the luxuries of life. Mr. Shaw is very hostile about this, very hostile. Yes. Yes.' His head receded as if the panther, momentarily baffled by its restricting chain, had paced back from its limit, and now padded from side to side trailing the slack metal, re-collecting its instincts.

'That's not true. That's not true.' Laura spoke confusedly. 'Everyone works.' She cast about. Floods of words moved in her seeking release. But how to select? And there was no outlet. And the injustice. None of it true.

Clare begged her, 'Don't argue with him.'

'What's that? What's that?' Sound without meaning had reached Felix on his platform. He stepped close to the edge and, eyes attempting to re-focus, thrust his face forward again saying, 'What's that?—*Vermin*. Gee, I'd like to see you all in strife. Bloody lazy, guzzling—'

If his vituperation left its objects unmoved, the purplish-red of his face and his teetering steps on the brink of the twelve-foot drop did not. Bernard leapt up the steps two at a time. It was obvious that Felix would descend alone at considerable risk to his neck.

Snarling dark-red face and dark disordered eyes jumped at him. 'Get away from me, *you*. Bloody gigolo. Sucking up to these things. Not like a man at all. Bloody rat.'

Bernard hesitated, his bright slanted eyes on Felix's. There was a slight silence. Everyone watched him. His hand was extended. Sunlight clear and gold as honey. Laura cried, 'At least leave the boy alone. He's had enough to put up with without this.'

'Please, Bernard. Don't listen. Take no notice. I've told you. Please.' Clare grasped the warm edge of the step on which he was standing.

Felix's attention was still hooked to the boy. Slowly he was growing calmer. The ape-like projection of himself which had appeared like lunacy to the frozen onlookers retreated slowly. Though still very drunk and possibly dangerous, he was no longer maniacal, and this was a relief. Bernard turned and bounded, loose-limbed, downstairs to the courtyard.

'You've found your ring.' Felix addressed his wife conversationally, and with something approaching sweetness, his heavy eyebrows raised in enquiry. 'I say—I take it you've found your diamond ring?'

He had the confidence of a barrister interrogating his social inferior.

'No.' Laura could feel his advantage, but its nature was obscure to her. 'No. Clare and Bernard are still looking for it.'

'Is that so?' Eyes greatly enlarged and concentrating on Laura with difficulty, eyebrows lifted higher. 'How considerate of them,' he went on with increasing sweetness, 'since they probably know where it is. I should imagine,' he paused as if to induce his tongue to even further punctiliousness in enunciation, 'that they are the best ones to look. Out of work. Hoboes. Big ideas. No cash. Why wouldn't they have an inkling where it might be?'

It seemed to Clare that a very long silence followed this speech, during which each word fell deeply into her, weighted like a bell. Half-smiling, she looked about at the others. He was traducing Bernard! But he was drunk. She knew better than to speak.

Approaching the ramp she asked, 'What do you think you're saying?'

He gave an odd laugh and kicked a small stone at her. It hit her shoulder and bounced off.

'What do you think you're *saying*?'

He scuffed some dust at her and grinned. 'You and your baby boyfriend. You could do with the money.'

She turned away and put a hand on her sister's thin arm. 'Laura, we'll go. From the house, I mean. You come, too. Why stay here?'

Bernard's young face was stern, the look he gave Laura fierce and purposeful. 'Clare's right. We'd better go. Will you come with us?—I'll leave you to talk, then. Collect my stuff. Call if you want me.' He went off towards the house.

Above them all, king of the castle, Felix was performing a little dance in his efforts to kick dust on their heads, and muttering.

Retrieving her arm from Clare's touch, Laura stared at her obsessively. 'You don't mean it, both of you. You're not going now, just because of what he said, are you? He's not responsible. He doesn't know what he's saying.' The skin of her face was a damp and bloodless white. The look her blue-grey eyes turned on Clare was at the same time tenacious, evasive and uncertain.

'I know that. It has nothing to do with this. You knew I'd go soon. "He's not responsible." I want people who are. There must be some. Leave all this. You're young. Nothing could be worse. Nothing could be worth it. You're young. You could do anything. All this—' Clare looked dazedly about—'senselessness. Don't waste your whole life.'

'I can't go.' Laura shook her head.

'Why?'

Up on the ramp Felix staggered, tried to regain his balance, failed and fell to the ground. The women paused, looking at him, somehow rested in the pause, estimating suddenly incalculably more than Felix's next move. He soon gave up his attempts to rise and rolled in towards the grass on the other side of the path.

Laura muttered, 'He's going to sleep.'

'Why can't you go? Look at me. Why can't you? I can't believe you want to stay,' Clare resumed mechanically. 'What is there here for you? Nothing but misery. He hates you. He tortures you. All of us. It's his only pleasure. For God's sake, Laura. Are you hypnotised?'

Dully, for the second time, Laura shook her sister's hands off. 'I couldn't go away,' she said, looking dully ahead. 'He wouldn't let me go. He'd find me. I wouldn't be safe. I'm safer when I know where he is.'

'You'd be afraid,' Clare whispered, staring at Laura's face with bitter sadness. So it was beyond discussion. There was nothing to be done. Because what Laura said was comprehensible, and even in some excessive way justified, reasonable. She was afraid herself, in a way. He was like a sorcerer. Not clever like a sorcerer, but wicked like one. 'Yes,' she agreed vaguely. 'But *I'll* go.'

'All right. If you want to.' Laura was stunned, indifferent. She added, 'I don't want a back room with a gas-ring. A home is something you can't give up just like that, when you've worked—You'll realise that if you have one of your own some day.'

As the two women spoke they glanced desultorily

over the garden as sick people might have looked at the forbidding lushness engulfing a sanitorium.

'I hope not,' Clare answered without expression, assessing the future. 'I don't believe so.' In a moment she asked, 'What about your ring?'

'Oh, the ring—' Laura lifted her head and gazed at Felix stretched on the path. 'Bernard might help me get him into bed before you go.'

'We wouldn't leave you with him like this.'

'All right.'

They looked at each other in silence for several seconds. Then Clare went inside and Laura picked up the tray and followed her.

Laura and Felix stood together in the doorway of the sitting-room, with the silence and emptiness of the house like a third and overpowering physical presence beside them. Almost haunted the place felt to Laura, and had felt all day. And now in the late afternoon, with its shadows and the loss of the sun's heat, a chill and empty melancholy was apparent in the separate rooms of the house, in the inimical stretches of sky and ocean to be seen through its windows; and the half-light of the clouds, the moody shade on the sea, was queerly menacing. Yet she was undisturbed by yester-day's departures. She felt a glacial calm.

Yet there was something sinister. The ceilings of the house were high. There was too much space above her. And even when the lamps were switched on, at this indeterminate time of day, large areas of enclosed space remained in dusk. Shady, white and silent, cool and dim, the house was like the shrine of some forgotten religion, overrun by barbarians, sacked, and overrun by time.

'There it is,' Felix asserted rather than said, pointing a tobacco-stained finger.

By the skirting-board under the windows, the diamond ring lay ingenuous, winking and blazing.

'I left it there so you could see where it was,' Felix again asserted. 'They couldn't have looked too hard, eh?'

Laura said nothing. Felix ambled over to pick the ring up, talking. 'Lucky I happened to come in here just now. I nearly stood on the flaming thing. Well, don't you want it?' he asked, aggressive, gravel-voiced.

'Of course I do. It isn't lost, after all,' Laura said with a composure that could have sounded like irony. 'They'll be glad.' Taking the ring from Felix's outstretched hand, she slipped it on her finger and raised her eyes to her husband's face. Felix's face: it would never change substantially except in the natural ways of age. Faces were intractable. They were what always made it hard to believe anyone could alter. Dispassionate, Laura took in his thick greying hair that he smoothed with coconut oil, his restless dark-brown eyes, the pores of his tough skin, his wrinkled sinewy throat and his, in some way, horribly incongruous, imported, impeccable clothes.

If he had crossed a frontier and plucked the least self-knowledge from this act (which was in no way outstanding by his lights) he could never be held responsible for the other Felix's deeds. If he understood his act, he literally would not be the man who had performed it.

Watching him steadily, Laura had a wordless perception that in human affairs in an absolute sense there can never be any victors, there is no such thing as self-interest, and no way of being right.

'So all the fuss was for nothing. Tearing off and everything.'

'Yes.' Laura saw signs of self-justification already struggling to express themselves about his mouth and eyes. She blew her nose and then said briskly, 'Well, I have to damp down the ironing,' and with the air of one about to tackle an important task, went away. But she only went to her bedroom, closed the door, and sat on the hitherto sacrosanct bedcover, hairbrush in hand, pressing the nylon bristles down and letting them spring up.

Left alone, Felix cleared his throat and patrolled the room, feeling sick, grimacing violently, glaring through the windows, his hands plunged deep in his trouser-pockets.

* * *

Central Station's sooty spaces reverberated with hollow booming sounds. Yellow luggage vans swinging trailers laden with suitcases and crates tooted past, startling travellers who hardly expected to be hunted down by motorised traffic even here indoors.

A bag in each hand, Bernard steered a path through the shifting crowds towards the restaurant. It was five days since he and Clare had left the house. Now she followed him bearing in the pocket of her waterproof jacket a ticket to a country town hundreds of miles distant, the first stop on a journey of no fixed duration.

'I wish you were coming to Europe.' Bernard watched the anonymous hands of the waitress place a battered coffee-pot on the table between them. 'You won't change your mind now, but you should think about going some time. I know I've chosen not to live there, but there's everything to see.'

'I suppose there is.' Rearranging the cutlery minutely with a forefinger, Clare went into mental battle, thinking: then people who like to look at things can go, but I only—

She agreed, '*Later*, it would be—' She lifted her cup and drank to gain time, for she had no inclination to force her intuitions through the sieve of language. But false, unreal, an act implying self-deception, she knew it would have been, to have left the country now. To the world you had to offer a disinterested self and had not only to be, but to appear to be so, though not an eye watched and no one cared. Every instinct rose even now to reject the idea of leaving the country, as though her course had still to be decided. A false gesture. As though pretending to believe what she did not: that the *real*, *significance*, existed in another country and might be found in a specific geographical position, like the Pyramids.

'Would be what?' Bernard prompted. All the changes, shocks, momentousness of recent times jammed his voice.

'I don't know,' Clare lied. For she had deduced long ago that no thrilling of the senses, no increase in wealth, social contacts or handsome objects would take her anywhere but further away from the state that would be natural to her. She hoped to be known, and she hoped to have to know to an extent that taxed, extended and outreached her powers. But if none of her hopes came to pass, it would be bearable. She knew from experience that everything was bearable because it had to be. All that happened was that people changed, and that was sometimes sad.

'Hullo. It's only me.' Laura stood beside their table, wrapped in a new coat of soft black-and-white tweed.

'Laura!' Clare jumped up to kiss her and stood back. 'My, you smell delicious. Sit down. Have some coffee.'

Laura patted Bernard's arm and sat down at the

table. 'No, I won't have anything, thank you. But aren't you having any breakfast? You have to eat, you know.'

Bernard smiled at this familiar message. 'You never set us a good example.'

'I eat as much as I need. But you're a growing boy,' Laura said solemnly, drawing off her French suède gloves, resting her lizard-skin bag on her lap. 'Now I'm not staying. I just had to tell you that Felix and I are going away. It's just decided. We're going for a trip to America and South America. We might even live there. You see! Everything's different now. Once I couldn't have come here like this to the station, and I know he's been funny about you talking to me on the phone these last days, but this morning I just said, "I'm going to run in for five minutes to Central to see Clare off on the train," and he said, "Right-oh! I'll drive you in." He would never have offered to do that before. So I'd better not keep him hanging about too long. The Jaguar's so hard to park. He was still having a bit of trouble with it when I left him, so he said he'd just drive round for a few minutes if that was all I was going to be.

'I don't know why you both rushed away like that. Felix was dreadfully upset to think you might think he *meant* anything that day you went away. When I told him what he said he was dumbfounded. He said he didn't think you thought so badly of him to think

327

he could mean a thing like that. He's fonder of you both than you give him credit for. He's always—with Clare—he would always do anything to please her. Much more than he'd ever do for me. She could have got him to do anything.'

Laura went on, 'It really jolted him when you went away, though. I think it's made him appreciate for the first time in his life that he mightn't like it if everyone left him. And he's getting very nervous suddenly. The other night the doorbell rang at eight o'clock, and do you know—he didn't want to open the door. It's so quiet in our district and nobody ever comes to the house at night. You know that long dim hall. I said, "I'll come with you," but he said, "Why should we open it? Who could it be?" But we crept down together and peeked through the curtains and it was that little plumber man coming to see about the sink. He does jobs for himself after work. We'd forgotten about him with all this turmoil going on.

'Oh, well. If you think,' she looked in Clare's direction but not exactly into her eyes, 'you'll be better off roaming about the countryside or driving some old car from place to place through the bush till you've used up all your savings—Doing hard jobs when you could have any number of good jobs here in the city. Be careful, though, Clare. I'm not joking. It's dangerous for a woman. You should take some sort of protection with you. I don't mean a gun—If you'd even gone to

Europe! It wouldn't cost you any more, either. Hills and rivers you want. I'm sure there must be better ones everywhere else than here. I loathe this country. The people are barbarians. They only think about money and horses and drinking. Really, I hope I can persuade Felix never to come back. I feel we'd make friends in another place. I'd like a different sort of life. There's no culture here. I'm not surprised you decided to go home,' she said to Bernard with partisan heat. 'To all your theatres and beautiful buildings.'

'But I'm coming back for the beginning of the university year.' He looked at Laura with surprise. 'I told you.'

'Oh?—I don't remember. Everything's been so topsy-turvy. You probably did.'

'No, the year doesn't start for five months.' Bernard explained, 'Max—the solicitor who's help-ing—thought that if I got work on a ship going home I could see my family and help to finalise the compensa-tion claim. With the money I earn going over I can pay my passage back. Or I might find work on a migrant ship as an interpreter.'

'Well!' Laura was flabbergasted by this degree of optimism and organisation. She said, 'At least you know what your plans are, which is more than Clare seems to do. But how did you manage to get your job on the ship? We had another presser before you who'd been a steward, and he said it was very hard.'

'It is. But Max arranged for me to meet a man he knows—'

'Ah!' Laura's exclamation was sage and bitter. 'That's the only way to get on. It isn't fair, really, all this pulling of strings. Probably many another boy in your position has tried to get home and had to give up in despair.' Laura's fellow-feeling for these disappointed lads was evident. 'I mean,' she added hastily, catching Clare's eye, 'that it's nice that *you* were lucky, but it isn't right that other boys aren't, too. Still, that's how the world goes. You need a rich father or influential friends. And Bernard,' Laura hurried on with propitiating politeness but no concentration, 'you're still going to do this botany course.'

'Yes. For sure.'

'And what will you work on when you finish, I wonder?' Laura's foot tapped out the seconds anxiously.

Bernard felt reproachful about something, but said, 'There's a good deal of scope for research, but it's a bit early to say.'

'Dear, dear!' Laura sketched a show of distress and indignation. 'Shut away in a little laboratory. Anyway, here we are, all off in different directions. I hope you're both going to write me nice long letters about all your doings?'

'Yes. But South America! Where will you be?' Clare asked her.

Laura exclaimed at her own foolishness and clapped the hand that wore the diamond ring to her chest. Extracting a notebook and pen from her bag she wrote several addresses out for Clare, who made copies of them for Bernard, who was writing out yet other addresses for Laura.

Exchanges made, instructions given, there was a sudden painful pause, then Laura stood up, her eyes going from one to the other unhappily, her hands busy smoothing on the fine suede gloves. 'I'd better get back to poor Felix. He hates driving in the city, but he came in specially so that I could say goodbye. He hasn't been very well,' she said gravely, looking out over the tables sprinkled with industrious and silent eaters, as she canvassed still, at this late hour, for disciples, hearts, minds, souls, to offer up to Felix. 'And he's had a tremendous amount to do—letters and 'phone calls in—connection with our trip.'

She kissed Clare. They both said, 'Look after yourself.' She took Bernard's big hand between hers. 'Now remember to eat up and keep well. I must go. But everything's quite different now.' She gave an odd little laugh. 'The worm's turned.'

Her desperation was such that the two she appealed to could only murmur good wishes and release her instantly to see her running off to the entrance in her pretty new shoes. She did not look back once.

Bernard sat down again and glumly refilled Clare's

cup and his own and clanked the empty pot back on the table. They drank in an armed silence, only accidentally giving each other the shadowed looks intended by their reflections for the absent ones.

Bernard looked at his watch and emerged in the moment, and as he regarded Clare's face and absorbed her presence for the last time for months or years, there began to emanate from him the least tinge of reproach: his trusted adviser and consultant was unseasonably casting him off.

Meeting his eyes, Clare felt disloyal, cagey, ashamed of herself and surprised. But there it was: she would be relieved to go. Nothing she had done had been with the surreptitious intention of attaching him to her side, dependent. On the contrary. Exclusiveness in personal relations, owning, being owned, being walled up, *exclusiveness*, she thought again, felt like a trap. To be bound, at this stage in her life, by any attachment, were it ever so well-phrased or congenial, felt as welcome as the prospect of strangulation—and rather similar.

She was fond of him. How could she not be? Because of him that futile, wasted, lacerated thing behind her—her life—was transmuted into an apprenticeship of infinite worth, undergone in surroundings of surpassing richness. Her hand had studied all those years, and each least part and facet of her had learned some small relentless task again and yet again in order to become the person who had been useful to this boy.

Life had agreed to find her useful. It knew, something knew, at last, that she was here. Anything was possible. Everything was true. People could indeed change out of recognition, permanently, between two breaths.

'I won't like Sydney without you.' Bernard's eyes looked and looked with static alarm and nostalgia.

'You'll be away in a couple of weeks yourself,' Clare rallied him. She had begun to suspect that affection, love, were things about which there was nothing to be done. People might love each other dearly, sleep together, live harmoniously or tempestuously together for years, but still, in a way, there was nothing to be done about it. She felt herself to have emerged at a point on the road she was in nature bound to have reached even at the end of decades of joyful living. It was a pity, perhaps, to have bypassed innocent happiness on the way—'You'll become a magnificent, great botanist, and you'll discover six new flowers the first time you go into the field. And you'll be sought after, but you'll remain simple and unspoiled and content in this quiet backwater.'

Bernard grinned. 'And you'll become a nursery gardener and watch the weather. At a vast distance from that house.'

'What a lovely idea!'

'A long way from that house.'

'No, no. That doesn't matter any more. And even at the worst it was very instructive.'

Scepticism was all over him.

'Really. It made me recognise things as they were. And that—I was supported by a sort of faith. I'm not sure in what. But I thought I saw bits of the true, if not of the good and the beautiful. That made most things bearable. That was my retreat. There was the external world—office, friends, amusements—And then there was *home*—so real it seemed to have six dimensions, fundamental as the floor of the world. Nothing at all from the outside could penetrate. The outside was a place of coloured tissue paper where people went about *not knowing about reality*.' She added, 'So you see—it was all—as they say—in a way—pure gain.'

'Yes.' Bernard blinked once or twice, and thought. 'Yes, I see that.' And he began to smile as people do in the instant of hearing very good news.

The train worked its way through the geometry of moving tracks, poles, overhead wires, cubes and squares of corrugated iron, black rotting terraces, narrow walls and fences leaning askew. Dismal relics of clothing blew damply on clotheslines. The outer suburbs marched up, crowded, formal and hard as nineteenth-century cemeteries.

More outer suburbs and more time: hills and valleys of roofs, grey-blue gravelled streets, blue-black tarred roads, square miles of brick, corrugated iron, gravel, concrete, hard dry substances, hard shapes, graveyard architecture and landscape. Still time and suburbs passed.

Abruptly the road by the train lines changed colour and character: it was a bush track—bright clay. And there were trees suddenly, swift-moving past—blossoming eucalyptus, pines. Alone in the compartment, Clare jerked the window up and leaned out into the day. The light was wonderful. Waves of air beat against her face, and it smelled of grass, or clover, or honey.

Whatever it is, I remember it, she thought, breathing in. Her eyes paused here on a line of willows as they glided past, and the willows were familiar, too. She remembered it all.

Yet it was funny that she should think so; for it did occur to her that she had only just arrived.

Text Classics

textclassics.com.au